# THE MEN OF 633 SQUADRON

633 Squadron, under **Commander Ian Moore,** was once more a unique fighting weapon—a close-knit team made up of a motley crew of individualists ...

**Millburn,** the dashing Yank who refused to transfer from 633. His girl-chasing exploits landed him in more trouble than chasing Me.109s— and twice as quickly ...

**Tony St. Claire,** the brilliant musician, and his girl Sue, the assistant Intelligence Officer who faced torment each time he went on Ops ...

**Paddy McKenny,** who'd lost both his girl and his religion, and was flying in a way that made him a dangerous menace to the rest of the squadron

... And, not in the squadron but attached to it —and its severest critic—**Ernest Lambert,** bestselling, virile novelist, now war correspondent. For him every man was a potential ploy in his vicious campaign to discredit the RAF ...

# 633
## SQUADRON
### OPERATION CRUCIBLE
#### BY FREDERICK E. SMITH

BANTAM BOOKS · TORONTO · NEW YORK · LONDON

**633 SQUADRON: OPERATION CRUCIBLE**
*A Bantam Book*

*PRINTING HISTORY*
*Originally published in Great Britain by Cassell & Company
in 1977*
*Bantam edition / May 1979*

*Bantam Books are published by Bantam Books, Inc. Its trade-
mark, consisting of the words "Bantam Books" and the por-
trayal of a bantam, is Registered in U.S. Patent and Trademark
Office and in other countries. Marca Registrada. Bantam
Books, Inc., 666 Fifth Avenue, New York, New York 10019.*

PRINTED IN THE UNITED STATES OF AMERICA

*To Mac, Boy, Pat and Monica*
*with love and happy memories of Clifton*

The 21cm rocket struck the B.17 full on its starboard inner engine. The explosion was followed by a ball of black smoke. A few seconds later the wing sheared away and the Fortress began spinning earthwards. Three parachutes blossomed out into the tracer-streaked sky. With seven men still trapped inside, the B.17 disappeared into the clouds that hid the earth.

The clear sky above was filled with the frenzy of battle. Over 150 B.17s, flying in three tight boxes, were pouring out contrails that spread back as far as the eye could see. Darting in front and around them like swifts avid for food were countless German fighters. Black threads of tracer criss-crossed the sky like some surrealistic spider's web. Columns of smoke, ephemeral monuments to shot-down comrades, shredded the winds of the stratosphere as the remaining B.17s fought for survival.

The enemy units attacking them, products of experience and German ingenuity, were formidable. The 21cm rockets, designed to create havoc among tightly-packed formations, were carried by Me.110D "destroyers". Mixed in with them were veteran units of Focke Wulf 190s heavily armed with 20mm cannon. Formidable enough on their own, these units were augmented by aircraft from the 3rd Air Force based in France. The Americans had made another penetration deep into the heart of the Fatherland. Every effort was being made to punish them for their temerity.

A new wave of destroyers was sweeping head on towards the B.17s. At 1,000 metres lances of smoke and flame darted from their wings. No attempt was made to aim at specific Fortresses: the enemy pilots knew, as with duck-shooting, that the laws of chance guaranteed some hits among such a dense target.

Struck just ahead of the pilot's cockpit, one B.17 swung off course like a blinded animal and crashed into the starboard wing of a companion. Locked in a tangle of broken spars and sheared metal, the two huge aircraft went spinning helplessly down. No parachutes emerged from the wreckage and a massive explosion before the aircraft had fallen two thousand feet made certain none would.

A second B.17 had ten feet of its port wing severed. Lurching perilously, it seemed about to slide to certain death when its desperate pilot brought up the wing by strength and prayer. Ignoring the danger of collision, his comrades on either side closed in to give him protection.

Since leaving their fighter escort on the Franco-German frontier the B.17s had been under constant enemy attack and during the long morning over half of them had sustained damage. Jagged holes let in icy blasts of air that froze bare hands to metal. Oil ran like black blood from severed pipe lines and formed slippery pools on the metal floor. Soot and blackened metal showed where frantic men had extinguished fires. As gunners strove to follow the lightning turns of the German fighters, their feet slipped on hundreds of spent shells. Above oxygen masks, paths of sweat ran whitely through the stains of cordite and oil. A few men found relief in cursing the leaders who had sent them against such massive odds. Most men, numbed by their discomfort and the fury of battle, fought on mechanically and doubted if safety would ever be reached. They had, they felt certain, already fought a thousand years.

Yet, in the way of air combat, the end came suddenly. At one moment the sky seemed full of deadly hornets, in the next it was empty as the German pilots, sighting the eager Spitfires and Thunderbolts at their rendezvous, withdrew out of range. Cowardice played no part in their withdrawal. Aware that the Allies were attempting to bleed them to death by attrition, the

Luftwaffe was under the strictest order to avoid contact with enemy fighters unless the occasion was justifiable.

Justification was clearly impossible here. A continuance of the attack that had carried the German fighters within range of the Spitfires and Thunderbolts would have resulted in as many losses to the Luftwaffe as to the Allies, and the mathematics of 1943 did not permit such extravagance. With the Allies still possessing no long-range fighter that could escort the USAAF on its raids into Germany, it was better sense to wait until the B.17s once again ventured into the Fatherland. The hundreds of B.17 wrecks that already littered Germany bore witness to the success of this policy.

Yet although the German withdrawal brought relief to the hard-pressed crews, for some the ordeal was not over, as wounded men fought to keep crippled aircraft flying. Back at an airfield in East Anglia two men were out on the field watching the grim assembly of crash wagons and ambulances. One of the men, bearded and wearing a greatcoat with the shoulder flashes of a war correspondent, was Ernest Lambert, American novelist.

A middle-aged man, short and stocky of build with a square aggressive face, Lambert's appearance did nothing to suggest he was one of America's lions of literature. His rise to world fame had been extraordinary. Until 1936 his name had been unknown to the public at large. Then MGM had filmed his fifth novel, *The Rains of Rajapur*. The film had been a massive success and from then onwards every book of Lambert's had received rapturous acclaim. With his work extolling the virtues of self-reliance and manliness, it was hardly surprising that the Hearst newspaper empire, for a fee that was said to be astronomical, had claimed his services for the duration of the war. The fact that most of Lambert's syndicated articles to date had either implied or stated that America's Allies were not pulling their weight appeared in no way to have affected his standing with the Hearst empire. Indeed suggestions had appeared in the American Press, brave suggestions because Lambert was a formidable adver-

3

sary, that this very chauvinism was the real reason for his engagement.

His companion was the Station Intelligence officer, George Hodgkinson. New to his appointment and awed by Lambert's reputation, Hodgkinson had felt it incumbent on him to offer Lambert a seat on the mission. His vague surprise at Lambert's curt retort that he had more to do than sit on his ass over Germany had not been assuaged by the constant sight of the correspondent propping up the Mess bar.

With the massing of the crash wagons and ambulances along the runways complete, an apprehensive silence had now fallen over the airfield. Taking his eyes off the eastern sky, Lambert turned to Hodgkinson.

"Why aren't they getting Mustang support?" His voice had the abrasive accent of a New Englander.

Hodgkinson, stringy in build and aware of it, showed some discomfort at the question. "We find they're underpowered, sir. The Alison engines only develop 1,150 h.p."

"I know that. But what about those fitted with Merlins?"

"They're O.K. In fact they'll outfly a 109. But we haven't enough to provide a worthwhile escort."

He received an agressive stare. "Maybe you haven't. But what about the British?"

Hodgkinson misunderstood him. "They've been providing escorts, sir. They're doing it now over France."

"What the hell's the use over France? It's over Germany we need them."

"Their Spitfires haven't the range, sir. They were built for Metropolitan defence, not escort duty."

"That's why I'm asking about Merlin-powered Mustangs. The British have enough by this time. Why aren't they using them?"

Hodgkinson, who had no idea and in any case had a couple of drinking buddies in the RAF, was grateful for the siren that took away the need for an answer. Harsh and portentous, it caused an apprehensive stir among the onlookers who were standing beside the

4

crash wagons. Engines began revving and a green Very light soared up from the Control tower.

Fifteen seconds later a far off drone could be heard. It grew heavier and men pointed at the eastern sky. Black specks, some trailing smoke, had appeared and became larger by the second. With at least half their number damaged, the intact B.17s began to orbit the airfield to give them landing priority.

The air was now shuddering under the impact of fifty engines. The first B.17 had gingerly manoeuvred to the western side of the airfield and was settling down to land. Airfoils whining, it swept past the two watching men and set its wheels on the runway. As its tyres screamed and screamed again, spray came up in clouds from the wet tarmac. As the pilot applied the brakes the B.17 slewed to the left and ran into the grass. It was the moment for two crash wagons and an ambulance to speed across the runway and halt alongside the smoking engines. Within seconds foam was spraying on to them and the danger of fire averted.

With a nod of approval Lambert turned his attention to the second B.17 which, wobbling perilously, was settling down on the same runway. As it drew to a halt, an ambulance and a crash wagon raced up. Asbestos-clad figures climbed into the rear gunner's shattered cupola and hacked their way inside. A minute later they lowered something in a sheet to the medical orderlies below.

The third B.17 was a grotesque sight. Half of its tail fin was shot away, huge holes gaped in its fuselage, and the entire port wingtip was missing. Moreover its undercarriage was hanging down like a bird's broken claw. Both men ducked as its shadow slanted obliquely over them. Frantic red Very lights from the Control Tower were calling for a second approach but the wounded crew, with a shattered radio, were in no condition to respond. Fighting pain, loss of blood, and an aircraft that seemed held together only by will power, they had reached home and could do no more. As the wheels missed the runway and touched the grass there was a scream of shearing rivets as the undercarriage collapsed. The aircraft was thrown into the air by im-

5

pact, only to crash down as heavily again. For fifty yards it skidded forward, throwing off mud and pieces of metal. Then its nose dug in and the huge machine stood on end. For a moment it appeared about to somersault, then the fuselage crashed back with an impact that shook the ground. As Hodgkinson muttered "Oh, my God", there was a coughing roar and a fireball that hid the entire wreck from view.

"Oh, my God!" Hodgkinson said again and began to run forward. Lambert caught his arm.

"Forget it. There's nothing you can do."

The fireball was swelling like a giant balloon. Incredibly, thin screams could be heard through the thunder of engines and the howl of sirens. Hodgkinson looked as if he were going to be sick. "Some of them must still be alive."

Looking as shaken as the Intelligence officer, Lambert turned away. "I want to use your Communications Room. Right now."

Hodgkinson looked embarrassed. "We never allow outside contact until the de-briefing is over, sir. It's standard procedure throughout the Command."

"I'm an official war correspondent, Major. That means I have a priority on communications."

Hodgkinson's glance in the direction of the Control Tower was a plea for help. "They'd never let you in without the C.O.'s permission, sir."

"Then get his goddamned permission. I've got a story I want in tomorrow's papers."

Hodgkinson's eyes were drawn back to the B.17 inferno. "He'll be busy right now. But I'll do my best."

"You do that, Major. Because there'll be some hard questions asked if this story isn't sent."

Smoke from burning rubber and oil made Hodgkinson gag as he hurried away. Lambert watched him for a moment, then started towards the Signals Centre. His walk suggested an incensed and revengeful bantam cock.

## 2

The camouflaged staff car pulled up outside the Administration Block of RAF Sutton Craddock with a squeal of brakes. The Air Commodore who jumped out was a small man with the alert movements of a squirrel. Wearing no overcoat although there was a chill in the late September wind, he nodded to his Waaf driver and marched briskly up the neat path that led to the door. A sergeant and a corporal, watching him from the safety of the Guardhouse, grimaced at one another. The appearance of Air Commodore Davies at Sutton Craddock rarely failed to denote trouble of one kind or another.

Trousers flapping round his legs, Davies hurried down a corridor. An Aircraftman Second Class, on his knees scrubbing the linoleum floor, saw him coming and hastily drew his bucket aside. Ignoring his salute, Davies strode past and halted outside the C.O.'s office. Seeing the door was ajar, he gave it a single rap of his knuckles and pushed his way inside.

There were three men inside the office and it was clear they were all expecting Davies. The big, broad-shouldered man who stepped forward was Henderson, the Station C.O. Nicknamed "Pop" by the squadron at large, he was a middle-aged, benign Scot who had taken command of the station after the death of Barrett in the Swartfjord. He was experiencing his usual ambivalence at the sight of the choleric Davies. The Air Commodore's terse phone call that morning had by implication warned him that Davies was coming up with some specialist mission for the squadron. Henderson could find no complaint in that: his élite unit of Mosquitoes existed for that purpose and Davies brought with him a devotion to duty and a single-mindedness that the Scot, a professional airman himself, could only

7

commend. His one reservation was that sometimes Davies could be over-zealous in achieving his objectives.

The other men were a contrast in types. The portly officer in his middle-forties was Frank Adams, the Station Intelligence officer. With his build and thick-lensed spectacles he could not be accused of looking a military figure, a fact the self-critical Adams had long accepted. Not a professional airman, and blessed or cursed with a vivid imagination, Adams' feelings towards Davies were more loaded. Although he shared Henderson's respect for the man's drive and enthusiasm, he occasionally deplored the ruthlessness that could weigh success against the lives of men who were his friends. At the same time Adams knew it was those very objective qualities that made Davies such an effective field commander.

The third man, considerably younger than his two fellow officers, was Ian Moore, Squadron Commander. With a small combat scar on his right cheek, Moore was slimly-built with a fresh complexion and fair, wavy hair. As always his uniform was immaculately tailored. The recent inheritor of his father's chain of footwear shops, Moore was not short of money and more than a penny of it went into keeping him the best dressed officer on the station. Yet his was no case of the frills outmatching the package. Moore was an ex-Pathfinder and the ribbons of the DSO and Bar, and DFC, and the more unusual American Congressional Medal of Honour beneath his pilot's brevet testified to his outstanding combat record. Davies, by pulling strings as only the wily Air Commodore knew how, had worked his transfer from Pathfinders and given him command of 633 Squadron after its near annihilation in Swartfjord. Although at this time internal strife had been bringing the squadron to the point of disintegration, by the use of charm that could only be described as charismatic and leadership that had been inspired, Moore had welded the squadron into an élite unit again that had eventually destroyed the notorious Rhine Maiden establishment in far-off Bavaria. It was a feat that had gained for Moore a respect from the crews that had previously been given only to Roy Grenville, the leader of the Swartfjord raid who was now a German prisoner of war. The destruction of the Rhine Maiden plant had also earned Moore and the squadron the gratitude of American bomber crews who were only too aware of the losses they would have suffered had the proximity-fused rockets ever reached production.

Henderson's voice had a slight Highland burr. "Good morning, sir. You're looking well."

It was not Davies' way to indulge in formalities when the pressure was on. Pulling a newspaper from his briefcase he slapped it down on the desk in front of the Group Captain. "I don't suppose you've seen this, have you, Jock?"

Henderson picked up the newspaper curiously. "The *New York Daily Mirror?* No, I haven't. They don't stock it around these parts."

Davies ignored the gentle sarcasm. "Take a look at page three."

As Henderson opened the newspaper, Moore and Adams saw him give a slight start. As he began reading, Davies moved impatiently forward and tried to regain the paper. "You can read the details later."

The big Scot was not a man to be hurried when he chose otherwise. With his eyes still on the print, he moved away from Davies. A full six inches shorter than the Scot, Davies realized that in a confrontation of this kind he was outclassed and, like the good soldier he was, he turned his attack elsewhere.

"You two have heard of Ernest Lambert, haven't you?"

Both officers nodded.

"Did you know he's become a newspaper correspondent?"

Moore answered him. He had a laconic, cultured voice. "Yes, sir. Doesn't he have a roving commission?"

"Too right he has. And he's roving around the U.K. at the moment." From the corner of his eye Davies saw Henderson lift his head and was on him like a flash. "Well! Have you finished?"

Henderson relinquished the paper at last. "Not all of it. But I've got the drift."

"Bloody disgraceful, isn't it?" Davies demanded.

The big Scot gave an indifferent shrug. "Isn't it just the usual sensational rubbish the newspapers dish out?"

Davies stared at him. "You know who Lambert is, don't you?"

"Yes. He's an American novelist."

"Do you know what books he's written?"

Henderson was beginning to look resentful. "Yes. They filmed one of them a few years back, didn't they?"

"They've filmed damn nearly all of his work, man. He's the biggest name in the business." Davies transferred his stare to Adams. "You must have read his books, Adams?"

Noticing Henderson's expression, the highly-sensitive Adams shifted uncomfortably. "I've read one or two, sir."

"Which ones?" Davies demanded.

Cornered, Adams tried to avoid Henderson's aggrieved eyes. "I think one was called *The Rains of Rajapur*. Another was something to do with the Middle East."

*"The Desert of God?"*

Adams brightened. "That's the one."

Davies gave an impatient grunt. "Stop being so coy, Adams. You've read the lot and so has Moore. Even I've read three of 'em. And to be fair they weren't bad." He turned back to the red-faced Henderson. "He's known as the hairy-chested novelist. Hard, tough, but also literary. I suppose that's why he's been enrolled for the duration, so he'll keep the lads marching and the factories humming. The only snag is, if he keeps this up America won't have any Allies left." Seeing the other two men's curiosity, he thrust the newspaper at Moore. "The article's a direct attack on the RAF. He's sniped at us before but this time he's gone too far for us to ignore it."

With Adams peering over his shoulder, Moore was trying to get the gist of the article and to listen to Davies at the same time. Thirty seconds later he handed the paper to the curious Adams. "I assume it's the political implications you're worried about, sir?"

Davies nodded. "You can say that again. There

are always plenty of people on both sides of the Atlantic eager to find faults with the other, and this character's playing up to both. Only this time he's working on a particularly sensitive nerve. I don't suppose any of you have heard of Operation Pointblank that the Heads of State drew up at Casablanca early this year?" When all three men shook their heads, Davies continued with a grunt: "Nor should you have done. Basically it set out two principles. One was that Allied operations should start in North Africa to take pressure off the Russians. The second—and this is the one that concerns us—the strategic bombing of Germany was to be intensified. In June this year this order was broken down into specifics. Both Harris and Eaker were told to seek out and destroy factories devoted to enemy aircraft production. You know something about that—the B.17s who gave you cover on your way to Bavaria last month were after the Messerschmidt factories in Regensburg."

Seeing he had fully captured the attention of his listeners, Davies walked over to a large map of Western Europe that hung on the office wall. "This new directive didn't please Arthur Harris. As you must have gathered by this time, he believes area bombing can win us the war by itself. The Yanks have different views: they think they can hurt Jerry much more by bombing specialist targets in daylight. How much these different views are governed by necessity I'll leave you to guess. In the early years of the war we suffered so heavily in daylight raids that we turned to night bombers and now, with our factories tooled to produce them, we've no alternative but to continue their use. The Yanks are in exactly the opposite position. Lacking our experience of '39, '40, and '41, they came into the war as we did, believing the day bomber could always get through. Which is true as far as it goes but, as we learned the hard way, only at a hell of a price. So they're as committed to their B.17s as we're committed to our night heavies and neither side can turn back now."

The faces of the three listening men were a study as Davies paused. As in any war in history, unit commanders in 1943 did not enjoy the confidences of their Commanders-in-Chief, and overall strategy could only be guessed at by intelligent observation. That Davies, a stickler for military security, seemed prepared to lift a veil or two made the moment one of high significance. Adams found himself giving a nervous cough as the Air Commodore continued.

"I'm not going into all the pros and cons because most of 'em don't concern you. But there's no denying that until recently the Yank daylight raids have pleased the boys at the top because one of the objectives of Pointblank was to destroy as many fighters as possible before the invasion, which we all know must come soon. Jerry's being clever in not committing his fighters to our own fighter sweeps over France but when the Yanks penetrate in daylight into Germany and attack big cities or vital factories he is forced to react. Of course he attacks our night forces just as energetically, but at night and with our .303 armament we can't hope to destroy as many of his fighters as the Yanks can with their ten .5 Brownings per aircraft. In theory, then, the Yanks can do heavy damage to his numerical strength but in practice they're the ones who are suffering the most. You know what their losses were the other day? Thirty-five B.17s with another fifteen damaged beyond repair. And sixty partially damaged. All that out of an initial force of one hundred and sixty aircraft."

Henderson let out a shocked whistle which Davies answered with a grim nod. "Terrifying, isn't it? Eaker's blaming the losses on insufficient front-line strength and he's probably right. Eight hundred or a thousand B.17s in one raid could probably out-gun Jerry fighters. But let's get back to Lambert. One of his bleats is that Harris should be co-operating more with Eaker in twenty-four-hour raids on specific targets. That way he argues the German defences in each area would be over-stretched. But now he's grinding another axe. Rumour has it that General Arnold over in the States is complaining our Fighter Command isn't doing enough to defend the B.17s and Lambert is making the complaint in public. In fact, as you see, he's saying our intransigence is costing American lives.

"We know Fighter Command's problems—the

Spitfire was designed for short-range interception and even with wing tanks and modifications it can't reach further than the German frontier. But Fighter Command do have a number of modified Mustangs and Lambert's also complaining we're not releasing enough of them to the 8th Air Force. I can't say how true or false this is, but I do know the RAF has been receiving bad publicity in the States recently and for all kinds of reasons this is causing both Portal and Eaker headaches. Something must be done quickly to bring back the old love affair and you're the unit chosen for the job."

The atmosphere in the office was one of high expectancy as Davies' eyes moved from one man to the other. "It's not difficult to understand why. Firstly, you're not part of Bomber Command whose policy of area bombing has lost favour with the Yanks. Secondly, you're not associated with Fighter Command either. Thirdly, and the best reason of all, your Swartfjord raid and your recent destruction of the Rhine Maiden Project made you the blue-eyed boys of the Yanks." Davies, whose comments on the Americans had so far been a model of objectivity, backslid for a moment into jingoism. "And so it bloody well should. If you hadn't wiped out those anti-aircraft rockets, Christ knows the state they'd be in by this time."

It was Henderson's turn to cough. "Can I ask a question here?"

Davies frowned. "If you want to."

"Are these criticisms of the RAF coming from the American crews themselves or only from General Arnold and his staff officers? Because we've not found any resentment among the American boys we know."

Disliking interruptions when he was in full flow, Davies tended to slide into sarcasm. "I thought I'd just explained that. Next to Betty Grable, you're the Yanks' favourite pin-ups. It's the poor bloody artisans of Bomber and Fighter Commands who're taking all the stick." Seeing Henderson's expression, Davies modified his tone. "No, I don't think the average Yank crewman thinks any of this. He knows we're just doing the job we're told to do, the same way he does his. But who is he compared with the Pentagon, Ernest

13

Lambert, and the public at large who don't know an aileron from a joystick? Our job is to discredit Lambert by showing the American public how wrong he is."

Henderson was looking doubtful. "And you've got an operation for us that can do this?"

"I'm expecting to have, Jock, if things turn out the way we're hoping. And I ought to know that by Friday at the latest. In the meantime don't be surprised if you get a visit from our newspaper friend. Rumours are going around he wants to see the set-up here."

The Scot looked horrified. "Lambert? Here?"

Davies grinned. "Why not? He can hardly visit RAF units without taking a look at us, can he? Don't look so worried. Give him plenty of whisky and you might even win him over without a shot being fired."

"I'll get some warning when he's coming, won't I?"

"Oh, Christ, yes. I'll contact you as soon as they request permission for his visit. In the meantime you can stand your boys down. Not that I want 'em swigging beer in the Mess all day." Davies switched his gaze to Moore. "Get 'em on the ranges and give 'em plenty of low-level practice."

Henderson's ears pricked. "Low-level?"

Davies picked up his briefcase from the desk and took the newspaper from Adams. "No luck, Jock. Security's as tight as a bull's arse in fly time on this one. It has to be; there are Allied lives as well as our own involved. You'll get all details as soon as permission is given." The spry Air Commodore moved to the door where he grinned again. "Cheer up, Jock. If we pull this off, you might get Veronica Lake sent over as a squadron mascot. And the rest of us might get a spare tin or two of Spam."

With a wink Davies disappeared, leaving the three officers staring at one another.

## 3

Milburn grinned at the girl behind the desk. "Hiya, kid. How's life this morning?"

The girl, a pretty Waaf with freckles, eyed the dark, tousle-headed Millburn with some caution. Of Irish descent, the good-looking American had a reputation with women that was a legend on the Station. "Life's fine, thank you—sir."

"It is? That's great. Let's keep it that way." Millburn lowered a leg over the corner of the desk. "How about doing a movie with me tonight?"

The girl drew hastily back. "No, thanks."

The American slid another six inches across the desk. "What is it, honey? You still holding a torch for that Limey boy friend of yours?"

"What if I am?" she asked defiantly.

"It's a waste, honey. He's two thousand miles away in Africa. You're losing precious flying time."

"And it wouldn't be a waste if I went out with you?"

Millburn's grin broadened. "That's for sure, honey. You'd be getting experience. And that's money in the bank for a girl."

The girl opened her mouth, glanced at the closed inner door, and dropped her voice into an exasperated whisper. "Tommy Millburn, you are the most conceited man I've ever known."

"You've got the wrong word, haven't you, honey? You mean confident. There's a world of difference."

"Not to me there isn't."

The grinning Millburn lifted his six-foot, well-proportioned frame from the desk. "You'll see the light sooner or later. And when you do, you know who'll help you."

The girl gave a sniff. "That'll be the day. Will you see the Wing Commander now? Or have you something more important to do?"

Millburn waved an indulgent hand. "No. If he promises to hurry it up, I guess I can fit him in."

Hiding her smile, the girl opened the door. "Squadron Leader Millburn is here, sir."

Moore, who was sitting at his desk signing papers, glanced up and smiled. "Thank you, Tess. Show him in, will you?"

Millburn's entry typified the informal atmosphere of an RAF operational squadron. "Hello, skipper. Teddy Young said you wanted to see me."

Moore indicated for him to draw up a chair. "Yes, there are a couple of things. Did Teddy tell you that we're standing down for a few days?"

"Yeah. What's the reason? Have we something big coming up?"

"We might have. But there's nothing definite at the moment. So if your boys start asking questions, let them think they're being given a rest."

Millburn grinned. "They're not fooled as easily as that."

"All right, tell them they're getting sloppy and need some practice. Take them over the gunnery range and let them have a go at the low-level targets."

Millburn looked disappointed. "How many sessions?"

"Just the mornings. You can take the rest of the day off."

"Great. They'll think it's Christmas." The American pushed a packet of Lucky Strike across the desk. "What's next on the list?"

"I've had news of Harvey. He phoned me this morning. He's made such a good recovery the hospital's discharging him in a couple of days."

"You're kidding. He's had three operations, hasn't he?"

Moore nodded. Although busy lighting his cigarette, he was studying the American's expression. "He has to convalesce for a while, of course, but he ought to be back with us around the middle of October."

"That's great," Millburn said. "I wonder if the nurses down there have mellowed him."

Moore smiled. "I wouldn't think it's likely, would you?"

"Not much. He'll probably give me a bollocking as soon as he gets back for not keeping his office tidy."

Moore exhaled smoke. "You do realize I'll have to give him his flight back?"

To his gratification the American looked surprised rather than upset. "What else? Hell, he practically destroyed that rocket plant single-handed. You know something? The boys'll be pleased. He's a better mother hen than I'll ever be."

"We all agree he's a fine flight commander. But you've done a good job yourself. That's something else I want to talk about. You're a cert for the job if you do what the Yanks want and move over to them. In fact, with your experience you might get a squadron command. I know you've flattered us before by staying here but this time the situation's different. We can't hang on to you at personal cost to yourself."

Millburn's affability turned to wryness. "Let's get it straight, skipper. Are you trying to get rid of me?"

"Don't be a damn fool. I'm trying to be fair to you."

Looking embarrassed and defiant in equal parts, the American took a few seconds to respond. "One thing I'd like to make clear, skipper. I think my guys are doing a great job."

Guessing what was coming, Moore tried to hide his amusement. "So do I. So do we all."

With that important point made, Millburn's tone changed. "So it's not that. It's just that a guy gets used to one unit." Terrified of appearing sentimental, Millburn searched for a more harmless reason and found one. "What about girls? A guy can lose out if he's always moving around."

"That's true. Mind you, there are plenty of girls in East Anglia. And from the stories I hear, they don't exactly dislike the Yanks."

"But the ones I've got here are house-trained. And that saves a man a lot of time."

17

Moore lifted his shoulders expressively. "Why didn't we think of that?"

Millburn grinned as their eyes met. "So I stay. O.K.?"

The young squadron commander made no attempt to hide his satisfaction. "Of course you stay. The last thing I want is to lose you."

"Then do me a favour, skipper. Don't do me any favours. Just let me soldier along as before."

Moore's laugh reached the Waaf in the anteroom. "All right. But don't let me hear you moaning when Harvey gives you that bollocking. And don't get prickly when one of your war correspondents asks you what a clean, upright American boy is doing in the RAF."

"War correspondent?"

"Yes. We've got one visiting us any day now. Ernest Lambert, the novelist."

Millburn whistled. "Lambert? Has it to do with the Rhine Maiden job?"

Realizing he could say little about Lambert's visit without endangering security, Moore prevaricated. "If it is, he's a bit late. The dust from that settled a month ago."

"Maybe he's just getting round to it."

Moore nodded. "I suppose it's possible." Changing the subject, he picked up a form from his desk. "I see you've put through McKenny's request for leave. You don't know he's still got two months to go?"

"Yeah. Only he's been pressing me hard and he's been hitting the bottle recently."

"What is it? Girl trouble?"

"Search me. He won't talk about it."

"Has the M.O. seen him?"

"I made him take a medical last week. The M.O. says there's nothing wrong with him physically. He says he's a bit highly strung but then who isn't?"

Moore glanced down at the form again. "If I authorize this I'll have every man jack on the squadron slapping applications in. Try to find out what's troubling him, will you, and then we'll see what we can do."

"Fair enough. Anything else?"

"No. That's the lot for the moment."

The American nodded and stubbed out his cigarette. As he reached the door and the Waaf appeared, he turned. "You know the real reason I'm staying here, don't you, skipper?"

"No. Tell me."

Millburn winked and patted the cheek of the girl who was holding the door open for him. "It's Tess here. She's driving me wild, skipper. A woman like her's worth anything. Even flying with a tribe of Limeys."

The girl's expression told she had forgotten the presence of the laughing Moore. Before she could vent her feelings, the ebullient American had pulled the door closed and vanished.

The small officer standing beneath the naked light bulb that hung from the billet roof was trying to put a shine on his service cap badge. Halfway through the operation he turned and scowled at Millburn who was lying full-length on one of the beds. "If you used Harvey's quarters instead of still kipping in here, maybe that lazy young sod Wilkinson would give me better attention."

Millburn lifted his head. "It's not rank that does it, mush. It's personality."

"What do you mean—personality? You've got more cash to bribe him with, that's all."

"Jealousy'll get you nowhere, my little Welsh blinder. Why don't you accept that some guys have it and some don't? Anyway, what's all this moaning about? I thought you'd be happy to get a couple of days off duty."

The small officer was in no mood to be placated. "Don't worry; we'll pay for it. I saw Davies coming out of the Admin Block this morning. When he pays us a visit there's always trouble."

Johnnie Gabriel, nicknamed Gabby or The Gremlin because of his wiry frame and sharp features that could look either comically old or young at will, was one of the Squadron's characters. Somewhat older than his aircrew colleagues, with a thirst for excitement that was insatiable, he had enlisted in the Thirties as a fighter pilot for the Government in the Spanish Civil War. Before crashing into enemy territory he had shot down three Fascist planes. Threatened with execution by the Falangists, Gabby had volunteered to fly for Franco and by some miracle of persuasion had been accepted. On his first solo mission he had flown straight out of Spain into France.

On the outbreak of World War Two he had not unreasonably expected the RAF to accept him as a trained pilot. Instead his offer to fly had been rejected and he had been kept waiting eighteen months before he was offered training as a navigator. His disgruntled acceptance had eventually led him to a Mitchell squadron where he had become Millburn's navigator. Set alongside the powerful American with his devil-may-care features and shock of black hair, the Welshman looked more like a gnome than ever. Yet the two ill-assorted characters had become inseparable friends and notorious in every squadron in which they had served for their mad pranks and tireless pursuit of women. To date they had been in 633 Squadron just over four months. In spite of their wild reputation on the ground, they were a highly capable crew and had been an almost automatic selection to lead A Flight after Harvey had been wounded and hospitalized.

Millburn yawned. "What's wrong with a bit of trouble?"

"What are you looking for?" the Welshman gibed. "Another DFC to show those Yank buddies of yours?"

"Coming from you, that's really something," Millburn grinned. "Who's the guy I once found polishing a scratch on his arm with a toothbrush so he could show it to his dames?"

Gabby, who had been wounded during the Rhine Maiden operation, gave a sniff of indignation. "Some of us have had more than scratches, mate. You forgotten I was a stretcher case when we got back from Bavaria?"

"You've never let anyone forget. From the line you shot in the hospital, the nurses thought you'd captured Hitler and brought him back in the bomb bay."

"So what? I got some dates for you, didn't I?"

"Yeah, you did. And I haven't got over 'em yet."

Back on his favourite topic, Gabby tried blandishments. "Change your mind and come tonight. Both of those kids have fallen for you."

"Not a chance, mush. You're on your own."

"But Betty's friend's not that bad. A bit skinny, perhaps, but she's got good legs."

"A bit skinny? She's like Olive Oyl in one of those Popeye movies. I know why you want me along. So you can use my car."

"It's not that at all. Four's more company than two."

"You mean more company than three. I'm on to you, you little bum. That dame of yours won't go out with you unless Olive Oyl tags along and I don't blame her. So I'm supposed to provide the car and pick up the bills."

Gabby looked hurt. "You've got it all wrong. We've just more fun when we're out together, that's all."

"More fun for who?"

"At least you could lend me the car," the Welshmen muttered.

"That's more like it. Well, I could but I won't. I'm going out myself on a recce after dinner. So the car's out."

"Sod," Gabby muttered, putting on his forage cap. Millburn guffawed as he watched him set it at a jaunty angle. "You're wasting your time, mush. With Olive Oyl keeping a beady eye on you all night, you're never going to make it."

"I'd do it for you, Millburn. You know I would."

"Like hell you would. What about the time I picked up that dame in Scarborough? You ran out on me as soon as you saw her friend and I was stuck with the two of 'em for the rest of the day."

"That was different. She had bad breath and bow legs."

"At least she had legs. This dame walks on sticks."

Gabby had a last try. "So I've got to take the transport into town?"

"That's right. And back. You've got a tough night ahead of you."

21

The small Welshman quivered with indignation. "I've never picked up a girl yet without asking if she had a friend for you. And this is the thanks I get."

"That's right. I've been stuck with so many plain Janes it's starting to affect my morale. From now on you take the rough with the smooth, boyo. Starting from tonight."

Seeing it was hopeless, Gabby started for the door. He threw his last punch from the step outside. "Now I know why you're still in our mob, Millburn. The Yanks are too smart to have you."

Millburn's guffaw reached the Welshman before he slammed the door closed. "You've got it wrong as usual, kid. The girls here won't let me go."

## 4

The Mess was unusually quiet that evening. With no operational flying that day, the crews were making the most of the occasion. Teddy Young, seasoned Commander of B Flight, had proved himself a dinkum Australian by going to the last of the season's flat races and taking a party of ten with him. Other airmen were visiting their girl friends in the local market town of Highgate or farther afield in Scarborough. Older and senior officers would arrive late but at this moment Timber Woods, the barman, was yawning and wishing he had something to read.

When Adams appeared in the doorway only two men were propping up the bar. One was Jack Richardson, the heavily built, ginger-headed Equipment Officer, the other was Paddy McKenny of A Flight. Neither was in conversation: in fact they were standing at opposite ends of the counter. The sight came as no surprise to Adams. Richardson, who drank heavily and told particularly dirty jokes, was not the most popular man on the station and his usual drinking partner, Marsden, the Signals Officer, had gone to the races with Teddy Young. McKenny was one of the many Irish volunteers who resented their country's neutrality. A strong-featured man with the abundant black hair and fair complexion that favoured so many of his race, he had been posted to 633 Squadron shortly after its near annihilation in Norway. Bernard Ross, a member of the original squadron whose pilot had been killed, had been teamed up with him. Both men having received training for the role, they were recognized as the squadron's photographic specialists.

With McKenny not one to wear his heart on his sleeve, Ross, a Scot from Ayrshire, was probably the only man on the station who knew of the sensitive streak that ran through the Irishman. To the squadron at large, McKenny was a rugged man who, having volunteered to fight the Nazi menace, was playing his part with skill and tenacity.

In the four months the Irishman and the Scotsman had been crewed together they had developed the kind of comradeship that men would look back on with nostalgia in the days of peace ahead. One common link was undoubtedly religion. Both men were Catholics and although neither paraded his faith before his less pious colleagues, they both observed their religion's more important conventions.

Nothing therefore could have emphasized more the change in McKenny's personality than his ceasing to attend Mass and Confession. In addition, he had started drinking heavily and, to Ross's secret hurt, begun showing a preference for his own company. The Scot's absence that evening was a result of this. An uncle of his, visiting Scarborough on business, had invited both men to have dinner with him. With McKenny having repeatedly rejected the invitation, Ross had been left with no option but to go alone.

To date this change in the Irishman had not affected his combat efficiency and so it had been noted by his fellow officers but no more. Adams, however, who had protective leanings towards the young aircrews, had made discreet enquiries of Ross, only to learn the Scot was as mystified as anyone at its cause. Inevitably rumours were beginning to circulate among the ground crews that McKenny was losing his nerve.

Two other officers shared the room. One was Sue Spencer, Adams' assistant Intelligence Officer, a willowy, graceful girl, gentle of disposition but highly efficient at her work. Her companion was Tony St. Claire, another of the squadron's pilots. St. Claire was sitting at the piano in the far corner of the room; the girl was standing at his elbow.

Adams was unashamedly envious of St. Claire. An ex-student of the Royal College of Music, the young pilot had been making a name for himself on the concert platform before the war had called him into service. He was unquestionably the handsomest man Adams had ever seen: tall and slim, with a Byronic head and an artist's hands. Waafs went faint at the knees at the sight of Tony St. Claire and yet he had eyes for no one but the girl at his side. In turn she showed a devotion to him that sometimes gave Adams nightmares. One of the girl's tasks was to help him de-brief the crews after an operation, which meant they shared together the excruciating wait before the surviving aircraft landed. In Adams' experience the girl's disciplined face had never betrayed her dread, nor had she ever expressed it to him, and yet to the sensitive Adams it seemed to fill every corner of the Nissen hut that served as his Intelligence office. The fact that Sue Spencer happened to be the kind of woman Adams' lonely nature admired did nothing to help him at such moments. Gentle, understanding, undemonstrative, she was the antithesis of the waspish and unsympathetic woman his wife had become.

As Adams paused in the doorway he saw Richardson was throwing hostile glances at McKenny. A man who needed company to fulfil himself, the Equipment Officer clearly resented the younger man's unsociability. Not wishing to disturb the couple at the piano and so forced to choose between lasciviousness and moodiness, Adams chose the latter and made towards McKenny. A black mongrel dog that had been sniffing at the Mess entrance padded after him across the stained carpet. Before the Rhine Maiden operation Adams had

24

promised to look after Harvey's dog if anything should happen to the Yorkshireman and by this time the lonely Adams had come to need the dog perhaps more than it needed him.

Contenting himself with an amiable nod at Richardson, Adams leaned against the bar at McKenny's elbow. His tone of false heartiness jarred him. "Hello, McKenny. So you haven't gone to the races with the others?"

Although clearly resenting the intrusion, the young pilot straightened himself. "No, sir. I'm not keen on horse racing."

The electric light glinted on Adams' spectacles as he nodded. "That makes two of us. And anyway I always lose." Seeing the barman waiting for his order, Adams glanced furtively at the Irishman's face. All the signs indicated he had drunk enough already and yet Adams did not see how he could deny him a round.

"I'll have a beer," he told Woods. Then: "What about you, McKenny? Do you want another?"

"I'd rather not if you don't mind, sir."

Although aware why his offer was refused, Adams felt relief. "I don't mind. It keeps my Mess bill down. Are you staying on for dinner?"

"I don't think so."

Adams proceeded cautiously. "You're going out, then?"

"No, sir."

Adams pulled out his pipe and knocked it against the bar. "From what I've heard it's not a bad meal tonight. Lamb, mint sauce, and all the trimmings." At the pilot's indifferent shrug, he went on: "What's wrong. You're not off colour, are you?"

The stare he received was decidedly hostile. "No, sir, I'm not. Why?"

Hiding his embarrassment, Adams began packing his pipe. "Isn't it the most obvious question when a man misses his meals?"

McKenny muttered something and turned towards the bar. "There's nothing wrong with me, sir."

Conscious he was making a hash of things and uncertain what to do next, Adams took refuge in a sip of beer. "I'm glad to hear it. How's that kite of yours? You've been having an engine problem, haven't you?"

The pilot's expression suggested that he could not care if the engine fell out of its mountings. "It keeps losing revs. Chiefy hasn't pin-pointed the trouble yet."

"It must be a tough one if Chiefy can't find it," Adams offered.

He received a morose nod. Adams had a last try. "I suppose you've heard that Squadron Leader Harvey is now convalescing."

"Yes, sir."

"With luck we ought to have him back with us in three or four weeks. The boys are planning quite a party."

There was no reply. Aware he had run out of conversation, Adams put a match to his pipe. The clouds of smoke he emitted brought a cough from Woods behind the counter and an injured glance. In the silence Adams heard the soft notes of the piano. Half-hidden in the shadowy corner of the room, St. Claire was playing a melody of singular beauty that Adams could not place. As he ceased playing Sue Spencer bent impulsively down and kissed his cheek. Richardson, also watching the couple, gave a grunt of disgust. Why, Adams thought, did men with minds as prurient as Richardson's always gibe at demonstrations of affection? He was turning back to McKenny when Sue caught sight of him and waved him to join them. Adams hesitated, then tapped McKenny's arm.

"Excuse me, will you? Sue wants a word with me."

The young Irishman had difficulty in hiding his relief. "Of course, sir."

Adams picked up his beer and crossed the room. The black mongrel, which had curled up at the foot of the bar, rose and padded after him. Sue, who was looking excited for one so disciplined, caught his arm and led him towards the piano. "I didn't see you come in. Have you been in long?"

"Only a few seconds," Adams lied.

"Why didn't you come over and join us?" Before Adams could reply, the girl went on: "Tony's just finished playing part of a concerto he's written. It's beautiful."

Adams waved the young pilot back into his seat. "I heard the last few bars of it. I'm impressed."

The girl, whose hand had been drawn back to the pianist's shoulder as if by a magnet, laughed happily. "You see! I told you." She turned back to Adams. "It's Teddy Young's birthday next Tuesday. I want Tony to play the concerto at the party the boys are giving him."

The handsome young officer glanced up at Adams, one eyebrow quizzically raised. "Can you imagine it, sir? A concerto at an aircrew party? She can't wait to get me drawn and quartered."

Perhaps because of his own complex nature, Adams found the mixture of art and masculinity in St. Claire one of the pianist's most attractive features. "It is chancing your arm a bit," he grinned. "And anyway, it sounds too good for those young barbarians. Why don't you give a recital to us more mature, more civilized types? It shouldn't be difficult to reserve the Mess for an hour or two one evening."

Sue showed her pleasure. "Would you do that?"

"Why not? We're the ones who'll enjoy it." Then Adams noticed St. Claire's expression. "That's if you're willing, of course."

"If you don't mind, sir, I'd rather not."

Sue gave a cry of disappointment. "Why?"

St. Claire lit a cigarette. "I'd rather not, darling. Just leave it there, will you?"

It was a refusal Adams understood and respected. While the young officer could not avoid using the Mess piano—his only opportunity to keep in practice—for him to have given a recital might have suggested to some men that he was parading his talent. To lighten the moment Adams bent down to pat the dog that was nuzzling his foot. Seeing an escape in his action, the girl took it without thinking. "I wonder how Sam will react when Harvey gets back."

"He'll do cartwheels and somersaults," Adams told her.

The sensitive girl was already regretting her words.

27

"He'll be glad to see him again, of course, but he's also grown very fond of you."

Hiding a sigh, Adams gave the dog a final pat and straightened. "No. We've got along all right but he's really a one-man dog. You'll see what I mean when Harvey appears."

A shout made all three of them look round. Richardson, whose resentment at his isolation had been growing by the minute, was staring with hostility at McKenny. "You! McKenny! What's the matter with you tonight?"

Adams noticed the young pilot had another drink in front of him. Sensing the danger, he gave the couple at the piano a warning look and crossed the floor. "How about a drink, Jack?"

The belligerent Equipment Officer gave him a scowl. "I've got a drink. I was talking to that toffee-nosed kid over there. Doesn't he know it's rude to stand in the Mess and ignore everybody?"

Adams kept his voice down. "He doesn't mean to be rude, Jack. Forget about it and have a drink with me."

Spoiling for trouble, the beefy Richardson pushed him aside. "I'm not having a bloody pilot officer ignore me. He needs a lesson in manners. McKenny, come over here!"

The pilot hesitated a moment. Then, face pale, he moved along the bar. "What do you want, sir?"

"You've been standing there over half an hour without saying a word to anyone. Don't you know that's bad manners?"

"I'm sorry, sir. It wasn't intentional."

"Wasn't intentional? I heard Squadron Leader Adams invite you to have a drink and you refused him. Yet the moment he walked away you ordered one yourself. What kind of behaviour do you call that?"

"It didn't worry me," Adams said. "In fact I never noticed it."

"Well, I did. And I don't like young kids being rude to senior officers." Richardson swung back on the pale McKenny. "You've been acting this way for weeks

28

now and drinking like a fish. For Christ's sake pull your socks up and start acting like a gentleman. Don't you realize that's what you're supposed to be?"

The Irishman stiffened. "Is that all—sir?"

His delayed use of the title was all that Richardson needed to turn hostility into outright aggression. "Don't try to be funny with me, McKenny, or you'll be in serious trouble!"

"I'm not being funny—sir."

Adams threw a fervent glance at the door, hoping against hope to see newcomers whose presence might break up the scene, but the Mess remained disturbingly empty. The hoarseness of Richardson's voice told he had lost his self-control. "Don't think I don't know what's wrong with you, McKenny. Just as everyone else on the station knows."

For a moment the wrought-up pilot looked puzzled. "I don't know what you're talking about."

"Come on, McKenny. You're a bad actor. But I suppose your nerves have something to do with that too."

Adams heard a gasp from the watching Sue. It was a sound that brought perception to McKenny. As he gave a violent start and took an agressive step forward, Adams seized his arm. "That's enough! We're going outside."

The young Irishman was deathly pale and breathing hard. Fearing he might be unable to restrain him, Adams felt relief as St. Claire ran up and grabbed his other arm. "Get a hold of yourself, Paddy," the pianist muttered. "Do as the Squadron Leader says."

For a moment it seemed McKenny might resist them both. Then he pulled away and made for the door. Giving Richardson an expressive look, Adams followed him.

They reached the path that led to the junior officers' billets before Adams, who was conscious his role so far had been an inept one, felt it was safe to speak. "He was half-drunk, you know. And he had no one to tell his filthy jokes to."

In the evening gloom the Irishman looked grim

and shocked. Although Adams felt fulminate of mercury would have been safer to handle, he tried again. "All the same, he was right in saying you haven't been yourself these last few weeks. Wouldn't you like to talk about it? I promise it won't go any further."

He received an aggressive glance. "What is it, sir? Have you got the same idea he has?"

"Of course I haven't," Adams protested. "But any fool can see something's bothering you. Sometimes it helps to talk. That's all I meant."

"It's not important enough to talk about, sir."

"But if it affects you so much, it must be important." Then, seeing the futility of argument, Adams compromised. "At least promise me one thing. If you do feel like having a chat about it, come and see me."

To his surprise McKenny halted. "There is one thing you can do for me if you want to help."

Adams felt gratification. "What's that?"

"You could try to get me some leave. Even a couple of days would be better than nothing."

Adams felt disappointed. "Have you put in an application?"

"Yes. And it's been rejected."

"Did you give a reason for requesting it?"

"No."

"There you are," Adams muttered. "No one can get special leave without a reason. If you'll give me one I'll have a talk with the Squadron Commander." The bitter glance he received made Adams frown. "I'm sorry but I didn't draw up the rules, McKenny."

"No, sir. May I go now?"

"I'm not stopping you. There is just one thing, though. I'd keep out of Richardson's way for a while if I were you."

McKenny was already walking away. "I tried to do that, sir, but it didn't help very much."

Adams opened his mouth, then desisted and watched the Irishman disappear into one of the wooden huts ahead. The complex Intelligence officer had long felt that men were the victims of their stars and those who tried to help them achieved little but disappointment. At the same time it was a hypothesis that in no way repressed his better instincts.

With a sigh he started back for the Mess, with Sam pattering somewhat mournfully after him. A late September fog was drifting in from the airfield and was already diffusing the dim lights of the Control Tower. Autumn was arriving early this year, Adams thought. In earlier wartime years he had tended to prefer autumn and winter, feeling that war in the gold of summer when the earth was burgeoning with its fruits was too monstrous a sacrilege. Tonight, however, with the damp fog settling down and the leaves dripping moisture, the combination of autumn and war seemed an unholy alliance.

He led Sam back to the Mess, only to pause again in the doorway when he saw how it had filled up during the last few minutes. With two general duty officers to share his jokes with, Richardson was now oozing bonhomie at the far side of the room. Another group of officers were clustered round the tall figure of Henderson. Driven from the piano by the invasion, St. Claire and Sue Spencer were lost in a world of their own by the window. As he watched them, Adams suddenly experienced a feeling of isolation. With a sigh he called Sam to heel and made his way towards his office.

## 5

The red telephone on Henderson's desk rang just before ten the following morning. Waving back his Waaf typist, the Scot picked up the receiver. The somewhat high-pitched voice that greeted him could have belonged to only one man. "Henderson? Listen! I was right about that fellow Lambert. They phoned here a few minutes ago to ask permission for him to visit you. When will suit you best? Today or tomorrow?"

31

Henderson was showing dismay. "If he has to come, today is better, I suppose."

"Then it'll probably have to be this afternoon. That O.K.?"

"Yes, sir. But what's he coming for?"

"How the hell do I know? Because you're one of our most famous units, I suppose."

Henderson glanced at the Waaf, who had resumed typing, and lowered his voice. "It couldn't be about this operation you're planning, could it?"

Davies' hesitation suggested he had asked himself the same question. "It's possible someone in Staines' outfit might have leaked it out. These Yankee Pressmen are powerful and this one's bound to have collaborators everywhere. But I wouldn't think it likely. So not a word unless he brings it up and even then play it canny."

"I can't be anything else seeing I don't know what it is, can I?"

"Then you're lucky," Davies said caustically. "You don't have to watch your tongue."

Henderson grimaced at the rebuke. "What do you want me to say to him?"

"Keep off politics. Just give him plenty of spiel about the squadron's achievements, stressing the Swartfjord and Ruhpolding raids." At times like this Davies could sound like a malicious elf. "Rub it in that if we hadn't destroyed that Rhine Maiden plant, the Yanks mightn't have an 8th Air Force left by this time. Then, when you've softened him up, show him round. Only keep him away from the SCI dump. We don't want him giving Jerry the impression we're about to drop mustard gas on him."

It was clear from Henderson's expression that he would rather face three Me.109s single-handed than the redoubtable Lambert. "Will you be able to get here, sir?"

"Not this afternoon. I'm meeting Staines. But you can cope. Give him plenty of bullshit: it's important he goes away impressed. And whenever you can, steer him towards the Mess. They say he likes tanking up and the more drinks the fewer questions he'll ask. All right?"

"Yes, I suppose so."

"For God's sake, cheer up, Jock. It's not the C.-in-C. visiting you." When Henderson did not answer, Davies went on: "There's one thing. If all goes well with Staines this afternoon, I shall want you all briefed and ready to go from the first light on Friday onwards. It's going to be one of those operations. So don't let your boys out on Thursday night. All right?"

"Yes, sir. Is that all?"

"All for the moment. I'll be in touch as soon as I get the all clear. In the meantime, good luck with Lambert."

Henderson replaced the receiver and sank somewhat heavily back into his chair. His Waaf sergeant, a healthy-looking country-bred girl from Dorset whose vital statistics were enough to make any middle-aged officer reflective, pulled a letter from her typewriter and laid it on a pile of others on his desk. "That's the lot, sir. Is there anything else you want?"

At any other time her question would have appealed to the Scot's sense of humour. Instead he nodded at a cabinet that stood near the girl's desk. "What's the whisky situation like?"

She opened the cabinet. "The bottle's almost empty sir."

"It is? Then be a good girl and slip along to the Mess for another, will you? I think I'm going to need it."

The Waaf smiled as she moved towards the door. "Are things as bad as that, sir?"

"They're a damn sight worse," Henderson said gloomily.

The billet door swung open, letting in a shaft of weak sunlight. The man who entered, freckle-faced and ginger-headed, was Bernard Ross, McKenny's navigator. Coming straight in from the morning sunlight he did not immediately notice the man lying on the bed.

"You in here, Paddy?"

McKenny rose reluctantly on one elbow. "Yes. What do you want?"

"Moore's buying the boys drinks to celebrate stand-down. Don't you think you ought to come over?"

McKenny dropped back on his pillow. "He won't miss me."

"He might. In any case it's a bit rude, isn't it?"

McKenny did not answer. Ross threw down a letter on the blanket that was covering the Irishman. "This came in the morning post."

McKenny sat up with a jerk. "Why the hell didn't you give it to me straight away?"

"I've only been in the billet ten seconds," Ross pointed out.

Tearing open the envelope, McKenny pulled out a single sheet of notepaper. As he began reading it, Ross tried again.

"Then what about going to Scarborough with us this afternoon? We might as well make the most of this stand-down: they'll probably change their minds tomorrow. We're doing a movie, then having a meal afterwards. Millburn says he'll find room for us in his jalopy."

Devouring the letter, McKenny showed no signs of hearing him. Although good-tempered by nature, Ross began to show irritation.

"You could answer me, couldn't you?"

When the Irishman still ignored him, the young navigator shrugged and made for the door. "All right; make yourself unpopular. Why should I care?"

A muffled curse as McKenny reached the end of the letter made him halt and turn. Seeing the Irishman crushing the letter in his hand, Ross approached his bed again. "What is it, Paddy? Bad news?"

McKenny's bitter eyes lifted up to him for a moment, then he sank back on his pillow. Seeking a way of reaching him, Ross gave a start. "It's nothing to do with that recent Baedeker raid, is it?"

It took a moment for his question to sink through the Irishman's misery. "What raid?"

"The one on Lincoln. I thought you knew about it."

"Was it a heavy one?"

"Nothing like we're handing out to Jerry. Only thirty or so kites. So I don't think you need worry too much about Joan or your sister."

To his surprise the Irishman was now looking excited as he swung his feet to the floor. "Are you sure about this?"

"Of course I'm sure. We're claiming five were shot down."

Cramming the letter into his pocket, McKenny slipped into his tunic. Ross watched him in bewilderment. "Are you coming to the Mess, then?"

The Irishman snatched his cap from a peg on the wall. "No. I'm having another go at getting a 24-hour pass."

"But I thought you'd just been turned down?"

"I have. But I'm going to try again."

Ross showed concern as McKenny tried to pass him. "You can't try twice in two days. You'll get all their backs up."

"Who cares about their backs? I want a pass."

Ross tried a last time before he was pushed roughly aside. "You know you won't get it. So why make trouble for yourself?"

There was no reply. McKenny was already outside and hurrying down the path that led to the Administration offices.

The large American staff car was already parked in the courtyard of the country house when Davies' more modest Hillman emerged from the tree-lined drive. The challenge the Air Commodore received at the entrance was his third since entering the estate. As the Hillman moved forward again and parked near the American car, a young lieutenant, waiting at the foot of an imposing flight of steps, hurried forward and snapped a salute at the emerging Davies.

"Good afternoon, sir. The Brigadier's in the library. General Staines is with him."

Nodding, Davies pulled his briefcase from the car and made for the steps. The young lieutenant, who had caught the eye of the Air Commodore's pretty Waaf

35

driver, hesitated a moment before following him. The Waaf lit herself a cigarette. In the world in which Lynne Barker moved, second lieutenants were ten a penny.

Davies reached the top of the steps and turned right along a terrace. As the courtyard fell back, lawns and flowerbeds appeared below him. Among the elms that surrounded the gardens, rooks were cawing angrily at a pigeon that had settled in their midst. Smoke from a bonfire gave the afternoon air the scent of autumn. A jackdaw, perched on one of the large flower pots that lined the terrace, watched his approach with bright, curious eyes. Its hop on to the wall as he drew level was its only concession to his presence. Davies' thoughts were quizzical as he heard the second lieutenant hurrying after him. Security at High Elms was so tight that even the birds felt safe.

The lieutenant led him down a panelled corridor patrolled by an M.P., tapped on a side door and opened it. "Air Commodore Davies is here, sir."

The room Davies entered was all hide-bound books, panelled walls and dark oak furniture. At the far end french windows gave a view over the terrace and gardens. As the lieutenant withdrew, Davies saw two men occupied the room. One of them, sitting at a long table that ran down the centre of the room, was wearing the uniform of an American Air Force General. Ed Staines had once played quarterback for West Point and it showed even today in his fifteen-stone, granite-hard body. Beneath spiky, iron-grey hair, he had a leathery face with bushy eyebrows and a solid chin. In one tobacco-stained hand he was holding an object that resembled a toy airship but in fact was a cigar.

The English Brigadier who was his companion could hardly have provided a sharper contrast. Elderly, slimly-built with a sensitive face and trimmed moustache, he had an appearance that was both military and distinguished. An Officer in Special Operations Executive, he had been working on and off with Davies ever since the Swartfjord raid in the spring of that same year. Although he was by nature a quiet, reserved man and Davies was nothing if not volatile and quick-tempered, the two men had discovered, secretly to their surprise, that their natures were complementary rather than conflicting and that they worked well together.

The Brigadier was approaching Davies with outstretched hand. "Hello, Davies. General Staines got here earlier than he expected, so I've been able to give him the outline of our plan."

Davies, whose last encounter with the American General had been during the Rhine Maiden affair, saluted, then took the huge hand that reached across the table to him. The American was grinning cordially. "Remember me, Davies? I'm the guy you conned into sending one hundred and fifty B.17s all the way to Bavaria to cover sixteen of your Mosquitoes."

Davies was heartened by the greeting. "You have to admit it was worth it, sir."

Staines dropped his bulk back into his chair. His gravelly voice had a strong Texan accent. "I think you can say that. If we had those rockets to contend with on top of our other problems, I'd be in the bread line by this time. Davies, where the hell are those Heinies getting their ships from? Every time we go over, there are more of the bastards."

The speed at which Staines moved on to this highly sensitive ground told Davies something of the big American's urgency and he chose his reply with care. "I suppose it's due to their policy of avoiding our fighter sweeps and conserving their strength until we penetrate into Germany itself."

"That's right. We haven't fighter escorts, so we get clobbered. And how we're getting clobbered. Do you know what our losses were on our last mission?" Although Davies nodded, the American told him regardless. "That's nearly a thirty per cent loss rate, Davies. And that's about it. We can't go on much longer until we get more B.17s or adequate fighter cover."

Davies gave a start. "You're not thinking of suspending operations, sir?"

"What goddam choice do we have?" Staines demanded. "No Air Force can take those kind of losses for long." As the shaken Davies dropped into a chair, the American went on: "You can see now why certain characters back home are asking why your Fighter Command, with its thousand of front-line ships, isn't giving us escort protection."

Uncertain of Staines' stance in the controversy, Davies prevaricated. "I take it you're referring to this campaign Lambert, the novelist, is leading, sir?"

The Texan scowled. "Who else? The sonofabitch saw some of our ships coming back from Munich and the articles he sent back to the States were almost hysterical."

Davies took heart from this attack on Lambert. "What can Leigh Mallory do? The Spitfire was designed for short-range defence, not escort duty."

The Brigadier was offering Staines another glass of whisky. The American nodded his acceptance before turning back to Davies. "No one's arguing about that. But we can't ignore public opinion back home. Everything's at stake here, including our allocation of B.17s. We haven't half enough already: we're going to get fewer if Congress decides they're throwing good money after bad. Don't forget we've a powerful body in the States who want us to concentrate on the Japs first, and this propaganda of Lambert's is playing right into their hands."

Although Davies seldom drank before dinner, he felt a need for the whisky the Brigadier was now offering him. "It's even more serious than I thought."

"You'd better believe it. It's turning into the kind of disillusionment that could spread throughout all the Services and even affect decisions in the White House itself. That's why I'm interested in this idea the Brigadier has put up to me. If you could pull it off, you'd be guaranteed the kind of publicity that would knock Lambert's campaign to hell."

Davies threw a delighted glance at the elderly Brigadier. "Then you're prepared to give us the green light?"

Staines's raised cigar checked him. "Not until you've cleared up two points for me. How are your boys going to escape detection on their way out? To me it looks damn nearly impossible."

38

"They're all specialists at low-level flying, sir. And don't forget they've already done it once."

"What do you mean—already done it?"

"When they bombed the servomechanism factory at Hoffenscheim. They'd be flying at least two-thirds of the way along the same track."

The Texan seemed about to say something, then shrugged instead. "All right. They'll be the ones who'll get clobbered if they're picked up. But what about my boys? What guarantee can you give that half of 'em won't be killed?"

Davies had already decided to make no rash promises. "Naturally we can't promise there'll be no casualties. For one thing we don't know what the German reaction will be. But my boys are experts at this kind of attack and we don't think the risks are very high."

Staines studied his face for a moment, then turned to the Brigadier. "Can we rely on your partisans?"

The Brigadier's quiet voice was an assurance in itself. "We've used them before, sir, and they've always proved trustworthy."

There was the sound of sandpaper on wood as Staines rubbed his chin. Then, giving a grunt of decision, he nodded at Davies. "All right, show me the nuts and bolts." As the delighted Davies dug into his briefcase and began pulling out photographs and statistics, the Texan checked him. "As you're doing this as much for our sakes as your own, let's get one thing straight. This is a political mission as well as a military one. Which means that if it turns out a shambles, Lambert will skin you, your squadron, and the entire RAF alive. As I've sanctioned it they'll probably have me shovelling snow for Christmas too, but at least I know what I'm doing."

Davies glanced at the silent Brigadier before answering. "We're aware of the risks, sir. But if you're prepared to take them, so must we. Without allowing things to get worse, I don't see what alternative we have."

Staines gave a grin of appreciation. "I'll order a couple of shovels, Davies, just in case. Now fill me in with the details."

## 6

The large American car halted outside the wicker gate. The driver, a young and loquacious G.I., turned in his seat. "The Black Swan. I guess this is the pub, sir."

His passenger, the bearded Lambert, was gazing at the old country inn alongside the road. Solidly built with white-washed walls and a grey slate roof, it was reached by two gravel paths, one leading through a garden to a private porch, the other to the saloon and public bars. A large crab apple tree, bearing its September fruit, stood just behind a picket fence.

The G.I. was grinning. "You know you won't get a drink? The Limeys have this crazy thing about licensing laws."

"I know." Climbing out, Lambert surveyed the airfield opposite. Hangars and the Control Tower could be seen over the long wooden fence that served as its perimeter. Fifty yards down the road a 25-cwt transport emerged from the main entrance, paused outside a sentry box, then accelerated towards Highgate. The autumn sun was already low in the sky and a sullen bank of cloud on the horizon hinted there would be fog again that night. Hiding a shiver, Lambert walked down the private path to the front porch. Finding the oaken door locked, he swung down a heavy iron knocker. About to knock a second time, he heard the sound of a bolt being withdrawn and a couple of seconds later a girl appeared in the doorway. "Good afternoon, sir. What do you want?"

Lambert's eyes flickered over her appreciatingly. She was a big handsome girl with bold features and dark hair. The sweater she was wearing and the short apron beneath it, drawn tightly round her waist, accentuated her large breasts. Seeing Lambert's interest, she lifted a hand and touched her hair. Maisie, the barmaid of the Black Swan, as generously natured as she was well-proportioned, was a girl whose feminine instincts were triggered automatically when a man entered her orbit. When one appeared with the flashes of an American war correspondent on his greatcoat, Maisie's reflexes were as acute as a seismograph.

"My name's Lambert," the correspondent told her. "Ernest Lambert. Are you Maisie?"

The girl looked surprised. "How do you know my name?"

"You were engaged once to a Canadian, weren't you? A pilot who won the VC."

Maisie's expression changed. It was only six months since Gillibrand had been killed defending the airfield and the reminder was still painful to her. Before she could reply Lambert nodded towards a field that lay alongside the inn. "You can still see scars in the stubble over there. Is that where he crashed?"

As the girl nodded there was a shout from inside the pub. "Who is it, Maisie?"

"An American," Maisie shouted back. "A war correspondent."

"A what?"

"An American war correspondent."

A man wearing braces and an open-necked shirt appeared in the hall and came to the girl's side. Joe Kearns, the genial owner of the inn and a friend of Adams, was in his middle fifties with a countryman's ruddy face and thinning white hair. He gazed curiously at the bearded Lambert. "What can we do for you, sir?"

In spite of being a New Englander, Lambert had never been able to take cold weather and was secretly cursing the chilly afternoon that no one appeared to be feeling but himself. "I'm visiting a few RAF stations. Can you spare me a few minutes?"

Pushing forward, Kearns saw the man's shoulder flashes. Although looking puzzled, he nodded. "I reckon so, sir. Come inside." He turned to Maisie. "Take him into the private lounge, lass, while I find my jacket."

The room Lambert entered had a mullioned window set in an alcove. The walls were oak-panelled and

41

blackened beams crossed a low, whitewashed ceiling. With shadows gathering in the corners and the thick stone walls defying noises from the airfield, the atmosphere was that of a bygone age. Lambert's nod expressed his approval.

"This is all I expected. How old is the inn?"

Maisie had all the indifference of her kind to her heritage. "I dunno. Hundreds of years, I suppose. Won't you sit down?"

Lambert settled into a high-backed chair and pulled out a packet of Camel cigarettes. "Will you have one?"

Maisie examined the packet as he offered it to her. "Gillie used to smoke these."

"Sit down and tell me about him."

Maisie accepted a light, then dropped somewhat reluctantly into a chair at the opposite side of the window recess. "What do you want to know?"

"Tell me how he won his VC."

"It was the morning the Jerries raided the camp. Gillie was waitin' to go on a met. flight and managed to get his plane off the ground. He shot down two, maybe three of 'em and then he must have run out of ammunition because he crashed into a Jerry who was goin' to bomb the Control Tower." The girl lowered her head and pretended to adjust a high-heeled shoe. "They both crashed into that field over there."

"He was alone in his ship, wasn't he?"

"His ship?"

"I mean his aircraft."

"Yes," Maisie muttered. "His regular navigator, Jimmie, had been killed a few days before, and he left his new one on the ground. I suppose he didn't want him killed as well. Not that it made any difference. He was killed later when they did the raid in Norway."

"That's how it's been for years, sir." The voice came from Kearns in the doorway, now wearing a tweed jacket with leather elbows. "We just get to know 'em and then they're killed. Sometimes you forget who's dead and who's alive."

"You must have known Grenville," Lambert said.

"Of course, sir. He's the squadron leader who led

42

the raid to Norway. He got the VC too, you know. Would you like a drink?"

The American saw Kearns had a glass in his hand. "I thought you English weren't supposed to serve drinks in the afternoon."

Kearns put the glass beside him. "We can't sell 'em, sir. But there's nothing to stop us giving one to a visitor."

Lambert discovered the drink was whisky. "Aren't you two joining me?"

"If it'll make you more comfortable, sir, we'll have a small one." Kearns glanced at Maisie. "I opened a new bottle, luv. You'll find it under the counter in the saloon."

With an inviting swirl of her skirt and a backward glance at Lambert, Maisie withdrew from the lounge. Lambert watched her go, then offered Kearns a Camel. The innkeeper shook his head. "No thanks, sir. I'm a pipe smoker myself."

Lambert's tone was casual as he put his cigarettes away. "I guess the boys use this pub as much as they use their Mess?"

"Yes, sir, I think they do. And we try to make 'em feel as much at home as we can."

"In other words you're almost one of the family?"

"That's one way of putting it, sir."

"So you must know as much about them as anybody?"

"I'm not quite sure I follow you."

"They come and drink here. So you'll hear both their private and professional problems."

Kearns, who for all his amiable exterior was nobody's fool, was instantly on his guard. "What we hear we forget, sir. It's wartime, you know."

A quick learner himself, Lambert realized he was not talking to some country pushover. "We have that problem in my job every day—what it's safe to publish and what we should hold back. So don't get me wrong. I don't want any state secrets but I'd appreciate one or two harmless stories for my newspaper."

"Is that why you're here, sir? To write about the squadron?"

Lambert lifted an eyebrow. "What else? 633 Squadron's a big name in the States. People can't read too much about it."

With his affection for the squadron on a par with Davies', Kearns was mollified by the flattery. At the same time he was too much of a Northcountryman to lower his guard that swiftly. "They deserve a bit of credit. I've never met a finer bunch of lads."

"Tell me about their new squadron commander. How do you reckon he stands up alongside Grenville?"

"Mr. Moore?" Kearns hesitated to find the right words. "He's a different man in one way and yet he's alike in another. If you know what I mean."

"I'm not sure I do."

"Well, Mr. Grenville was more forceful in his ways whereas Mr. Moore is quieter like. But from all I hear he's every bit as good a leader. The lads have come to think the world of him."

"He's got a bit of money behind him, hasn't he?"

Kearns was instantly on guard again. "I wouldn't know much about that, sir. All I know is he hasn't any side and treats everyone the same."

"What about Frank Harvey, the guy who was wounded bombing that ammo factory? Did you know him?"

The phrasing of Lambert's question was deliberate. With the need to hide from the public the Germans' lead in rocketry, the Allied Governments had instructed the Press and radio to describe the Rhine Maiden exploit as a raid on a huge enemy ammunition factory. Kearns, who because of his friendship with Adams knew more than he was supposed to know, was equally cautious in his reply. "Aye, we knew the lad well. He was one of us."

"One of you?"

"Aye. A Yorkshireman. His home isn't that far from here."

"What sort of a guy is he?"

"A big feller. Dour but as straight as a die. And a hard man to stop if he gets the bit into his teeth."

"Didn't he have a girl friend staying here?"

Kearns was wondering how much the war cor-

44

respondent knew. Anna Reinhardt, the German girl working for the Allies, had stayed a week in the Black Swan before returning to Europe to organize the Mosquito raid. The innkeeper decided the Yorkshire dictum of "when in doubt say nowt" was the wisest course.

"He might have had, sir. But plenty of lads bring their girl friends here."

An expert on interrogation, Lambert could see he was getting nowhere with the canny innkeeper. Downing his whiskey, he rose. "I'd like to stay longer but the C.O. might show me round the airfield today and there isn't that much light left. Can I have a room if I need one tonight?"

Maisie had just appeared in the doorway and answered for Kearns. "Yes; we're empty at the moment. Aren't we , Joe?"

Kearns could do nothing more than nod his head. At the front door the American turned to him. 'I"ll phone you from the airfield as soon as I know the score. In about an hour's time."

He gave a shiver as Maisie opened the door for him. "Is it always as cold around here in September?"

"We can get early winters," the innkeeper confessed. "This looks like being one of 'em."

Maisie watched the American climb into his car before withdrawing from the porch. Kearns frowned at her as she closed the door. "Why did you tell him we'd plenty of room? If he stays the night he's going to be asking us more questions."

Maisie shrugged. "So what? He's a war correspondent, isn't he? What can we tell him he can't find out somewhere else?"

Kearns was wondering at his unease. "I don't know. But be careful what you say to him until I've had a word with Frank Adams."

Back on the road the G.I. had reversed the car and driven through the station gates to the guardroom. As a young S.P. conferred with him, an enormous shout made a nearby puppy drop its tail and run for its life. A massive middle-aged sergeant had emerged from the guardroom and was making towards the car. "You, lad! What do you think you're doing?"

The young S.P. stiffened and turned an embarrassed face. "It's the American war correspondent, sergeant?"

"And you're telling him how you're winning the war, are you? Get back to your duties, lad, and leave this to your betters."

As the red-faced youngster backed away, the sergeant bent down to the driver's window and pointed at a gravel strip opposite. "That's where you park, lad. You can wait there while I take your gaffer to the C.O." Turning, he threw open Lambert's door. "Mr. Lambert, sir?"

Lambert's bearded face gazed out. "Yes, sergeant."

"The C.O.'s expecting you, sir. Follow me, please."

Curious eyes followed the two men as Lambert obeyed. Six feet three inches tall, without one speck of mud on his white gaiters and polished boots, the sergeant was a figure straight from the War Manual. Behind him the forty-six-year-old Lambert, at least nine inches shorter, was finding his hairy-chested image suffering from the contrast. In an instinctive effort to compensate, he was walking with longer strides than usual, with his iron-grey beard thrust forward like a cow-catcher of a Western locomotive.

The sergeant marched off the road, opened a door, and stood like a granite statue while Lambert passed through. The N.C.O. then led the way down the corridor, the impact of his boots bringing Lambert visions of typewriters leaping into the hands of startled Waafs. His rat-tat-tat on the C.O.'s door sounded like a burst of machine-gun fire. A second later he threw the door open, whipped up a salute like a karate chop, and made his announcement.

"Mr. Lambert—sir!"

Henderson, who seemed singularly unruffled by this display of military efficiency, rose from his desk and came forward. "Thank you, sergeant. Please come in, sir."

The impassive S.P. whipped up another salute and vanished. Shaking hands with Lambert, Henderson closed the door. "Welcome to Sutton Craddock. Shall I take your coat?"

46

Lambert's eyes were on the small coke stove that served to heat Henderson's office. With fuel in short supply at this stage of the war, general orders forbade fires until October 1st and the Scot was not one to steal a march on his men. "No, thanks, Group Captain. I'll stay put for a while."

Henderson drew up a chair for him. "Would you like a cup of tea?" Then, remembering. "Or a cup of coffee?"

Lambert hid another shiver. "Make mine coffee."

Henderson opened the ante-room door. "Get us a couple of coffees, will you, Laura?" He glanced over his shoulder. "Black or white?"

"Black and strong," Lambert told him. His gaze followed the big Scot as Henderson returned to his seat behind the desk. With Americans generally the taller of the two races and yet with the first men he had encountered at Sutton Craddock both dwarfing him, Lambert felt it was not one of his better days. Shaking his head at the cigarettes the Scot was offering him, he pulled out his pack of Camels. "I like 'em toasted. You care for one?"

Henderson reached out amiably. "It'll make a change. We used to get these in our Mess at one time but they seem to have dried up recently."

As the men lit their cigarettes they took the opportunity to size one another up. Too goddam easy-going like so many of the other Limey's he had met, was Lambert's assessment. And this was supposed to be one of their crack units. When the hell were they going into top gear? Or hadn't they got a top gear?"

Henderson's impression was even less favourable. A professional airman, he had found it distasteful that a civilian should have the power to investigate and criticize the force he served in. That the investigator should also be a foreigner and a scribbler of fiction to boot seemed the final insult to the Scot. Although conscious of his prejudice, he liked neither the man's aggressive manner nor his somewhat protuberant eyes. As for his untrimmed hair and beard, the clean-shaven Scot decided they epitomized the undisciplined Press world from whence he came.

The smoke both men exhaled suggested a certain satisfaction with the assessments. Lambert moved his gaze round the austere office with its large wall map of Europe, its charts, graphs, and photographs of aircraft and airmen. "So this is the unit that received a special commendation from Congress! That doesn't happen every day of the week."

Henderson was wondering if there was any irony in the abrasive New England voice. "We're aware of that. Naturally it's something we're very proud of."

"They gave you a lot of coverage in the States. More in fact than they gave our own boys. Did you know that?"

"No, I didn't. If it's true your Press were at fault. It was a joint operation and we certainly appreciate the help your boys gave us that day."

The correspondent gave his characteristically impatient nod. "What are your views on those rockets, Henderson? Were they the menace they were made out to be?"

Henderson shrugged. "I can only go on what the boffins say. According to them no daylight formation would have stood a chance once they were in full protection."

"You think they'd have done more damage than their fighters are doing now?"

It was a question that reminded Henderson he was dealing with a professional interrogator, and he proceeded cautiously. "I'd say a great deal more. They would also have left Jerry's fighter force intact for the invasion when it comes."

The correspondent leaned forward. "Do you know what I find particularly interesting about the Rhine Maiden mission, Henderson?"

"No. What?"

"I'm fascinated by the escort job you did on our B.17s on their way back. All the crews I've spoken to said if you hadn't given them fighter cover until they reached our Thunderbolts, their casualties would have been twice as high."

Henderson almost relaxed his vigilance. "It's generous of them to say so. But then we've always had good relations with your aircrews."

With his victim lured over the trap, Lambert pulled the trip lever. "I'm sure you have. But it does raise a question a lot of folks back home are asking. If your unit was able to give such effective fighter cover on the Rhine Maiden job, why can't it be done more often? The Mosquito is in full production now and you're getting more and more squadrons equipped with them."

Annoyed at the way he had been trapped, the Scot almost over-reacted. "That's just what amateurs would think. Made of wood as she is, the Mosquito is something of a miracle plane but her main strengths are her speed and her high-altitude performance. If she had to take on German fighters in daylight at the altitude your B.17s fly at, she'd be at a disadvantage, particularly if she had to carry auxiliary tanks."

For one so aggressive, Lambert was looking almost bland. "And yet I've got dozens of witnesses who say she was a match for the Heinies over Bavaria."

It was not like Henderson to brag about his squadron but the moment seemed to call for it. "You're forgetting this is one of the RAF's specialist units. Many of my boys are on their second tour of operations and some are on their third. That's the reason they did so well."

"Couldn't other squadrons receive the same training?"

"It's not just training—it's experience. And experienced men are in short supply. Most die before they can get it."

"So you don't think Mosquitoes are the answer to the losses our boys are suffering?"

"I'm sure they're not," Henderson said bluntly. "What you want is a long-range, single-seater fighter that can go all the way there and all the way back. Failing that you need more Forts in your formation to increase your fire power."

Lambert's smile was innocuity itself. "I see you're quite a strategist."

Henderson knew he ought not to retaliate but the

49

temptation was too great. "Aren't we all? At least I've got the excuse that flying is my business."

It was the moment when the Waaf sergeant brought in the coffee and for that Henderson blessed her. "Thanks, Laura." Guiltily remembering Davies' orders not to get involved in arguments, Henderson hastened to his cupboard and brought out the new bottle of Scotch. "What about a shot to keep out the cold?"

Lambert shrugged. "Why not?"

Somewhat surprised the correspondent was showing no rancour, the Scot poured a generous shot into both cups. "If you want to take a look round the station, we'd better start in a few minutes or it'll be too dark."

Lambert picked up his cup. "Is it all right with you if we go round tomorrow?"

Henderson stared, dismayed. "Are you staying overnight?"

"I can't very well get back to London tonight, can I?"

The Scot recovered with an effort. "No, I suppose not. All right, let's do that. Do you want us to find you a billet now or later?"

With an eye on the empty stove, Lambert reacted quickly. "There's no need. I'm staying in that pub across the road, the Black Swan." Before the Scot could show his surprise, the American went on: "If it's O.K. with you, I'd like to attend your briefings tomorrow. What missions have you lined up?"

The embarrassed Henderson felt aggrieved that Davies was not there to handle his own chickens. "I'm afraid that won't be possible. We're on stand-down at the moment."

The correspondent stared at him. "Stand-down? I thought things were at crisis point right now?"

"We only got the order yesterday." Unable to give the true reason, the pink-cheeked Henderson could only curse inwardly at the flaccid excuse he had to make. "They must have decided the boys needed a rest. They're been on maximum effort for nearly a month."

Lambert's silence seemed to say it all. Fumbling inside his greatcoat he pulled out a notebook. "I'm told you've got an American pilot on your establishment. A guy called Millburn."

"That's right. He's acting as flight commander at the moment. He's one of our best men."

"I'd like a talk with him. Can you arrange it?"

"Yes. In any case you'll probably see him in the Mess tonight." A malicious vision that embraced violent aerobatics and air-sickness brightened Henderson's expression. "If you'd like to take a closer look at the Mosquito, why don't you ask Millburn to take you up? I can't think of anyone who could demonstrate its performance better."

## 7

Condensation gave the carriage window the texture of frosted glass. McKenny felt its chill as he rubbed it with the palm of his hand. The autumn evening was almost over and night was settling over the flat Lincolnshire fields. The train rattled over a bridge and the young pilot caught sight of a car with blinkered headlights passing along a road below. A solitary house with darkened windows swept past. Then the fields returned with their trees and fog-shrouded hedges.

McKenny blamed the shiver that ran through him on the unheated train. With rolling stock neglected by the demands of war, its progress suggested that the driver was afraid that any higher speed than 20 m.p.h. would result in its disintegration. To the young Irishman, whose failure to keep the appointment he had made for that evening would mean the waste of his hard-won leave, the dragging minutes were torture. As the train halted for the umpteenth time at a country station, he forgot the elderly couple sharing the compartment and muttered a curse. Glancing round, he saw

51

neither the man nor the woman had taken any notice of him. Grey-haired, tired-faced, both looked too occupied with their own problems.

The clatter of boots made him turn back to the window. A sizeable party of American airmen, hellbent for a night out in Lincoln, had burst into the dimly-lit station and were boarding the train. Half a dozen of them clustered outside his door, then saw the elderly couple and moved into the next compartment. As the hiss of steam quickened he could hear their voices and laughter. Their gaiety seemed to mock him and he huddled deeper into his greatcoat.

It was another half hour before the train pulled into Lincoln. Grip in hand, McKenny was waiting at a door and leapt down to the platform before the train stopped moving. Even so a party of Americans were first at the barrier and before he reached the taxi rank every cab had gone. A big American top sergeant left behind gave a friendly grin. "Hard luck, bud! But it's always this way on pay days."

McKenny realized now that he was going to be late no matter what happened. Fighting back panic, he lowered his grip to the pavement. The light had long gone and wisps of fog were drifting into the forecourt. The American gave a shiver. "Jesus, it's raw. Why the hell had they to post me to a dump like this?"

McKenny was watching the fog and wondering if it would add to his problems. The American, who by this time had recognized his gaffe as well as McKenny's rank, tried to make amends by offering him a cigarette. "This your home town, sir?"

Behind McKenny a dozen other Americans were assembling.

"No," he muttered. "I'm Irish. My sister lives here."

The sergeant relaxed. "They told me it didn't start getting cold in these parts before October or November. So what's wrong this year?"

McKenny sucked in smoke. "It happens this way sometimes. It could warm up again in October or it could be an early winter."

"Jesus, I hope it warms up. I come from New Mexico and . . ."

To McKenny's relief a taxi entered the forecourt. "Maybe we can share," the American offered. "Which way are you going?"

"The Western Hospital."

"Is that near the American Services Club?"

The Irishman thanked God. "It's on the way."

"Then jump in and let's go."

The taxi drew away. With the recent raid having enforced a blackout, traffic was at a crawl. The American noticed the glances McKenny kept giving his watch. "Does your sister work in the hospital, sir?"

The pilot's voice was curt. "No. I'm seeing her later."

About to ask a further question, the American noticed his expression and gazed out of the window instead. Five minutes later the taxi halted and the driver glanced back. "Is this all right, sir, or do you want to go inside?"

McKenny saw the taxi standing outside the hospital entrance. Dragging out his grip, he began fishing into his pockets for money. The distant sound of traffic was muffled by the settling fog. His urgency made the good-natured American tap the driver's shoulder. "I'll see to it, bud."

Thanking him, McKenny ran across the road to a pub that stood on a street corner. Pushing aside a blackout curtain he entered a large saloon bar with a long counter and glass-partitioned alcoves. Girls and servicemen, many of them Americans from East Anglian bomber bases, packed the floor and clamoured for drinks at the bar. The alcoves with their leather window seats were occupied by civilians, most of them elderly.

The impact of glare, smoke and noise halted the Irishman for a second before he started forward. To his relief he caught sight of the girl when he was halfway across the bar. Wearing the uniform and cape of a staff nurse, she was sitting in one of the alcoves with her back to a window. As McKenny struggled towards her a young American corporal, with a crew cut and a face like a newly-picked apple, left his grinning friends and edged by an elderly couple into her alcove. The girl's reply to his invitation was a smile and a shake of her head. When the American's second attempt failed he grinned bashfully and returned to the bar.

The youngster's friends were chaffing him as McKenny pushed past. By this time the girl had seen him and her look of relief matched his own. "Thank God," he muttered, bending down to kiss her. "I was afraid you might have given up by this time and gone back."

"What happened?" she asked.

With a groan he dropped alongside her. "Nothing really. Just the damn train took twice as long to get here than it should."

"You're looking thinner," she said. "And very tired."

His gaze was devouring her, moving from her short dark hair to her large expressive eyes, and down to her shapely mouth. McKenny, who was as deeply in love as a man can be, had long ago decided he would never anywhere see another girl as beautiful as Joan Williamson.

"I was afraid I was going to miss you," he muttered. "How long can you stay?"

"Only until nine. It was difficult enough to get an hour off at such short notice."

"I couldn't phone you earlier—I only got the 24-hour pass this morning. And then I had to use the excuse I was worried about my sister."

"How is she?"

It was a measure of McKenny's infatuation for the girl that he had hardly given a second thought to his sister during the journey. "Haven't you phoned her to find out?" she asked when he did not answer.

"She's not on the phone," he muttered.

"Couldn't you have phoned one of her neighbours?"

He shifted guiltily on the window seat. With the minutes as precious as jewels, his love begrudged every moment spent on anything but their problem. "Can't you stay until ten?" he urged. "Surely the girls would cover up for you."

"I can't, Paddy. We're hopelessly under-staffed and we've got air raid casualties and casualties from the bomber bases as well as our normal intake. We're working fourteen and sometimes sixteen hours a day. So how can I take another hour off?"

"You can't or you won't?" he asked bitterly.

"That isn't fair, Paddy."

"Why isn't it fair? I'm as sorry as the next man for those poor devils over there but I don't think a bit of feeling for me would come amiss. I'm in the Forces and I bleed too, you know."

Her dark head lowered. "I know how hard all this is for you. And I'm desperately sorry."

"I don't think you do know. I happen to be so much in love with you that the stinking world isn't going to be worth living in if I lose you."

In a world at peace she would have chided him for self-pity. In a world at war, with him in one of its most dangerous occupations, she could feel nothing but apprehension. "You mustn't talk like that."

"Why not? Don't tell me you care."

"Of course I care. I care very much."

"You've a strange way of caring, haven't you? Is it true what you said in the letter I received this morning? That you're going overseas soon?"

She gave a hesitant nod. "Yes. We hope to leave sometime in the middle of November."

His exclamation drew the attention of the elderly couple at the far side of the table. "You *hope* to leave. And yet you've just been telling me about all the casualties you're getting in. What are you trying to do? Escape?"

Her eyes lifted. "You can't believe that of me."

"How the hell do I know what to believe? When we got engaged six months ago you told me you'd never been so happy in your life. Now you can't get away from me fast enough. What have I done? I've hardly seen you in that time."

"How often must I tell you that you haven't done anything? I can't help what has happened to me. I've even tried to fight it but it's no use."

There was a torment in his bitterness that made

her wince. "So I have to be dumped like a load of ballast. My Christ, it turns you people callous. You don't give a damn what you do to people who love you."

Before she could protest a middle-aged couple pushed past, forcing both of them to their feet. When they dropped back she fumbled for his hand beneath the table. "It has nothing to do with you, Paddy. You must believe that."

When he did not answer she saw he was staring down at her hand that no longer wore his ring. At his look her voice broke. "What else could I do? I can't let you go on hoping. It's too cruel."

He snatched his hand away. "Cruel? What do you think this is?" Pain made him want to hurt her as he was hurt. "Do you know what I think? You're not satisfied to be like the rest of us, doing our small bit to win the war. You have to be the Lady with the Lamp, shining it through Darkest Africa. Have you ever thought of that?"

The girl turned pale. Alongside her the middle-aged woman nudged her husband to listen. "I know how it must seem to you. But that's the problem. Until one's had the experience it is difficult to understand."

There was no reaching him in his bitterness. "You couldn't put it better. You're something special now. I'm just one of the cattle who isn't worth a damn to anyone."

For a moment she showed anger. "That's a wicked thing to say. You're just as important as I am. Perhaps much more important."

"Who to?" he sneered. "God?"

She flinched. "Don't talk like that, Paddy."

"Why not? It's a fair question, isn't it?"

She tried to catch hold of his hand again. "Talk to your priest about it. Why didn't we think of that before? Tell him everything and I'm sure he'll make you understand."

His laugh sounded like a file on metal. "That old hypocrite? All he'll give me is a mouthful of cant. Anyway, what makes you think I still go to Church?"

"You haven't stopped going?"

"Of course I've stopped. I haven't been since you gave me my cards."

She was showing more distress than she had shown all evening. "You mustn't do that, Paddy. You were brought up in the Church. You need it more than people over here."

His eyes burned at her out of his dark, embittered face. "If you do this to me I shall never go near the Church again. Never!"

Her voice dropped into a whisper. "That's blackmail, Paddy."

"If it's blackmail, it's what you're doing to me."

"Speak to your priest," she begged. "At least try it."

He saw he had found a way of hurting her. "Since when do you go to enemies for help?"

A shudder ran through her. "Don't talk that way, Paddy. Please don't talk that way."

"Why not?" he jeered. "Are you afraid a thunder-bolt might strike me down?"

She rose to her feet. "I'm going to get you a drink. Wait here for me."

He pulled her down. "I don't want a drink. I want you to postpone that trip until you can see things more clearly. It's only a few months' delay. You can always go next year."

Biting her lip, she allowed her eyes to touch the clock over the bar. Instantly he leapt to his feet. "You can't get away from me fast enough, can you? Come on then—let's get it over!"

Turning, he pushed his way through the crowd of servicemen. The middle-aged woman, her face alight with vicarious excitment, leaned towards her husband as the girl ran after him. "Paddy, please! Don't run off like this!"

He halted only when they were outside in the dark street. Two slow-moving cars went past with a hiss of tyres, then there was only the muffled murmur of traffic in the city centre. She hesitated a moment, then pulled him round to face her. "Keep quiet and listen to me for a moment. You're wrong in thinking I don't want to marry you. I know you'd make me happy and I've always wanted children. That's why this is the hardest thing. . . ."

It was a mistake. Before she could finish his arms were around her, crushing her as if to fuse flesh against flesh. "Then let's get married right away. I'll make the arrangements as soon as I get back."

Relief made his words brittle. "God, you've had me frightened these last few weeks. Don't frighten me like that again."

Voices sounded behind them as the pub door opened. A soldier and a girl, their arms wrapped round one another, walked past. Watching them go over his shoulder, she knew that if she lived a hundred years nothing would be harder to say.

"You didn't let me finish, Paddy. I have to go through with this. I have to because it's so much stronger than I am. Won't you try to understand and not think badly of me?"

She felt she had driven a knife into his unguarded body. The white blur of his face stared at her, then he pushed her roughly away and started down the road. In the distance the cathedral clock was chiming the hour. Frantic for his safety, she ran after him. "You can't just walk away like this. First you have to promise to take care of yourself. And you mustn't give up the Church. Please promise me you won't."

He snatched his arm away. She knew the look he gave her would haunt her for the rest of her life. Sobbing, she followed him. "Now you're being cruel. How can I help what has happened? Paddy, please! Say something."

Hands driven into his greatcoat pockets, he was walking faster and faster. She ran another dozen yards after him, then halted. Behind her there was laughter as a party of servicemen filed out of the pub. As they moved in the opposite direction she realized the clock had stopped chiming. Ahead of her McKenny had not looked back and was beginning to merge in to the dark shadows that lay across the pavement. She watched him a moment longer and then turned away. Her young face looked blinded with grief as she crossed the road and walked towards the hospital entrance.

---

# 8

Henderson was chatting to Adams and Lambert in the Mess when he saw Millburn enter. Leaving Adams to hold the fort for a moment, he walked over to the American pilot and lowered his voice. "Remember what I told you. Watch what you say."

The tousle-haired Millburn grinned. "Take it easy, sir. In a couple of days they'll be featuring us on the cover of *Time* magazine."

Henderson was in no mood for jokes about Pressmen and publicity. "The only pictures he's likely to publish are you lot clustered round the bar downing double Scotches. So don't go getting dreams of glory."

He led the American to the bar. "Lambert, this is Millburn, my American flight commander that you asked to meet."

Lambert held out a hand. "Glad to meet you, Millburn." He indicated the ribbons of the DSO and DFC on Millburn's chest. "It looks as if the British are taking good care of you."

Millburn squinted down at the ribbons and grinned. "We play poker for these. And I'm the best poker player on the squadron."

Henderson scowled and intervened. "I hate to say it but he did win them the hard way. Mind you, if he had ribbons for the women he's laid he'd look like an American general."

Adams winced at the gaffe. Wondering what masochistic kink in his subconscious had let the words loose, Henderson did his best to make amends.

"It gets a bit expensive in pregnant Waafs. At the same time, if you were to offer me a half a dozen

more Americans like him I'd think it fair exchange."
When Lambert made no comment, Henderson gave it
up and made for his whisky that was standing on the
bar. After conferring a moment with Millburn, Lambert turned to the Scot. "You don't mind my having a
private word with him, do you?"

Henderson motioned Adams towards him. "No, go
ahead. You can use my office if you like."

Declining the offer, Lambert led Millburn away
from the bar and pulled a couple of cigars from his bat-
tledress pocket. "Havanas! I picked up a box yesterday."

Millburn shrugged and took one. "You been over
here long?"

"Three weeks. Ten days in London and the rest of
the time at our bomber bases in East Anglia. It's murder
down there, Millburn. We're getting shot to hell."

"Yeah," Millburn muttered. "We've heard about
it."

"They've got to have the same fighter protection
you gave Staines' bombardment group down in Bavaria.
If you could do it, why can't other Mosquito squadrons?"

Millburn's spontaneity owed nothing to the few
words Henderson had slipped to him earlier. "It's a
long range fighter's job. There's no other answer."

"And yet you held them off. Why?"

Millburn had no effete English inhibitions about
singing his unit's praise. "Because the boys here are the
best in the business. Haven't you done your home-
work?"

"Is that why you haven't moved over to the
Yanks?"

The directness of the question made Millburn
frown. "I don't know. I haven't thought about it."

"What else could it be?"

"Maybe I like the girls here!"

"Don't make a joke of it, for Christ's sake."

"What do you want me to say? That I make more
money here?"

O.K. I'll spell it out to you. You've got years of
60

combat experience. You ought to be giving the fruits of that experience to your own country. Period."

The hot-tempered Millburn was showing resentment. "What difference does it make? We're fighting the same enemy, aren't we?"

"That's not an answer and you know it."

"Why do I have to give you an answer? I've nothing against my own guys: they're doing a great job. But I've been over here nearly three years and a man makes friends in that time. Anyway, what would I do on a heavy bomber unit? I'd be a fish out of water in a B.17."

"You might get more respect in one," the correspondent said dryly.

Millburn's black eyebrows came together. "What does that mean?"

"There's a strong feeling back home that the RAF isn't doing all it could to protect our boys. As a member of the RAF you have to share that blame."

"Blame? This is the outfit that destroyed the Rhine Maiden plant and got a Congressional commendation. You forgotten that?"

"That was an isolated incident. In general the British don't appear concerned about our losses. In fact some of us believe they're not sorry."

"Not sorry?"

"That's right. It helps them to argue their night bombing policy is the correct one."

Millburn was beginning to breathe hard. "That's the biggest load of bullshit I've heard in years. Everyone here is as concerned as hell for our boys."

"All the same, that's what's being said in the States. From the top downwards."

Obeying Henderson in his own way until this moment, Millburn broke free of the leash. "If it is, you're one of the guys who's handing out the poison. I've heard all about you, Lambert. You're the sonofabitch who's trying to split the Allies down the centre and give the Heinies the war on a plate."

All conversation in the Mess ceased as men turned to stare at the incensed Millburn. Henderson, who had been keeping an anxious eye on him during the dialogue gave Adams a horrified glance and hurried forward. "What's all the shouting about, Millburn?"

The American was too irate to mince his words. "Nothing, sir. I just hadn't met a Fifth Columnist before, that's all."

Henderson's shocked face was a study of emotions. Half of him wanted to kiss the American on both cheeks and pin another medal on his chest; the other half was trying to imagine Davies' reaction if news of the incident reached him.

"You gone out of your mind, Millburn? Mr. Lambert is a guest of the squadron. I want an apology immediately. And it had better be good."

To the Scot's surprise, the bearded correspondent shook his head. "Forget the apology, Henderson. I represent the free Press. That means any man's entitled to his views."

Henderson damned his need for gratitude. "That's very generous of you, sir." He glared back at Millburn. "In that case you'd better go to your billet and get your good manners back. Bloody disgraceful behaviour!"

Still angry, Millburn made for the door. Hesitating a moment, the Scot followed and caught him outside. "What the hell are you trying to do, Millburn? Get us drawn and quartered over there?"

"Didn't you hear him?" the American demanded. "He thinks we're glad when the Yanks have heavy losses."

"He's not going to change his mind if we accuse him of being a Fifth Columnist, is he?" Henderson grunted. "Pull yourself together. Things are bad enough as they are."

Millburn relaxed as his temper cooled. "I'm sorry, sir. But no guy should say things like that."

Henderson felt a grin coming, battled hard, but it broke through. "There's one good thing. Being a Yank yourself, he can't say it's Limey prejudice. But no more arguments with him, Millburn, or I'll bounce you all the way to East Anglia!"

Davies came on the telephone next morning while Henderson was showing Lambert round the airfield. Leaving the correspondent in Adams' care, the relieved Scot jumped into the jeep sent for him and was in his office four minutes later.

"Hello, sir. Sorry to have kept you waiting but I was out on the airfield with Lambert."

Davies' voice was full of suppressed excitement. "He arrived, did he? How are you getting on with him?"

"Not too badly, I suppose. Although in one way it's a pity we're on stand-down. I've the feeling he thinks we're a pack of scroungers."

Davies could contain his news no longer. "He won't be thinking that for long, Jock. The job's on tomorrow morning. I got clearance from Intelligence ten minutes ago."

The Scot felt his pulse quickening. "Do I cancel all passes, sir?"

"Yes. And make sure any lads who're already out are back by 18.00 hours. I'll want your senior officers this afternoon. We'll also need the advice of your armament officer on what stores to carry."

"What about Lambert? He's sure to want to attend."

Davies' grunt betrayed how his decision hurt. "Seeing one purpose of the exercise is to move public opinion in the States I suppose he has to be. All right, Jock, let him come. But don't let him leave the station afterwards. He's subject to the same security regulations as the rest of you."

"What time can we expect you, sir?"

"I'm waiting for the last of the photographs and then I'm on my way. Say around 15.00 hours."

In fact Davies arrived half an hour earlier. Henderson escorted him to the Operation Room where his senior offices were assembled. Among them were Moore, Teddy Young and Millburn. Lambert, more curious than anyone, was talking to Adams when the two men appeared. Waving everyone closer, Davies climbed on to the platform that stood beneath the huge

63

map of Europe. The two red spots high up on his cheeks told those who knew him he was more than usually excited.

"Good afternoon, gentlemen. I've called you to this preliminary briefing because I've got a rather special operation for you tomorrow." For a moment Davies' eyes rested on Lambert before sweeping round the arc of curious faces. "It won't be news to you that our American colleagues have been suffering heavy casualties in recent months on their deep penetration raids into Germany. They've stuck at the job with all the guts in the world but without fighter escorts their losses have been frightening. Last week alone they lost over four hundred men." As somebody whistled Davies nodded grimly. "It doesn't take long to run up that score when every B.17 carries a crew of ten. We wish to Christ we could help them but the only fighter capable of escorting them is the Mustang and until enough of them get the Merlin engine, the Yanks are having to go it alone."

With that punch delivered at Lambert, Davies changed his tone. "However, there are more ways of killing the cat than shooting it. Our agents in France tell us that it's Jerry's practice these days to take all aircrew prisoners shot down in northern Europe to a special compound north of Paris where they've assembled a team of interrogation experts. Because this interrogation is very thorough, men are sometimes kept there for weeks. When they are finally released they're shipped away by special train to prison camps deep in Germany or Poland. Some of these trains carry two or three hundred prisoners." Seeing Lambert give a start, Davies gave his imp-like grin. "That's right, gentlemen. We're going to give one of these trains our special attention."

Taking a pointer from the desk, he moved to the large map of Europe. "Our agents in France informed us about this compound and the trains six weeks ago. When we expressed interest they began a detailed surveillance. All the trains so far have taken this route, Noyon to Guise, then through the Ardennes to Liége, Aachen, and so into Germany. We believe they're using this secondary route because of the attention our fight-

64

er-bombers are giving to the main-line tracks. We've now been informed the largest shipment of prisoners to date is moving out tomorrow. So this is your mission. To halt and disable this train so that a large band of partisans assembled close by will be able to free the prisoners and through their escape network help them to return to this country."

A buzz of excitement filled the room as Davies walked back to the desk and picked up a pile of photographs. "I want you to pass these round. They were taken by our agents of the stretch of line where your attack will take place, a valley deep in the Ardennes. We've chosen it because the Ardennes is both mountainous and heavily-wooded: ideal country for an ambush and an escape because communications are relatively poor." He passed the first photograph to Henderson. "You'll see the stretch of line ends in a tunnel. Two flak posts guard it. Your first job is to knock out these posts so that the partisans can block the tunnel with explosives without incurring too heavy casualties. Then, when the train is forced to halt, you'll disable the engine and knock out the flak wagons that protect it. Once you've done this the partisans will break open the wagons and with any luck get the prisoners well away before Jerry can react. As the partisans are bringing transport with them, we're hoping this shouldn't be too difficult. Any questions so far?"

There was a short silence as the photographs changed hands. Millburn was studying a blurred, long-range photograph of a train. "What's the armament on these trains, sir? Do you know?"

"LMGs and 37mms," Davies told him. "One wagon in the front and one in the rear."

"No 88s?"

"No."

Moore and Young were conferring. A few seconds later the squadron commander's quiet voice stilled the buzz of conversation. "It's difficult to judge from these photographs how wide the valley is. I take it the agents know we need plenty of width to make a broadside attack?"

With Moore having put his finger on the item that

was worrying him most, Davies frowned. "Of course they know."

Young, knowing nothing of the politics behind the operation, put his foot in it with typical Australian aplomb. "Let's hope they've chosen right, sir. Because I wouldn't like to be those prisoners if we have to attack fore and aft."

It was all Lambert needed. "I have a few questions, Air Commodore. Are all these prisoners Americans?"

Davies' dislike of the man betrayed itself in his reply. "Not all, Mr. Lambert. The RAF suffer losses too. But as it seems most of our survivors are sent to a compound near Rheims, we can expect the majority to be your countrymen."

"Isn't this a rather unusual operation?"

Davies gave himself time to think. Although both he and Staines had known all along the correspondent was too shrewd not to guess the raid had political aspects, both had gone to considerable lengths to ensure he could not prove it. Davies' reply when it came was appropriately innocuous.

"Not for this squadron, Mr. Lambert. They are specialists in precision operations."

"All the same, it seems odd you're going to all this trouble to free our boys and doing nothing for your own down in Rheims?"

"It's not odd at all, Mr. Lambert. There isn't a railhead near our boys' compound: they have to be shipped away by motor transport."

Lambert shrugged. "O.K., so you want to free our boys. But then why don't you attack the compound instead of the train? Wouldn't that be safer for them."

At this juncture Davies realized he was enjoying himself. "It would certainly be safer for the prisoners, Mr. Lambert. Unfortunately it would also be pointless because with German troops everywhere, the partisans couldn't assemble to get them away."

The correspondent seemed unshaken by the grins of the airmen around him. "As it's a job that concern American lives, I can take it our own people have given you permission to go ahead?"

66

"Right from the top, Mr. Lambert. General Staines himself has authorized it."

Lambert threw a glance at Teddy Young. "Then, although one of your flight commanders appears to have doubts, you yourself are quite confident no prisoners will be harmed?"

"Only a damn fool would make a promise like that," Davies grunted. "This is a war operation and like all war operations, it is a calculated risk. A few men might be injured or killed but many others might escape. General Staines is aware of this and prepared to take the gamble. So would the men on the train if you were able to ask them. That's what being a soldier instead of a civilian is all about, Mr. Lambert."

Someone let out a low whistle that was instantly suppressed as Davies glared round. Seeing Lambert still appeared unmoved, Davies decided to open up with all his guns.

"For an important representative of the American Press you seem remarkably unenthusiastic about our plan to help your boys escape, Mr. Lambert."

With the question pushing Lambert right out on a limb, the watching Henderson silently applauded as for the first time the correspondent hesitated. "Not at all, Air Commodore. With the reservations I've made, I'm all for it."

Like the good soldier he was, Davies pushed his advantage home. "I'm glad. Because we do care about your boys, you know. If we pull this off I'd like the American public to know that."

Lambert's expression told Henderson beyond doubt that the correspondent knew the name of the game. "If you pull it off, Air Commodore, the public will certainly hear about it. Why shouldn't they? It's my job."

With the majority of the officers present knowing nothing of the politics behind the operation, there was more than one puzzled face. Feeling he had won one small victory, Davies turned to Moore.

"As Jerry's unlikely to neglect you the way he neglects our fighters, I've got plenty of diversions laid on for you. The Banff Wing will be out over the coast of Jutland and II Group have promised to play hell over Northern France. So one way and another Jerry's defences should be well stretched. As far as the route goes, I thought you could use the Hoffenscheim one you used last month, although that's for your navigational officer to decide."

"I take it you're not thinking of giving us a fighter escort, sir?" Young asked.

Davies had not yet forgiven the Australian for his gaffe. "How the hell can I? The essence of this operation is to keep below Jerry's radar detectors. A gaggle of Spitties above you would be a dead giveaway. When you get over the target you'll have to provide your own cover." When no one spoke, Davies turned to Lindsay, the Armament officer. "I suppose you'll have to use rockets?"

"I'm afraid so, sir. Those flak wagons are cannon-proof."

Davies' question betrayed his fear of a faultily-aimed rocket. "You couldn't use armour-piercing shells?"

Both Lindsay and Moore shook their heads. Seeing Lambert's expression, Davies let the point drop. "All right, let's move on to the flak posts. To be on the safe side one of your sections had better carry a couple of 250-pounders apiece. You can always jettison 'em later if you don't need them."

Moore was studying a photograph of the valley again. "Does anyone know if the gunposts have radios, sir?"

Davies was quick to guess how the squadron commander's thoughts were running. "No. We don't know about the train either. But it shouldn't matter if our timing's right. By the time the crew can stop the train they'll be in reach of the partisans anyway."

"I take it they won't be able to see the explosions?"

"The partisans say not. The track winds through the hills like a snake before it enters the valley. With any luck they won't see or hear anything."

As Davies had feared, Lambert was not through with him yet. "You've told me this unit specializes in this kind of mission, and of course I take your word for it. But I'm still not clear how they can take out those flak wagons without doing unacceptable damage to the rest of the train."

Davies' patience was beginning to run out. "I haven't the time to give you a lecture in aerial tactics, Mr. Lambert. Perhaps later on one of my specialist officers will go into details for you."

"All the same, this is what the mission is all about. Suppose for example the Heinies change the make-up of the train and put a flak wagon in the middle. Will your boys still go ahead?"

"In all operations of this kind the squadron commander makes the final decision. If on seeing the train he decides the risks are unacceptable he is allowed to abort and return home. Does that make you any happier?"

"I'd be a lot happier if I knew what you consider an unacceptable risk, Air Commodore."

Davies kept calm with a superhuman effort. "I must be wrong but I keep on getting the feeling you don't want us to try to rescue your boys. If I'm right, as you've attended this briefing you might want to put your objection in writing. I'm afraid we shall still go ahead because High Command still controls these decisions but at least it will ensure your objection is made public."

The intimidation his words contained angered even the case-hardened correspondent. "No one's objecting to an attempt to rescue our boys, Air Commodore, and you know it. All I'm doing is objecting to any risks being taken with their lives."

"And I've told you no unnecessary risks will be taken. Now do I have your permission to continue with this briefing?"

The two men's eyes held for a full five seconds before Lambert turned and made for a row of chairs along one side of the room. As he sat down, Davies glared round the arc of whispering men. "Perhaps we can get down to business now. Lindsay, how many AP rockets have you got in that store of yours?"

## 9

The only light shining in his Intelligence Room when Adams returned that evening was one near the door. With the far end in deep shadow and his myopic eyes taking time to adjust from the dusk outside, he was a moment before he noticed Sue Spencer sitting at her desk.

"Hello. What are you doing sitting in the dark like this."

Her uncharacteristic embarrassment told him immediately something was wrong. "I've got most of the material over to the Operations Room. I've been waiting for the Photographic Section to finish the extra prints."

"Are they done?"

"Yes. They came a few minutes ago." The girl rose. "I'll take them over now."

He waved her back into her seat. "There's no hurry. Davies has just put the briefing back half an hour. There are still a few technical details he and Moore can't agree on. I left them to it." As she sank reluctantly back he pulled out his pipe. "It wasn't a bad meal tonight, was it?"

She shook her head, appeared about to say something, then changed her mind. Without quite knowing why, Adams said it for her. "But then they always do put on a better meal before an operation, don't they?"

Her eyes met his own in the shadows. "Yes. I suppose it's the Eat, Drink, and Be Merry philosophy."

Sinking down behind his desk, Adams began packing his pipe. "What do you think of Lambert?"

He had the feeling only a part of her was talking to him. "I couldn't make him out. At one moment I felt he was genuinely concerned about the American

70

prisoners and in the next that his real objection to the operation was the harm it might do his case."

"You were probably right both ways. He'll be like the rest of us: good in parts and bad in others. I think he is concerned about the American losses and he does believe we're dragging our feet in providing escorts."

"He's not right about that, is he?"

"Not from all the information I've been given or found out. But it's easy to imagine how it must appear from the American viewpoint." Adams' shrug told why he had always found it difficult to find a niche in life where he could operate without doubting his integrity. "Anyway, how can any of us, Lambert included, ever know what goes on at the top? They probably don't know themselves."

She managed a smile. "You can sound quite cynical sometimes, Frank."

As Adams gave a somewhat shamefaced grin, the scream of an electric drill could be heard. With the strike imminent, fitters were working throughout the night. The girl turned away with a shiver. "Why do men fight, Frank?"

Tempted to give a bitter answer, Adams took another glance at her and thought again. "Because the human race is stupid, I suppose."

"Is that what you call it—stupid?"

Adams put a match to his pipe. "It's as good a word as any on a dismal autumn evening."

He sensed her resentment as she turned to him. "Am I embarrassing you, Frank?"

"No."

"I think I am. I'm sorry."

Adams chose his words carefully. "You don't have to be sorry. You've every right to be worried about Tony. You wouldn't be human if you weren't."

"But I shouldn't show it when I'm on duty, should I?"

"You don't. You're astonishingly brave."

"But I'm showing it tonight, aren't I?" When he did not answer her voice rose. "Aren't I?"

"If you say so."

71

"Why, Frank? Why tonight?"

"Because you can't hide fear all the time. Because you're human like the rest of us."

She appeared not to be listening to him. "They've done operations like this before. Often. So why am I so afraid tonight?"

"You're probably tired. Off you go and rest. I can manage without you at the briefing."

She refused almost angrily. Then her tone changed. "How much longer is it going on, Frank?"

"You mean the war? Oh, it can't last much longer. Not once we invade and we all know that's coming soon."

"You mean it can't last more than another year? Or two years?"

"Stop being such a pessimist. Once we've got troops into Europe they could crack quickly."

"The Germans? Never. They'll fight all the harder once we get near their old frontier."

Adams, who had said much the same to fellow officers in the past, felt the odds were stacked against him that evening. "We can't see into the future, Sue. So it's better not to try."

Once again she appeared not to hear him. "It's my own fault. I shouldn't have fallen in love. Only fools fall in love in wartime."

Adams cleared his throat. "Sue, be honest with both of us. Would you like to be posted?"

Her eyes widened. "Posted?"

"Yes. You can't go on being tortured like this. Nobody can."

She was staring at him as if he had suddenly become an enemy. "Do you think it would be better not to know? To spend every minute fearing the worst?"

"It wouldn't be like that, Sue. Millions of people have loved ones in the war but they don't suffer the way you're suffering here."

"How do you know that?"

"It's obvious they don't. And it's equally obvious why."

"It's not obvious to me. I'd go out of my mind if I didn't know what was happening." She was looking almost panic stricken as she gazed at him. "You won't do it, will you, Frank? Please say you won't."

Adams sighed. "I ought to. In the long run it would be the best thing for you."

The way she pulled herself together was a measure of her fear. "Don't be silly. You said yourself everyone gets a bit depressed now and then. Now we've had a talk I feel better already." Jumping to her feet she picked up a pile of photographs from her desk. About to carry them away, she paused. "You won't do anything, will you, Frank?"

Adams sighed. "No. Not if you don't want me to."

Glancing down the hut to make certain it was empty, she bent down and kissed his cheek. "Thank you, Frank. You're a wonderful person. Now I'll take these photographs over."

Smiling at him, she tripped down the hut and deposited the prints in a cardboard box. Carrying the box to the door she turned and gave him another smile before disappearing. Adams, who could still feel the imprint of her kiss on his cheek, sat a minute before switching on the light. The irony of the kiss had not escaped him. She was afraid of him now.

The morning of the 27th was in keeping with the rest of that autumn week. A light drizzle of rain during the night gave way to a dark and grey dawn. The Met. Forecast promised some improvement in visibility later but with a depression anchored over the Low Countries there was no likelihood of clear skies that day.

With the operation scheduled for low-level, most of the aircrews were delighted: a low cloud base greatly diminished the chances of fighter interception. Senior officers, Davies in particular, were less pleased. Poor visibility meant difficult target identification, and that could affect the exact timing on which the mission rested.

Visibility notwithstanding, the squadron made its preparations with its usual high efficiency. With Davies expecting his "scramble" call at any time after 09.00 hours, the Mosquitoes were already tuned and airworthy when the aircrews arrived at 07.30 to test them. After the pilots and navigators went off for breakfast, final checks were made and the aircraft were handed over to the armourers. Bombs were hoisted into bomb bays; rockets slung beneath wings. Magazines were snapped on to the 20mm cannon; shiny belts of .303 shells fed into the ammunition tanks. In a final act as significant as the closing of a visor, the safety pins of both bombs and rockets were withdrawn and the bomb doors closed. When the aircrews returned equipped with parachutes, revolvers, survival kit, foreign money and all the other paraphernalia they carried, their Mosquitoes had been turned into sophisticated and deadly war machines.

By 08.30, to Davies' great relief, the cloud base had lifted enough for the poplars at the far end of the airfield to be clearly visible. At 09.05 a terse call on the red telephone in Henderson's office sent a green Very light soaring up from the Control Tower. Within seconds the first Merlin gave its characteristic cough and fired. Other engines began firing as A-Apple, Moore's Mosquito, rolled from its dispersal point and began taxi-ing down the north-south runway. As other Mosquitoes followed it, the concentrated roar of thirty-two Merlins made every loose window on the airfield rattle.

At 09.09 a second green Very light soared up from the balcony on the Control Tower where Davies, Henderson and Lambert were standing. Immediately A-Apple's engines went into a higher octave and water began spraying from its tyres as it gathered speed. Heavy with its load of rockets and bombs, it dipped its wheels twice on the runway before breaking free and lifting with a crackling roar. As it banked away from the Control Tower the rest of the sixteen Mosquitoes followed at six-second intervals. All circled the airfield once. Then, slotting behind one another's starboard wings, the squadron headed south over the poplar trees. As the deep drone began to fade, Lambert glanced at Davies.

"They look good. I'll give you that."

"They are good," Davies declared. "Complete professionals." He turned to Henderson "Isn't that right?"

The undemonstrative Scot wished Davies would keep his pride to himself. "We like to think so."

"You are," Davies assured him. "No question about it."

Lambert was pointing at the aircraft that were now little more than dots against the grey sky. "Why are they flying in echelon like that?"

Davies was only too happy to emphasize his unit's expertise. "We've found out that Jerry's long-range radar can pick us up almost as soon as we leave our airfields. By flying in echelon our images superimpose themselves on his radar screens and give him the impression we're heavies. When the boys dive down at Manston on the south coast and fly ultra low level, he'll think we've just been air-testing and we've landed again."

The bearded Lambert gave a grimace of respect. "Who thought that one up?"

"It's one of the tricks Moore brought with him from Pathfinders."

"You think highly of Moore, don't you?"

Davies glanced at Henderson, who nodded his agreement. "If anyone can do this job, he's the man."

Lambert opened his mouth to say something, then closed it again. A morning breeze, fresh from the North Sea, was gusting into the balcony. "You think we can go somewhere a bit warmer now?"

For an embarrassed moment Henderson believed the correspondent's discomfort was going to bring a grin from Davies. To his relief the Air Commodore stifled the impulse. "Why not? There's nothing we can do for the next two hours. Let's go and have coffee in the Ops. room."

## 10

Hopkinson jabbed a finger at A-Apple's windshield. "Hallé, skipper! Eleven o'clock."

Moore took a quick glance at the crenellated skyline and eased A-Apple a couple of degrees to starboard. Adams had warned him there were heavy flak defences guarding the town's industries. Behind him the line of fifteen Mosquitoes curved like a piece of string and then straightened again. As the haze of smoke fell behind, a road appeared flanked by trees. At Hopkinson's nod Moore latched on to it, his wingtips no more than fifty feet above the tree tops. A man on a bicycle, seeing the aircraft were Allied, wobbled alarmingly as he tried to wave to them. A convoy of enemy transports coming in the opposite direction braked and white faces stared upwards. Moore caught a split-second glimpse of a soldier throwing a rifle to his shoulder but A-Apple's speed swept the image away.

The road went past a farmhouse and ran straight as a die for a couple of miles. With a slip in concentration at that height meaning certain death, pilots had to keep their eyes focused at an imaginary point half a mile ahead. Images leapt into vision and swept as rapidly away: a stretch of cobblestones, two schoolgirls skipping excitedly, a narrow canal. A thump on Moore's arm was followed by Hopkinson's yell. "Power cables ahead!"

A-Apple waggled its wings and switchbacked over the cables like a car in a funfair. Ahead, Moore saw a large bridge approaching. Hopkinson jabbed out a satisfied forefinger. "There's the river, skipper."

Moore was already swinging towards it. Striking the railway line that ran close to the river a few seconds later, he squatted A-Apple down on the track. "How are we for time, Hoppy?"

The navigator glanced at his watch. "Just about bang on. We should reach Namur in three minutes."

The thin-faced but sprightly Hopkinson was a Cockney who had been Grenville's navigator. Having missed the Swartfjord raid because of a wound received earlier, he had been one of the survivors of the old squadron when Moore had been sent to take Grenville's place. Shocked by the loss of his friends and in particular his skipper, Hopkinson had at first resented Moore and made it clear he did not want to fly with him. Moore, who was never one to give orders when he could use persuasion, had not forced the Cockney to become his navigator but instead had pointed out how his exceptional navigational skills could save the squadron lives as well as wasted missions. His patience had been amply rewarded. Today Hoppy, as he was universally known, was as much an asset to him as he had once been to Grenville.

The railway track and its telegraph poles were blurred by speed as the sixteen Mosquitoes headed down it. Freed for the moment from the tyranny of dead reckoning, Hoppy was able to examine the grey sky above. Since they had left Sutton Craddock the cloud base had been steadily lifting and on the navigator's estimate was now at least 3,000 feet high.

The track sank into a cutting. Moore was now flying only a few feet above the trees that grew on the high banks. A startled crow, trying to escape, struck his port wing and was flung away, a tangle of bone and feathers. A road bridge ahead brought a signal from Hopkinson and he eased back on the wheel. The superbly trained pilots behind him reacted as one man and the line of Mosquitoes rose and dipped again. With 633 Squadron existing for precision operations of this kind, Moore had put his men through many hours of exacting practice and it was doubtful if there was another squadron in the Allied Services that could have flown at such a height for so long. Without doubt they were too low for radar detection and yet Moore was only too aware of the efficiency of the German Observer Corps. If they flew much longer down the railway track, fighters would be vectored on to an interception course.

Hoppy's ETA for Namur was only seconds adrift. As chimneys and then buildings appeared ahead, Moore banked away from the track and flew south of the town. For a few seconds puffs of black smoke burst among the Mosquitoes as an alerted battery of 37s alongside a marshalling yard opened fire, and T-Tommy flown by Millburn shuddered as a piece of steel tore through its fuselage. Then green and brown fields were flowing below again as Moore's flight path took him out into the country. Hoppy nodded at his quick glance. "Any second now, skipper."

Although their height prevented them seeing it, the crews knew the great plain of Liége lay on their left, with the forest-clad foothills of the Ardennes ahead. As the town's skyline disappeared behind them, Moore again took the Mosquitoes down to ultra low level. Startled cattle reared and fled as the sixteen thunder-bolts roared past. Grass shivered and flattened under the air-blast of propellers. A clump of high trees appeared ahead. Like a line of horsemen taking a fence, the Mosquitoes soared over it and down. Hundreds of starlings, feeding in a freshly-ploughed field, rose in a startled cloud and swept away. In T-Tommy Gabby leaned toward Millburn. "What's he trying to do, boyo? Turn us into moles?"

Millburn grinned. "You know something? I always thought you were a mole."

Gabby glared at him. "You think that's funny."

Millburn grinned again. "I'll lay odds a mole wouldn't think so."

Ahead in A-Apple Hoppy was jabbing a finger upwards. Nodding, Moore rose a hundred feet to extend the navigator's field of vision. Peering out, Hoppy checked his watch again. Five seconds later he gave a nod "O.K. skipper."

Moore waggled his wings four times. Behind him, with Young in the lead, the fifteen Mosquitoes swung away north-east. The plan was simple; the timing complex. To avoid making the train crew suspicious, Moore would fly alone along the track, survey it, then turn north-east towards the tunnel, so completing two sides of a rectangle. Teddy Young would lead the squadron to the Meuse east of Namur and follow the river almost to Liége, when he would turn south-east, thus completing the other two sides of the rectangle. With distances and speeds precisely calculated, the squadron would be able to rendezvous with Moore the moment he broke radio silence. In later years sceptics would sneer at the suggestion that men could achieve such accuracy after flying hundreds of miles from their base. In fact it was quite common for aircrews to be within seconds of their ETAs.

Fields gave way to forests of pine as the lone A-Apple swept into the Ardennes. Compelled to fly higher than he would have liked because of the need to find the rail link between Namur and Marche, Moore could only hope the hill tops were screening him from the vigilant radar detectors. With both men keeping a wary eye open for fighters, an anxious minute passed before Hoppy gave an exclamation. Following his pointing finger Moore saw a double thread of steel running along the foot of a steep valley. The note of the engines rose half an octave as he put A-Apple's nose down.

Levelling off two hundred feet above the track he followed it round a wooden hill spur. Beyond the spur the valley widened and a small hamlet appeared. A man digging in a garden recognized the aircraft and waved his spade. Beyond the hamlet a column of white smoke was rising from a sawmill. Hoppy, among whose jobs was the monitoring of the aircraft's speed, tapped Moore's arm. "You haven't allowed for the dive, skipper. Throttle back a bit."

Realizing he was right, Moore obeyed. Ahead, the track ran around another wooded spur. As A-Apple swept over it Hoppy gave a grunt of satisfaction. "Marche ahead, skipper."

Skirting the town, Moore made contact with the railway again as it swung north-east. The floor of the valley they entered was dotted with small farms fed by a meandering stream. As they rounded a shallow hill Hoppy gave a yell. "There she is, skipper. Just as the Old Man said."

A mile or so ahead a train was steaming eastwards. Moore had already banked to port and was flying along the pine-covered hills that flanked the valley to the north. A lone Allied aircraft close to a prisoner-of-war train might arouse suspicion. One flying a couple of miles away could be dismissed as a chance encounter.

Hopkinson had his binoculars to his eyes. "She's the one all right, skipper. Only she's got two flak wagons at the back instead of one."

"Two? Are you sure?"

"Yes. The rear one seems to be carrying an 88. The other two look as if they've got 37mms and LMGs."

By this time Moore could pick out some details of the train with the naked eye. Although diminished by distance, it still had an air of brute power with its huge locomotive belching out smoke, its thrusting metal wheels, and the massive flak wagons at the front and rear. A sign its appearance did not belie its potential came five seconds later when a heavy explosion made A-Apple reel. Hoppy lowered his binoculars and gave Moore a wry grin. "It's an 88 all right."

Before Moore could reply flak began bursting all around the aircraft as the 37mm guns got their range. With all the information he needed, Moore swung into a tributary valley. Hoppy, watching the train until it vanished from sight, turned back to him.

"Everything seems O.K., skipper—it hasn't slowed down. But it's going to be a tougher nut than we thought."

"I'm afraid you're right, Hoppy," Moore replied dryly.

A minute later they rejoined the track. There was no risk of being sighted by the train crew: two hill spurs now separated them. Conscious they were now flying along the far side of the plotted rectangle, both men knew the tunnel must appear soon. Below, the railway track was leading them into wilder country. Rocky outcrops and fast-flowing streams mingled with forests of pines. A hawk was hovering over a scabrous hilltop. As the thunder of A-Apple's engines reached it, it dipped a wing and fell away.

The track curved round a bend and entered a wide valley. Three miles or so ahead the hills swept in and turned the valley into a cul-de-sac. Moore met Hoppy's eyes. "This must be it."

A-Apple went into a shallow climb. As the boulder-strewn floor of the valley swept past, the two men could see no sign of life. Hoppy gave a grimace. "Let's hope the partisans have arrived, skipper."

The words had barely left his mouth before something white fluttered among the thick belt of trees that clothed the northern side of the track. Nodding at Hoppy, Moore gave his attention again to the hill ridge ahead. Covered in trees, it appeared about five hundred feet in height at the point where the rail tunnel ran through it.

The branches of the pines shivered as A-Apple leapt over the ridge. Three seconds later the ground fell back to the floor of the valley and the railway track. Sweeping up the northern hillside, Moore banked steeply and flew back towards the tunnel. As the ridge passed below him an explosion made the Mosquito shudder. "See it?" Moore shouted.

Before Hoppy could answer a fork of tracer stabbing out from the southern hillside confirmed the gun post's position. It was sited high enough to defend the tunnel from both air and ground attack. Since the Mosquito had appeared, the crews of the flak posts on either side of the tunnel had been frantically stripping the covers off their guns and warming up their radar predictors. The western gun crew had won by a short head.

Both Moore and Hopkinson saw that Davies was right: the post had to be destroyed or the partisans could never reach the tunnel. As black puffs of smoke burst around A-Apple, Hoppy's voice sounded over the intercom. "O.K., skipper. Bomb fused. Left, left, steady . . ."

The gun battery was on a small rocky ledge half-hidden by trees. As A-Apple, with bomb doors open, swept towards it, the battery's LMGs opened up. Appearing to start slowly at first, the tracer suddenly accelerated like an unfurling whip. Forced to fly straight and level as Hoppy lined up his bomb-sight, Moore felt his toes clench up inside his flying boots as the steel lashed past.

The Mosquito's head-on approach was not lost on the German gunners. It was a simple situation of kill or be killed, and the barrels of the pom-poms were jerking like the head of striking cobras. To Hoppy, squinting down, it appeared that the gunners were giving a pyrotechnic display. Both he and Moore winced as a burst of LMG fire pierced the open bomb doors and ricocheted in a series of banshee screams from the bombs cradled there.

"Right a bit, skipper. Right . . . Steady, steady . . . bomb gone!"

The 250-lb. bomb, tail-fused with a five second detonator, fell away. With the vengeful flak still following him, Moore swung away immediately and dived down into the valley. Trying to look back, Hoppy was counting . . . "three, four, five!"

The explosion came half a second later, hurling trees and debris high into the air. It was followed by a minor avalanche down the hill. The black explosions and parabolas of tracer that had been following A-Apple were snuffed out as if by a magician's wand. On the intercom Hoppy's voice had a note of relief. "First time lucky, skipper!"

Moore drew an arm across his sweating face. "Let's hope so."

He put the Mosquito into a high climbing turn and gazed back. Gambling that the gun battery was completely out of action, six partisans had already run out of the surrounding trees and were urgently attaching explosives to the tunnel entrance. As A-Apple circled just below the hilltops a series of jolting explosions made its crew turn their eyes sharply on the stricken battery. A second later Hoppy gave a shout of relief. "It's O.K., skipper. It's the other battery waking up."

A parabola of LMG tracer, arching over the tunnel but falling well short of the orbiting A-Apple proved the Cockney right. Hidden from the battery by the ridge, the tough partisans continued their work. With the explosives in position, they ran out an electric cable to the side of the track. One man paused to wave at A-Apple, then all six disappeared into the trees.

Glancing back to ensure the train had not yet

entered the valley, Moore and Hopkins waited for the explosion that threw dust and rocks high into the air. When the smoke cleared, the tunnel entrance appeared to be partially blocked and earth and rocks covered a ten-yard section of track. Satisfied, Moore swung A-Apple towards the ridge.

"Let's put that other gun post out of action before the boys arrive."

It was a decision so typical of Moore that Hoppy made no attempt to argue although his expression was wry. The order of battle, as agreed between Davies and Moore, was that Moore would attack the western battery and then keep watch for the partisans on the train's progress. In the meantime Millburn, leaving the rest of the squadron orbiting in a valley two miles away, would fly in from the opposite direction and attack the eastern battery. Only if one of them were to lose his personal duel would the other Mosquito attack both gun posts. By using only two aircraft initially, it was hoped that neither the on-coming train nor the enemy radar detectors would be alerted.

As it happened, Millburn was the first to reach the surviving battery. With the American's natural aggressiveness stimulated by the prospect of aiding his compatriots to escape, he was nearly thirty seconds ahead of schedule. Seeing the battery squirting tracer at A-Apple, Millburn went at it bald-headed.

The post was a secondary one and unlike the crews of the western battery the gunners had no concrete bunker to protect them. With Millburn's attack coming from the lower reaches of the valley and with the crew concentrating on A-Apple, the American was able to fire two rockets before a shot was fired back at him. One rocket narrowly missed but the second smashed through the armoured shield of the pom-pom as if it were cardboard, killing the crew instantly. The LMG mounting was also damaged and its crew critically wounded.

With the valley now safe for the next phase of the operation, Moore and Millburn began orbiting the valley at the eastern side of the tunnel. From there they could see the train enter the valley without the likelihood of being seen themselves. As the long seconds ticked past, Moore felt tension winding like a spring inside him. The possibility had always existed that the train might carry radio and so have been alerted by the gun posts. A second, more lethal possibility was that the hill tops had not screened the two Mosquitoes from the enemy radar detectors. Intelligence believed the nearest fighter airfield was at Maastricht, fifty miles away. If the airfield's scramble system was efficient— and German defence systems usually were—this meant enemy fighters could reach the train approximately ten minutes after their initial warning. If all had gone according to plan, the Mosquitoes had that number of minutes to disable the train and free the prisoners. If the plans went awry, the valley would turn into a death trap for them.

Twenty more agonizing seconds passed before Hoppy's sharp eyes spotted puffs of smoke rising above the distant hill spur. Fifteen more seconds and the train appeared, a black-caterpillar crawling into the wide valley. Letting out his breath in relief, Moore signalled Millburn to close up behind him and spent the next minute making the two Mosquitoes as inconspicuous as possible against the vast backdrop of the hills. Alongside him Hoppy kept surveillance on the train through his binoculars. Puffing black smoke through its stack, it was hauling its bulk along the valley without suspicion of the obstacle ahead. When he estimated it was halfway down the valley, Hoppy tapped Moore's arm. Clicking on his R/T, Moore broke radio silence at last.

"Swordsman Leader to Zero Two. All obstacles cleared. Bring your boys over now."

As Moore heard Young's twangy voice acknowledge, he was conscious it was the crossing of the Rubicon. Whatever might have happened earlier, it was now certain sirens would be screaming and enemy pilots racing for their Messerschmidts and Focke Wulfs. Satisfied that the train's weight and speed must now carry it within range of the partisans, Moore swung A-Apple's nose westwards.

"Swordsman Leader to Zero Eight. While we're waiting for the boys, let's have a crack at that first flak wagon. The usual drill. Let's go!"

It was a snap decision that neither Hoppy, Millburn nor Gabby thought reckless. The quicker the train was attacked at this juncture, the less prepared its gunners would be. And the swifter its disablement, the quicker the squadron's escape.

As the two Mosquitoes swept over the tunnel, the train driver spotted the debris ahead of him and slammed on his air brakes. Long sparks flashed as, with a hiss of air, wheels locked and screeched along the rails. Prisoners in the central wagons were flung into heaps by the sudden deceleration and gunners in the flak wagons, hurled from their seats, hid their faces as loose shells slid murderously across the steel floors.

It was a moment of confusion that could not have been more fortuitous for the two Mosquitoes. As sparks flew from the train half a mile ahead, they separated, Moore climbing steeply to port, Millburn to starboard. It was a tactic Moore had made his crews practise many times and it was to prove invaluable today. Banking in unison they came plunging down from opposite sides of the valley, their targets being the engine and foremost flak wagon in which bruised and cursing gunners were only just climbing back to their feet. With the need for accuracy imperative, both aircrews came in at a slight angle to the train so that any overshoots would fly past the engine and not hit the central wagons.

With the flak guns not yet manned and the explosive content of their rockets small, both pilots were able to close well inside the prescribed safety distance before firing. As the rockets darted out like luminous lances, the two aircraft banked yet again to port and swept safely past one another. Moore's rocket, striking the now stationary engine, sent a huge column of steam and boiling water high into the air. Aft of the coal tender, Millburn's rocket pierced the flak wagon just behind and below its main turret. To Gabby, gazing back as T-Tommy rocketed upwards, the damage appeared to be slight. In fact the steel projectile, ricocheting around

85

the inner steel walls until its high velocity was exhausted, had smashed machinery and men indiscriminately and turned the wagon into a charnal house.

To Teddy Young and the rest of the squadron, now pouring into the valley, the sight was like two gannets attacking a huge snake. Catching sight of the aircraft as he levelled off from his climb, Moore wasted no time in giving orders. "Give us cover, Red Section Leader. Zero Nine—take the 37mm wagon. Ten—take the 88. In you go."

Young led his flight upwards and began his patrol at the base of the clouds. The two named Mosquitoes took station on either side of the valley and prepared to attack. Ideally Moore would have preferred to send in two aircraft against each flak unit but with the two wagons coupled together the danger of collision was too great. His compromise would at least ensure neither wagon could be certain from which side its real threat came. As the two Mosquitoes began to dive, Gabby, seeing no flak radiating from the wagons, gave Millburn a grin. "A piece of cake, boyo."

It proved a rash prophecy. The tough German gunners had now scrambled back into their seats and their menacing gun barrels were swinging round on their attackers. The 88, with its heavier shells but slower rate of fire, turned on the remainder of the aircraft orbiting above. The 37mm of the foremost wagon and the LMGs that both wagons carried shared themselves out between the two diving Mosquitoes.

Zero Nine was Andy Larkin, the rangy, satirical New Zealander, and Richards; Ten was Frank Day and Clifford, both survivors of the squadron. With the 37mm pointing in his direction, Larkin took the brunt of the flak; to the crews orbiting above, his Mosquito seemed to disappear into a rectangle of bursting shells. Miraculously it survived and went rocketing up the opposite hillside with no worse than blackened wounds in wings and fuselage. Not surprisingly, however, its rockets missed the 37mm wagon and lanced harmlessly into the trees.

Frank Day, having to face only LMG fire, was able to aim his rocket more accurately and it struck the revolving air-vent of the 88 wagon. It smashed the vent away but the tough armour prevented more damage and the projectile ricocheted away.

Shouts and curses on the R/T channel betrayed the crews' reaction to the defence the train was making. Moore's calm voice silenced them. "Your turn, Eleven and Twelve."

Eleven was McKenny and Ross; Twelve was Lester an ex-London University student, and Thomson, a building society clerk. As the two Mosquitoes began their dive Moore tried to draw some of the fire by flying lengthways along the train. Only one LMG gunner allowed himself to be diverted; the others concentrated grimly on the real threat above them.

Fire was now radiating from the two wagons like the quills of a porcupine. Although both Mosquitoes had to fly through sheets of LMG tracer, Lester had also to face the dreaded 37mm pom-poms. Before he could fire his rocket, a shell hit his starboard engine and another exploded an auxiliary fuel tank. Blazing fiercely, the entire wing folded back and broke away. The asymmetrical remains spun down and exploded among the trees. Emotion brought a curse from Hopkinson. "This is murder, skipper. Two kites at a time haven't a snowball's chance against that kind of flak."

His sharp reply betrayed Moore's own anger. "Keep your eyes open for bandits!"

For McKenny and Ross, now facing the combined fire from both wagons, it was like flying into an erupting volcano. Tracer clawed at the cupola and drummed viciously on the Mosquito's stressed skin. An explosion shattered the compass and ignited its alcohol. Kicking his rudder bar to make the Mosquito as difficult a target as possible, McKenny fought to get within range. As he levelled off to take sight on the 88 wagon, there was a jolt and a terrifying scream as the starboard propeller was shattered. As the Irishman cursed and switched off the engine, Ross saw his intention and gave a shout of protest. "That's enough, Paddy! Break away, for God's sake!"

Ignoring the Scot, McKenny flew on into the sheets of tracer and released his rocket at almost point-blank range. It flew straight and true, piercing the armoured side of the wagon just below its gun turret. The immediate cessation of fire from all its guns told its own story. Keeping control by will power as much as skill, the Irishman leapt over the train and struggled to gain height.

The shouts of triumph from the orbiting crews were stilled by Moore's urgent voice. "How are you, Paddy?"

"We're all right, skipper. But I've only got one engine."

"You got the 88 wagon, Paddy. Well done. Get off home and we'll try to catch you up later and give you cover."

"O.K., skipper. Thanks."

Up on the hilltops Thirteen and Fourteen were preparing to launch their attack. Thirteen was a blond young South African, Van Breedenkamp, and his English navigator, Arthur Heron. Fourteen was Tony St. Claire and Simpson. Witnesses to what lay before them, all four men were pale and grim. Orbiting above, Moore was acutely conscious that the stubborn defence of the last flak wagon was endangering the entire operation.

"Millburn! Let's share this one. You go in low after Van Breedenkamp and I'll follow St. Claire."

Aware how close enemy fighters must be and that the release of his compatriots below hung on a knife edge, Millburn could not have heard an order more to his liking. Breaking from his orbit almost before Moore had finished speaking, he made for the hillside from which the South African was preparing to launch his attack. At the opposite side of the valley Moore swept round to follow St. Claire. "In you go, Thirteen and Fourteen. We're right behind you."

The two leading Mosquitoes dropped their noses and began their dive. As the scream of engines and airfoils grew louder, the quadruple 37mms on the flak wagon opened fire on St. Claire. To the tormented partisans hidden in the woods its rhythmical pounding sounded like the drumbeats before an execution. Three seconds later the wagon's LMGs began firing at Van Breedenkamp. Both Moore and Millburn, flying half a mile back and only a hundred feet above the valley floor, were left unmarked as the enemy gunners concentrated on their nearest threat.

Van Breedenkamp was the first to release his rocket. It struck the wagon's armoured skirt, ricocheted on to the stricken 88 wagon, and made a fiery trail along the track. As the South African swung away, the LMGs immediately lowered their barrels on to the advancing T-Tommy. Coming in like a charging bull and totally ignoring the danger of collision with St. Claire, Millburn fired his rocket. It struck one end of the LMG turret and swung the heavy structure round on its axis. At the same moment the machine guns ceased firing. Millburn's yell of triumph made R/T earphones rattle. "See that, you guys! We've got the LMGs."

Yet although the impact of the rocket inside the steel hull must have sounded like the end of the world to the surviving pom-pom gunners, they ceased firing for only a couple of seconds. As they recommenced, the sky around St. Claire and his navigator turned into a hell of explosions and screaming steel. A red-hot fragment ripped a two-foot hole in the aircraft's port wingtip. Another lethal fragment ripped off an engine fairing and hurled it away. A third shell made a large hole in the nose cone housing the cannon and Brownings. Screaming like a banshee, air entered and flung an icy blast into the cockpit. One of the calmest men in the squadron, St. Claire still managed to steady the Mosquito and when a clear view of the wagon appeared through the bursting shells he fired a port rocket. Aimed at close range, it would almost certainly have hit its target had not a shell struck the starboard engine at precisely the same moment. Although half-stunned by the explosion, St. Claire managed to pull the nose up and the aircraft passed a few feet over the wagon. Trailing smoke and glycol, it staggered a few hundred feet up the hill. Then its crippled wing dropped and it fell among the trees.

The tragedy was visible to all the orbiting crews. With the 37mm shell swinging the Mosquito off course at the exact moment the rocket was fired, the rocket had struck one of the nearby wagons containing American prisoners. Although its explosive charge was small, it was sufficient to blow out almost all the opposite wall. As men spilled out on the track some clearly dead and others badly mutilated, Millburn let out a horrified "Oh, my God!"

At the opposite side of the track heavy explosions rocking A-Apple told Moore he was now the gunner's target. Before Machin, the last member of the flight, could grasp his opportunity, the revengeful Millburn stole it from him. Banking on a wingtip he headed straight for the wagon again. Seeing him coming, Moore held the gunners' fire until it became suicidal and then banked sharply away. As the pom-pom followed A-Apple, Millburn released two rockets. One ricocheted from the Wagon's armoured skirt but the second one struck it squarely and disappeared inside. The guns stopped firing immediately and a few seconds later smoke escaping from the turret told the battle was over.

There was no jubilation among the circling crews. The enemy gunners had died valiantly and down on the track the sight was harrowing as wounded men helped one another from the burning wagon. As one man paused to shake a fist upwards, the tough Millburn winced and turned his head.

Partisans, who had been anxiously scanning the sky for enemy fighters, now began pouring out on to the track. A dozen of them ran to help the wounded Americans, the rest, armed with tools and crowbars, began working frantically on the bolts of the intact wagons.

Their urgency was shared by Moore. Every professional instinct in him was screaming to pull the squadron out of the death trap while there was still time. Yet if he gave the order and the fighters came before the prisoners were released, the dead would have died for nothing.

To his relief the partisans appeared to have cracksmen with them because the locked doors were opened with almost magical speed. As the last one slid back and uniformed men leapt out and ran into the trees, a green Very light soared upwards.

It was a signal that came just in time. The light

had barely reached its full trajectory before Young's voice rattled in Moore's earphones. "Bandits, skipper! 190s."

Glancing upwards Moore saw a blunt-nosed shape diving at incredible speed towards his orbiting aircraft. It was followed by a Mosquito firing all four guns. Deciding it was wiser to wait for his comrades than lose height to aircraft as formidable as Mosquitoes, the 190 pilot swung past and disappeared into the clouds. Moore's welcome order came a second later. "Swordsman Leader to squadron. Line astern. We're going home."

Diving A-Apple to tree-top height he headed back up the valley. Peeling away, the survivors of his Flight followed him. Up aloft Teddy Young's flight gave a last snarl at the 190s that were harassing them, hid in the clouds for a few seconds, then dived into the valley themselves. Full of speed and at zero height, their camouflaged bodies merged into the green hillsides and the wolves who tried to follow them discovered only shadows on which to vent their fury.

---

## 11

The Mosquito leapt over a line of poplars and sank down on its belly again. Below an uneven grassy field flowed past. Half a dozen grazing cows reared up and then broke into a terrified gallop. A narrow stream and a cobbled road swept past in quick succession. A minute later a church steeple and a number of chimneys appeared on the skyline at two o'clock. Ross pointed a finger. "Calais!"

Instead of answering him, McKenny changed course a few degrees. Glancing ahead, Ross saw a major road had appeared on the flat landscape. Enemy transports preceded by a motorcyclist were making their way along it and McKenny was heading straight for them. Hiding his alarm Ross indicated a map strapped on his knee. "Forget the transports," he shouted. "Let's get back home."

Even within the terms of the RAF's code of practice, which since the days of Trenchard in the First World War had been attack, always attack, Ross's caution was justified. Although the Mosquito was an extraordinary aircraft capable of a high performance even on one engine, it was the pilot's duty in a damaged machine to do everything possible to return to base so that both valuable aircraft and its highly-trained crew could live to fight another day. To risk that achievement for a few easily replaceable transports was poor military judgment and made Ross grip McKenny's arm when the pilot took no notice.

"You're taking us among the flak posts, Paddy. Get back on course."

McKenny muttered something and flung his hand away. Staring at him, Ross's apprehension grew. Whatever the events that were changing the Irishman's character, one result appeared to be an alarming increase in his aggressiveness. Another, if one could analyse his expression, was a perverse desire to intimidate his navigator. Before Ross could protest again, McKenny lined up his reflector sight on the rearmost transport and opened fire.

The massive recoil of four automatic guns blurred both men's vision and seemed to halt the Mosquito momentarily in mid-air. As grey-clad figures leapt down from the transports and tried to reach the shallow ditches, they were cut down like grass before a scythe. A petrol tank exploded in a fireball of oily smoke that blackened the sky around the Mosquito as it went snarling down the row of transports. Cursing men flung themselves flat on the road; others rolled into the icy water of the ditch. A few, one of them a tough grizzled sergeant, knelt in the centre of the road and began firing back. Earth and sky swung dizzily as McKenny banked steeply and thumbed his gun button again. A second truck exploded, throwing flaming debris in all directions. As earth and sky tilted again, Ross let out a yell of anger. "What's the matter with you? You'll have fighters on us in a minute."

The horizon steadied and to his relief Ross saw they were heading for the coast. He jabbed an urgent finger to the south. "We can't cross here. Get back on our track."

If McKenny's revenge against the world was momentarily satiated, his self-destructive impulses were as strong as ever for he continued straight ahead. After trying twice more to dissuade him, Ross gave up and concentrated on pin-pointing flak posts they were approaching. Dunes of sand were appearing now in the grassy fields. Here and there were wooden bungalows, once occupied by summer holiday makers, now empty and abandoned. Other less innocent structures nestled into the sides of hillocks and sand dunes. Difficult to spot from the air because of their camouflage and low profile, they were as dangerous to aircraft as massed shotguns to low-flying pheasants. As the Mosquito flew past one of them, four lines of tracer leapt out and impaled it.

The swiftness of the attack took both men by surprise. One hose of bullets took half of the starboard aileron away. A second struck sledgehammer blows along the fuselage. Although the burst of fire swept from end to end of the Mosquito at lightning speed, Ross, whose navigator's seat was unprotected by armour, felt the blows lasted for minutes as his cringeing body waited for bullets to tear up through his buttocks and spine. As the Mosquito staggered away, a second bunker fifty yards away opened fire. Bullets smashed into the silent engine, tearing off a piece of cowling before ricocheting eerily away. Another burst of fire cut the stabilizing controls. Reeling like a drunken man, the Mosquito crossed the deserted beach with its coils of barbed wire and tank obstacles and flattened over the grey sea. Frustrated that their victim had escaped, gunners followed it with parabolas of tracer that splashed sullenly among the waves.

Ross, finding it hard to believe he was still alive, took a full fifteen seconds to find his voice. "What the

93

hell's the matter with you? Are you trying to get us killed?"

Although the nearness of their escape had turned McKenny pale, his face was as sullen as before. "What was I supposed to do? Go past those transports without firing a shot?"

Tension, spring-tight within Ross, had to find release. "Don't tell me that was for the war effort. You've been doing some odd things lately but that was the craziest thing yet."

McKenny's head turned. "What's all the fuss about? Did I scare you?"

The taunt added fuel to the Scot's anger. "If I was scared, I wasn't the only one. You know what Moore would do if he heard about this, don't you? He'd ground you faster than that."

It was a blow that struck home: McKenny's glance was a mixture of defiance and alarm. "What are you turning into? A bloody informer?"

"I'm your navigator, remember? And you're supposed to follow the track I give you when we cross the coast."

"Oh, for Christ's sake stop bellyaching! We got out all right, didn't we?"

Ross, whose training had kept him scanning the gauges and sky above even as he quarrelled with McKenny, gave a sudden start. "We're not out of the woods yet. Have you noticed our oil pressure?"

McKenny stared at the pressure gauge of the remaining port engine, then glanced sharply over his left shoulder. As he sank back, Ross tried to see past him. "What is it? A cut feed line?"

"I don't know. I can't see any spray."

Not for the first time that morning Ross blessed the grey sky that still stretched from horizon to horizon. Had it been cloudless there was little doubt fighters would have already pounced on them. As it was they were not halfway across the Channel. Only a few minutes from safety but the needle of the pressure gauge already on the fringe of the danger quadrant.

The white cliffs of Dover were distinct on the horizon when the men's sensitive ears picked up the sudden labouring note of the engine. With oil pressure down towards zero, the temperature gauge was in the red as friction began to heat up the oil-starved engine. Jettisoning his remaining rockets, which traced a fiery path over the wavetops before plunging into them, McKenny nodded at Ross's enquiry. "Yes, give them a fix. We're not going to clear the cliffs."

Praying the radio was not damaged, Ross called in Air/Sea Rescue and to his relief got a reply almost immediately. Giving them as accurate a fix as possible, he tightened McKenny's seat harness and then his own. The overheated engine was now thumping alarmingly and giving off smoke. With the wavetops snapping less than a hundred feet below them, the pale-faced McKenny gave Ross another nod. "I'm putting her down now. Jettison the hood."

With a series of bangs that threatened to tear the wing away, the engine seized and died. As Ross released the cupola, a rush of cold air and a scream of airfoils entered the cockpit. Handling the unstable Mosquito like a crate of eggs, McKenny put her nose down a few degrees. Gripping his seat tightly, Ross saw the choppy waves rushing towards him. As spray splattered against the windshield, McKenny hauled right back on the wheel. The Mosquito lifted her nose briefly, then dropped belly flat into the sea. The massive jerk threw both men forward against their straps. Alongside them there was a fierce hissing and a great cloud of steam as the white-hot port engine sank under the waves. Recovering his breath Ross snapped open his harness and pushed himself upwards. "Come on! Let's get out of here."

There was no answer from McKenny. His body was limp and blood was oozing down one side of his face. Dropping back, Ross unfastened his harness and with a superhuman effort heaved him out of his seat. By this time McKenny had opened his eyes but he seemed incapable of helping himself. Bending down, Ross somehow managed to get his head and shoulders under the pilot's legs. Bracing his arms against the seat he straightened his back and heaved McKenny to the cockpit rim. Steadying him there, he climbed on to the seat and pushed again. Tumbling like a limp sack over the rim, McKenny fell on the flooded wing and into the sea. Gasping from his efforts, Ross dropped on the wing himself and tried to grab McKenny's overalls as the swell washed him away. With the wing offering no handhold, the Scot was dragged into the sea himself. With their Mae Wests keeping them afloat, Ross was content for a moment to keep McKenny's head above the waves while he regained his breath. Recovering, he saw the wooden-framed Mosquito still afloat. Unsure how long it would remain that way but deciding it would be a better target for Air/Sea Rescue to locate, he struck out and dragged McKenny round to the tail section.

By the time he reached the tail the Irishman had recovered sufficiently to be able to help himself. Kicking and scrambling, the two men dragged themselves over the half-submerged elevators and clung to the fin. With their weight depressing the tail even lower, they had some difficulty in keeping their heads above the choppy waves. Blood was making pink rivulets down McKenny's face and both men were shivering from the cold. The Irishman coughed water from his lungs. "You think they'll be long?"

"They shouldn't be," Ross shouted back. "They've a base only a few miles away."

In fact rescue was already on its way. On permanent standby, an Air/Sea Rescue launch and a Lysander aircraft had been despatched within a minute of receiving the Mayday call. Spotting the Mosquito almost as soon as it crossed the coast, the Lysander had given the launch a radio fix. Already sniffing about like a wolf for scent, the power boat had changed direction and now, with a bow wave as high as her bridge, was bearing down on the sinking aircraft. Five minutes later, wrapped in blankets, McKenny and Ross were on their way to hospital.

"They should never have got us involved in politics, sir," Henderson muttered. "Something was bound to go wrong."

The Scot's criticism was aimed at Davies, who was

standing at the other side of the large desk in Adams' Intelligence Room. Moore and Adams were also present at the private inquest. Davies, who had just spent some of the most uncomfortable minutes of his life closeted with Lambert, answered, with a scowl. "Someone had to do it, Jock. And we were the obvious choice."

"I know that, sir. But it carried too many risks for the prisoners."

"Everyone knew that," Davies snapped. "And no one more than the Yanks. But they still gave us their permission. And they probably would again. You're talking as if the raid was a failure. Don't you realize two to three hundred valuable aircrew have escaped?"

Having made a point, the big Scot was not one to withdraw it without good reason, "I know that, sir, but how many will get back to the U.K.? Probably not more than a dozen or so."

"You're a bloody pessimist today, aren't you, Jock? If the Resistance play their cards right, they could get a hundred over to us. Maybe more."

Henderson looked sceptical. "I don't see Lambert stressing that, do you? It isn't as if he didn't warn us there was a risk of American lives."

"He's not the only one who issues bulletins! Staines is arranging for a Press release that will emphasize the hundreds of American boys we've freed. That can't look bad in the American headlines, can it?"

The Scot stuck to his guns. "Not if it goes in the headlines, sir. It's Lambert that's worrying me. After all, you said yourself he's the most influential correspondent in the States."

Knowing from all Lambert had told him that the Scot's fears were justified, Davies lost his temper. "What is all this, Jock? Are you blaming me for carrying out my orders? Or are you blaming me because a bloody flak shell hit St. Claire and spun him off target?"

Suddenly realizing that beneath his testy facade the Air Commodore was as upset as he was, Henderson turned contrite. "Of course I'm not, sir. It just seems so damned unfair that after all Moore and his boys did, they should get such a lousy break."

One of Davies' best qualities was his quickness to

forgive. "That goes without saying. It was a brilliantly-executed operation and everyone is to be congratulated for their part in it. The first man to say that was Staines when we spoke over the phone."

"I suppose he'll be one of Lambert's major targets?"

"He will be. But Staines can take care of himself. I gather he's already working on something that could put the ball right back into Lambert's court."

The Scot showed instant alarm. "We wouldn't be involved in this, would we?"

Davies' defiance was a giveaway in itself. "Why not? We're as keen to clear our name as anyone else, aren't we?"

"You suggested a minute ago we'd nothing to be ashamed about!"

"You know damn well what I mean. There's no question that Lambert's going to blow up this accident to further his own ends. So our job is to do something that'll K.O. him once and for all."

Henderson's alarm was manifest now. "I don't like it, sir. We're getting deeper and deeper into politics."

As apprehensive himself but seeing no way out, Davies became testy again. "Where the hell do you get this political stuff from? All we did this morning was try to free a few hundred American prisoners and we succeeded. All we'll be doing if Staines wins this additional job for us will be to work with the Americans instead of with our own forces. What's political about that? We're both on the same side, aren't we? To me these are war operations pure and simple and any political capital that comes out of them is just a fling-off."

Henderson half-opened his mouth to protest, then decided enough was enough. Self-guilt brought him a glare from Davies before the Air Commodore turned challengingly to Moore. "You've been very quiet so far, Moore! Don't you think the operation was worth while?"

Although Moore had bathed and changed, his good-looking face was still showing the strain of the fierce engagement. His answer was typically candid. "It's difficult for me to answer that, sir. I lost four of my men with another three in hospital. But if war is just a matter of mathematics, then I'd have to say it depends on how many Americans get back to the U.K."

"War *is* a matter of mathematics," Davies snapped. "And I've good reasons for believing a high percentage of 'em will get back." Noticing Moore's fatigue, his tone changed. "You did a great job, Ian. And I'm sorry about your men. Particularly St. Claire. It's a hell of a thing to happen to a man."

Standing just behind Moore, Adams thought of Sue Spencer and winced. When it had been confirmed St. Claire was missing, he had stood the girl off duty and taken the debriefing himself. Clearly in a state of shock, she had protested bitterly at his decision. It was the kind of courage that had gone straight through the defences of the sentimental Adams but when he had learned about the Americans St. Claire had killed he had been adamant. Hearing the grim details of how her fiancé had been shot down would be agony enough for her. Learning of the cruel trick fate had played on him might be too much.

Her absence had meant a long de-briefing session for Adams. An additional factor had been the condition of the crews. Flying long distances at low-level was always a heavy strain, and G.D. Waafs had been kept busy bringing in cups of sweet tea and sandwiches as the men had filed singly into Adams' "Confessional". All had carried in with them the smell of battle: the odour of cordite, burnt oil, sweat, petrol, and other less definable smells that Adams had grown accustomed to over the war years. As always, they had stirred conflicting emotions in him. Condemned by his age and poor eyesight to ground duties, Adams had never lost his envy of these young men whose missions brought hope to the oppressed people of Europe. At the same time his envy often disturbed and puzzled him because another side of Adams hated war with its waste of young and promising lives.

"When are you expecting to hear from General Staines again, sir?" It was Henderson, still worried about being drawn deeper into the world of politics and journalism.

"I'm seeing him tomorrow morning," Davies told him. "He's hoping to have some news for us then."

A tap on the door made all four men turn. As Sue Spencer appeared in the doorway, the room went quiet. Seeing the three senior officers with Adams, the girl drew back.

"I'm sorry. I thought Squadron Leader Adams was alone."

Henderson damned the heartiness in his voice. "That's all right, Sue. Come in."

For a moment it seemed the girl would withdraw in spite of his invitation. Then she closed the door and walked uncertainly towards Adams. Henderson pulled out a chair for her but she appeared not to see it. Adams, who had stepped forward, cleared his throat nervously. "What is it, Sue?"

The girl was clearly still in shock. Her face looked frozen as she gazed at him. "I want to know if it's true that Tony killed some Americans before he was shot down."

Davies cursed beneath his breath. "Who told you that?"

Her gaze turned on him. "I overheard two of the crews talking. Is it true, sir?"

For once Davies seemed to be short on words. Moore came to his aid and to the embarrassed men his cultured voice struck exactly the right note of sympathy. "It is true but it wasn't his fault, Sue. A shell swung him round just as his rocket was fired. It could have happened to any of us."

"But it didn't happen to any of you, did it, sir? It happened to Tony and everyone's going to blame him for killing those Americans."

"No, Sue. Nobody will blame him. Certainly not American aircrews. They understand how these accidents can happen in combat. That's something you don't have to worry about."

Her voice sounded as if it were struggling upwards through layer after layer of anguish. "A man loses his life trying to rescue others and he kills them instead. It's very ironical, isn't it?"

Henderson cleared his throat. "Aren't you looking too much on the black side, lassie? All we know so far is that they crashed into the woods. As the partisans would be near enough to give help, they could be as right as rain."

His words of comfort seemed to antagonize the girl. "As right as rain, sir? After going down with a wing shot away?" She turned to Moore. "They say you were just behind him when he was hit. Won't you tell me exactly what happened?"

Adams, who knew the girl better than any of them, was wondering if it might not be wise to tell her everything while she was in a state of shock. Moore's reply showed he was of the same mind.

"I think you're right not to hold out too much hope, Sue. Both of them were too low to bail out. On the other hand they didn't seem completely out of control. And they hadn't that far to fall."

If his words gave the girl any hope, she killed it immediately. "He's dead. They both are. You're all certain of it. But do you know what I believe? Tony's not going to rest. Not when he knows about the men he's killed."

As Adams felt himself stiffen, Henderson gripped his arm and put his mouth to his ear. "Get her out of here and take her to the M.O.! Tell him to put her to sleep. Go on—move it!"

The girl tried to resist Adams. Deciding it was one of those occasions when it was kinder to be cruel, Henderson turned authoritarian. "Flight Officer Spencer, you'll leave this office with Mr. Adams. At once. That's an order."

None of the three remaining officers looked at one another as Adams steered the white-faced girl outside. Grunting with relief, Henderson fished into his tunic for cigarettes. "Poor wee devil," he muttered. "What a hell of a thing to happen."

Davies was frowning heavily. "That's the trouble with having love birds on the same unit. Everyone gets hurt twice as much."

Taking the remark as a criticism and with his nerves still raw, Henderson responded with some heat. "They got involved after they were both posted here, and the regulations only apply to married couples. And it's never affected their work."

Seeing how feelings were running, Davies let the matter drop and glanced at his watch instead. "I've got to be moving. Try not to worry about what happened. You've all done a great job and I mean it. I'll be in touch again tomorrow. Probably in the afternoon."

Stiffening, the two officers watched his brisk figure march down the hut and disappear. With a groan Henderson sank into a chair. "Try not to worry! With Lambert sharpening his knives and he and Staines cooking up another operation for us." The Scot's aggrieved eyes settled on Moore. "Don't you think it's crazy involving us in politics like this?"

Moore hesitated. "If he's right in what he told us earlier, I suppose things couldn't have been allowed to drift."

"Yes, but why us? Hell, there are hundreds of squadrons in the RAF."

"We are his brain child, so we were a natural choice," Moore reminded him. "And I suppose the Rhine Maiden job did make us the most likely candidate for a public relations exercise."

Henderson sighed. "I suppose so. But if this is fame, give me anonymity. No one's quicker than the public to yank down their heroes and Lambert's sure to do a hatchet job now."

"It does look that way," Moore admitted.

"Then wouldn't it be wiser to cut our losses?"

"If that accident this morning made things worse, Davies can hardly do that, can he?"

"But has it made things worse? What about all those Yankee prisoners you helped to escape?"

Moore smiled. "That wasn't the way you were arguing a few minutes ago."

The scot groaned. "You're right. I'm so mixed up I can't tell my arse from my elbow." His tone changed. "Forget what you said to Sue just now. How do you think the Yankee crews are going to react when they hear about the men we've killed?"

"What would our reaction be if an American operation killed around twenty or thirty of our men?"

The Scot nodded gloomily. "Right. We'd say it was another Yankee cock-up. Let's hope they're more generous."

"They might be. But that's not likely to make any difference to what Lambert says to the American public, is it?"

Henderson made a gesture of distaste. "No, it isn't. So whether we like it or not we've got to take on another dicey job. Like kidnapping Eva Braun from the Eagle's Nest. Or towing the *Tirpitz* into Scapa Flow." An alarming thought brought an end to the Scot's sarcasm. "What if this one goes sour too? Christ, we could go down in history as the unit that split the Allies right down the middle and won Jerry the war. Have you thought of that?"

Tired though he was, Moore had to smile at the Scot's dour humour. "No. And I don't intend to until I've had some sleep."

A glance at the young squadron commander's face brought Henderson out of the realms of speculation. Heaving his bulk from the chair he took Moore's arm. "The hell with it. Let's go and have a quick whisky. Then you'd better get off to bed."

## 12

Halting the battered saloon by the kerb, Millburn whistled and turned to Gabby alongside him. "You're sure this is the place?"

Jumping out, Gabby walked towards a pair of large, wrought-iron gates. "Kashmir House. That's the address Wendy gave me."

Millburn joined him and peered through the gates. A circular drive, well-kept flowerbeds and a large house showed through the dusk. Millburn whistled again. "What did they say their Pappy is? A colonel?"

"A general," Gabby corrected. "Twenty-five years in India."

Millburn grinned. "A pukka sahib. I wonder what Mammy's like?"

"According to Wendy all Memsahib and Roedean."

"Roedean?"

"A posh girls' public school," Gabby explained, then showed impatience. "You going to talk here all night? The girls will be wondering what's happened to us."

Millburn took another glance through the tall gates. "You're sure there are no butlers or maids there?"

"No. They've all been given a half day. The girls have everything fixed."

"And Mom and Pop aren't due back until tomorrow afternoon?"

"That's right. What's the matter with you? You're not usually as cautious as this."

"I don't go to bed with debutantes every night in their Mammy and Pappy's stately home," the American pointed out. "If Pappy's an ex-Indian General he might have planted tiger traps in the drive."

Gabby swung open a gate. "All right. If you're worried, leave the car outside."

The small Welshman had met the girls two days ago. With Millburn on duty, Gabby had drifted into a charity dance organized by the local Women's Voluntary Service. Trained in observation, he had noticed two attractive girls helping out in the kitchen, and, ever the opportunist, had zeroed in. In no time at all he had discovered they were the high-spirited daughters of General Richards, ex-Indian Army, local J.P., and very much a part of the county society. On extended leave while repairs were being carried out to their private girls' college and with their parents away for a few days in Manchester, the two girls were clearly out to enjoy themselves and Gabby had taken full advantage of the situation. With self-assurance making up for his lack of inches and membership of the famous 633 Squadron to give him glamour, the navigator had quickly made a date for himself and Millburn. When Wendy had innocently suggested the men could come round to the house if they wished, Gabby's satisfaction had been immense. "We're in, boyo. For the whole night if we like."

Millburn, who found it hard to believe in fairies, had been more cautious. "Don't build on it. Kids like that are protected. Their idea of living it up is lemonade and snakes and ladders."

"Society kids? They're doing it before they go to school! I tell you, boyo, we're in. It's going to be bath salts, Bells Whisky, and bed, bed, bed."

The two airmen's shoes were crunching on the gravel. Halfway to the house, they heard the faint yapping of a dog. A few seconds later a light showed as the large front door was flung open. As giggles and upper-class voices could be heard, Millburn lifted a comical eyebrow. "Debretts? Or Burke's Peerage?"

Gabby grinned expectantly. "Probably both."

The girls had now appeared on the porch. A yapping Pekinese shot out after them, ran towards the two men, then scuttled back as Millburn tried to stroke it. Before either airman could speak, the taller of the two girls approached the American with an extended hand. "You must be Tommy Millburn. I'm Hilary and this is my sister, Wendy."

Millburn discovered Hilary's hand had a certain upper-class assurance. Wendy's hand had a more schoolgirlish wriggle. Millburn, caught more times than he cared to remember by Gabby's blind dates, was surprised to see how attractive both girls were. Hilary was tall and slender with long, blonde hair. Wendy, two inches shorter, had a slightly fuller figure and wore her hair in pageboy style. The family's wealth showed in their fashionable dresses.

Wendy had already taken possession of Gabby and was leading him into the house. Deciding the Welshman was starting to pay his debts at last, Millburn followed the delectable Hilary into the hall.

His feet sank into a deep pile carpet. On his right the crystal contents of a glass cabinet twinkled with the light from a huge ceiling chandelier. Ahead, a wide staircase ran up to a balcony. The panelled walls and balcony were lined with portraits of stern-faced soldiers with topees on their knees. A stuffed tiger's head and a huge Bengalese hallstand gave evidence of the family's background. A cocktail cabinet, a large sofa and two armchairs completed the furniture.

Giggling, Wendy pushed Gabby forward and dropped on the sofa with him. Giving her sister a sharp look, Hilary led Millburn to one of the armchairs. "I hope you find this comfortable."

Millburn hesitated. "What about you."

She drew up a leather stool and folded gracefully down on it. "I'll sit on this. I often do."

The Pekinese dog was sniffing at Millburn's leg. Reaching down to stroke it, the American drew back his hand just in time as the dog took a snap at him. He managed a smile. "What's his name?"

"Pouchi," the girl told him.

To Millburn's relief Pouchi took a last sniff at him and then moved petulantly away. His gaze returned to the girl. Her posture on the low stool showed him she had long and shapely legs. Unlike her sister, who had a fuller face, she had a slender chin and high cheekbones. With her blonde hair falling across her face in the fashion of the time, she had an enigmatic expression as she gazed up the American. "May I have a cigarette?"

Millburn began fishing in his tunic. "Sorry. I thought perhaps you didn't smoke."

She lifted a plucked eyebrow. "What on earth made you think that?"

When Millburn only shrugged, she accepted a cigarette and put it somewhat speculatively between her lips. Across on the sofa where Gabby was looking as smug as a cat with cream, Wendy turned. "Can I have one too, please, Tommy?"

Millburn lit both their cigarettes before dropping back into the armchair. As he lit his own, Wendy began to cough. "These have a funny taste, haven't they?"

"They're toasted. Don't you like them?"

Wendy pulled a face but persevered. On the leather stool, with her cigarette held elegantly in one slim hand, Hilary was eyeing Millburn again. "Are you really an American?"

"That's what my birth certificate says."

"But then what are you doing in the RAF?"

Millburn grinned. "Round about 1939 I got a hankering for a trip in a boat and it brought me over here. Then I met a guy in a pub one night and he told me the RAF would teach me to fly for nothing. He didn't say a thing about having to stop on and fight the war. Just shows you can't trust guys in pubs."

"I think it's wonderful you came over at that time to fight for us. Daddy would think so too."

Millburn blinked. "Would he?"

"Of course he would. Poor Daddy. He's been trying to get back into the Army ever since the war started but they won't have him because of his heart."

"That's tough," Millburn agreed.

"It upsets him because we're not doing more as a family. I know he'd give anything if we were boys. If we were, he'd have us in the Army tomorrow."

Millburn took another look at her shapely legs. "Sing hallelujah you're not."

"Not what?"

"Boys. There are too many boys around, don't you think?"

"We don't think so. Where we are in Harrogate they all seem to have been called up."

"There are still a few around," Millburn suggested. "Ready and rarin' to go."

She slanted a cool glance at him and then, with a flash of silken knees, rose. "Would you like a drink?"

"I wouldn't mind. What have you got?"

He received a stare. "Anything you want. Just say."

"Then I'll have a Bourbon."

"That's whisky, isn't it?"

"Kind of. Yes. Whisky'll be fine.

The girl turned to Gabby who was deep in puissant

conversation with the giggling Wendy. "What about you, Gabby?" When the Welshman did not hear her, Millburn spoke for him. "Women always do this to him. Give him a whisky too."

Jerking her head at Wendy, Hilary crossed the large room to the cocktail cabinet. Wendy, who, unlike Gabby, was missing nothing, hesitated a moment and then followed her. Watching the two of them whispering as they searched among the bottles for whisky, Millburn caught Gabby's eye and motioned him over.

"You're sure you've got the right age of these girls?" he muttered.

Gabby looked surprised. "Of course I have."

"Well, I'm not so sure. That upper-class stuff and sophistication can fool you but I don't put Hilary any more than eighteen or nineteen. And if there's two and a half years between 'em, that could put you into the red zone, mush."

Looking uneasy, Gabby glanced round at the whispering couple. "You're crazy. Wendy's got more on the top than Hilary."

"So what? They can have 'em as big as that when they're fourteen. You'd better watch it, boyo. I don't want you doing a stretch in Wormwood Scrubs."

Gabby glared at him resentfully. "Trust you to spoil it. Here we are, right among the fleshpots, and you have to give me a worry like that."

"You? Worry? That'll be the day. You check on her, buster, or the old man might do a tiger chase on us."

Across the room Wendy had found the whisky and was busy pouring it out. Seeing Hilary had noticed them talking, Millburn nudged Gabby who went back to the sofa. A minute later Wendy crossed the room carrying a tray. Giving a glass to Gabby, she approached Millburn. The way she eyed him made it clear she found the American's rugged good looks attractive. "We don't seem to have any Bourbon, so I've given us all Scotch whisky. Is that all right?"

The glasses on that tray, all half-filled, strengthened Millburn's suspicions. "Are those raw?"

"Raw?"

"Is that neat whisky?"

The nubile Wendy stared down. "Yes. Why?"

"You don't usually drink whiskies that size, do you?"

Looking uncertain for the briefest moment, Wendy glanced at Hilary who was at her elbow. With a light laugh the elder girl picked up a glass and sank elegantly on the stool. "Don't worry about us. There's always lots of drinking at the parties we go to. One gets used to it."

Waiting until Wendy had returned to Gabby, Millburn leaned forward. "How old is your sister?" he muttered.

"Eighteen. Why?"

"Are you sure?"

There was a sudden upper-class chill in the stare he received. "Of course I'm sure. What a silly question."

Lifting a hand, Millburn sank back. "O.K. O.K. I just want to be certain."

"Certain of what?"

"Certain she can handle whiskies of that size," the American countered.

"You seem very interested in Wendy."

Millburn decided he had done enough in the line of duty. "Wendy's Gabby's problem, not mine. Tell me about yourself. Have you got a boy friend?"

The girl's tone told him he was still not forgiven. "One or two."

"Here?"

"No."

Millburn grinned. "I always think it's here that counts, don't you? When do you expect your folks back."

He found the look she gave him difficult to interpret. "Somewhere around noon tomorrow."

"Is that a fact?"

"Yes. They're staying with my mother's sister in Manchester."

"They're taking risks, aren't they?"

"Why?"

"Leaving two beautiful daughters on their own."

He received that look again and this time wondered if it could be a challenge. "Why should that be taking a risk?"

Millburn shrugged. "Life being what it is."

"How is life with you?"

Millburn finished the last of his whisky. "It's getting better all the time."

She took the glass from him. "Then you'd better have another drink."

Millburn watched her graceful figure cross over to the cocktail cabinet where Wendy was already giving herself and Gabby a refill. Returning to the sofa the younger girl handed a glass to Gabby and then dropped giggling on his knee. Seeing the triumphant look Gabby gave him, the frowning Millburn, who liked to be second to no man, decided that different temperaments though the girls might have, this was the time to act. As Hilary returned and handed him another large whisky, he patted his knee. "How about sitting here for a change? You'll find it more comfortable than the stool."

Her smile froze. "On your knee? We hardly know one another."

"That's why, honey. Give my knee a try and we'll put that right."

She sank down on the stool with some hauteur. "I'm perfectly comfortable here, thank you. May I have another cigarette?"

Conscious he was getting the hot-and-cold treatment, the American consoled himself by remembering a full night lay ahead. Avoiding Gabby's grin, he prepared himself for a long siege. "O.K. Let's get to know one another. Were you born here or in India?"

"India," she muttered.

"Was Wendy born there too?"

"No. She was born in England."

Millburn made the comment without thinking. "You'd have thought it the other way round."

She stiffened. "What does that mean?"

"Nothing," Millburn said hastily.

"Yes, it does. You were hinting something."

110

"Was I?"

"Yes, you were. And I don't like people who hint things."

Never a man to be made a fool of, Millburn began to lose his temper. "There doesn't seem to be much you do like, does there?"

She was staring at the sofa where her sister and Gabby, with half a bottle of whisky inside them, were well past the need of conversation. The sight appeared to annoy her, for with an exclamation she jumped to her feet. "Would you like to look round the house?"

"You mean you're going to show me round?"

"If you'd like to see it, yes."

The American rose philosophically. "O.K. Let's go."

As they passed the sofa Gabby gave the American a licentious grin before sinking his face into the giggling Wendy's neck again. With heightened colour Hilary led Millburn into the library, the dining room and the kitchen quarters. As they came out in the hall again, she paused sullenly at the foot of the staircase.

"Would you like to see the rooms upstairs?"

Millburn shrugged. "Why not?"

Giving him another stare, the girl led him on to the balcony where he was introduced to her parents' rooms, Wendy's room, a couple of guest rooms and the bathroom. She passed by one door that stood in the centre of the balcony but on their way back she paused outside it. "I don't suppose you want to see my room?"

Puzzled by her behaviour but an eternal optimist, Millburn kept a low profile. "Why not? We've seen everything else."

With the balcony giving a clear view of the hall, Gabby and Wendy could be seen sprawled out full length on the sofa. As a loud giggle followed by a squeal floated upwards, Hilary gave an impatient exclamation and threw open the bedroom door. "I don't see any point in it but you can go in if you want to."

She did not switch on the light, giving Millburn only a glimpse of expensive furniture and a silken bed. As he walked forward across the thick carpet to gain a

111

better look, the door closed behind him. As he turned, a sullen voice sounded in his ear. "Well. Isn't this what you wanted?"

As Millburn stood there, too surprised to speak, the girl's voice came again. "What's the matter? You're not just all talk, are you?"

Coming to life, Millburn found the girl in the darkness and kissed her. The effect astonished him. With her sullenness falling away like an unwanted cloak, she pushed him towards the bed. As he dropped on it, she fumbled to unbutton his clothing while her mouth osculated against his neck and face. "Don't just sit there," she muttered impatiently. "Take your clothes off."

As he obeyed, Millburn could hear her heavy breathing and the urgent hiss of silk as she tore off her dress and underwear. Seconds later he was flat on his back on the bed again with the girl poised over him. In the darkness he could see the white blur of her face. When he tried to roll on top of her, she pushed him back, slid down, and lowered her head. The earth exploded for Millburn and bursting stars took its place in the heavens. A minute later her moist mouth returned and osculated against his own. He hardly recognized her throaty voice. "Now it's your turn, darling. Do anything you like. Hurt me if you want to. Only do it, do it!"

Grabbing her long, slender body, Millburn obliged. Her sobs quickened, then rose into a crescendo. "Yes, yes, yes . . . Don't stop . . . Don't stop. . . ."

When nature forced him to stop, the astonished Millburn found himself upturned once more. Lowering her head, Hilary caught the lobe of his ear in her teeth and tugged. As the American jumped, her hand slid down his body. Almost to his surprise Millburn discovered her squeezing, probing fingers awakened his passion yet again. The springs of the bed protested as the two of them rolled over and over. When he sank back at last, Millburn was panting as if he had run a marathon. As the girl put her arms around his neck, he pulled away. "Hold it, honey. You think I'm superman or something?"

Smiling, she drew his arms across her breasts and

snuggled herself into his thighs. Deciding the world was more full of surprises than a Christmas cake with currants, Millburn was about to fall into an exhausted sleep when he heard a car engine outside. He sat up sharply. Hilary's eyes opened. "What is it, darling?"

Leaping out of bed Millburn ran to the window but with the bedroom at the side of the house, he could see nothing but trees. He turned back to the startled girl. "Did your folks go to Manchester by train?"

"Of course. One can't get enough petrol for long journeys."

Millburn almost relaxed, then went tense again. "That means they'd have to take a taxi from the station."

Before the girl could answer he heard a door slam, followed by the sound of a departing car. Millburn began climbing frantically into his trousers. "They're back. They must be."

The naked girl leapt out of bed. "That's impossible. They definitely said they were staying until tomorrow."

Tucking in his shirt, the American slipped into his shoes. "Someone's arrived. And who else would it be at this time of night?" As the alarmed Hilary stared at him, Millburn remembered. "My God! Gabby and Wendy! They'll run right into them."

Motioning Hilary to keep quiet, he drew back the bedroom door. The chandelier had been switched off and only the faint glow of an electric fire stained the darkness below. Listening, Millburn heard voices outside, followed by the sound of a key in a lock. The yell of warning he was about to deliver Gabby died in his throat as the hall lights suddenly blazed on.

The scene that leapt out of the darkness was like a tableau for some blue comedy. Down on the sofa, where Wendy had proved that fast beginners are not always the quickest finishers, Gabby was starting to have his way at last. Naked except for his socks, he was poised over the pulsating Wendy, whose bare legs were wrapped passionately around him. To the horrified Millburn, the Welshman's white buttocks resembled some exotic mushroom against the green cloth of the

113

sofa. Frozen in nature's most ridiculous posture, Gabby in turn was staring back aghast at the intruders framed in the doorway.

One was a woman in her middle forties, amply-built and wearing a fashionable hat and coat. The sight of Gabby's buttocks leaping out of the darkness had brought a high-pitched scream from her. Now, hypnotized by the vision, she was clutching her throat. The florid General was alongside her, twelve to fifteen years her senior and sporting a white moustache, looked like a hirsute Victoria plum as he gazed uncomprehendingly at the sofa.

Time, which had stopped for all concerned, suddenly caught up with itself in a hasty whirring of cogs and dials. Confronted by Gabby's nether regions, the Memsahib had only one course open to her. With a muted sigh, she slid down to the carpet with elephantine grace and lay motionless. The General, looking more than ever like a Victoria plum about to burst, glared down at her. "Which one is it? Damn it, I can't tell from this end. Which one, woman?"

Memsahib kept her eyes tightly closed. Straightening, the General let out a bellow that made the crystals on the chandelier jingle. "You young scoundrel! I'll have you flogged. No, damn it, I'll have you shot! I'll shoot you myself."

Dancing with rage, he glared round for a weapon. Seeing nothing that would inflict the mutilations he had in mind, he charged for the library. Torn rudely from heaven to earth, Gabby rolled off the sofa and hopped frantically up and down as he tried to climb into his trousers. Wendy, panic-stricken, dragged down her skirt and fled weeping towards the kitchen. With the hall momentarily empty of all but the hopping Gabby, Millburn leaned over the balustrade. "Never mind your clothes, you moron," he hissed. "Get the hell out of there before he shoots you."

Taking the American at his word, the Welshman grabbed his clothes and bolted for the front door, leaping over the prostrate Memsahib in the process. Unsure whether the General had overheard him or not, Millburn withdrew into the bedroom. The panic-stricken

114

Hilary followed him. "He'll shoot you both! He's got a shotgun in the library!"

Aware there was no escape downstairs, Millburn threw open the window. To his relief a drainpipe ran down the wall a couple of feet away. Stuffing his socks and tie into his tunic pocket, the American climbed out on the window ledge. As more threatening bellows were heard downstairs, followed by the yapping of Pouchi, Hilary's white face stared out. "Hurry! In case he comes upstairs."

Suspecting the girl was more concerned for her own safety than for his, the sweating Millburn gripped the window sash with one hand and reached out gingerly with the other. To his relief the fall pipe seemed firm. Squirming round on the narrow ledge, he released the sash and grabbed the pipe with both hands. Shoes scrabbling against the wall, he began lowering himself down. He was passing a lower window when there was the crash of a shotgun followed by a startled yell. Aghast, he glanced up at Hilary who was leaning out the window. "My God!" he muttered. "He's shot Gabby."

She motioned him frantically to keep quiet. "Don't let him know you're here or he'll shoot you as well."

It was advice Millburn hardly needed. Yells and blood-curdling threats were followed by another thunderous blast from the shotgun. Feeling soft earth beneath his feet Millburn edged to the front of the house and peered round.

In total defiance of the blackout the lights of the porch were ablaze. They enabled Millburn to see the formidable figure of the General, shotgun at the ready, stalking along the left-hand-drive. Half-expecting to see a mangled body nearby, the relieved Millburn could see no sign of Gabby. Another roar from the General provided the explanation.

"Come and face your medicine, you scoundrel! I know you haven't got away."

Millburn realized Gabby could be hiding on either side of the circular drive. For his part, the trees and shrubs that flanked the right-hand drive were his nearest cover. As he wondered how he was going to cross the lighted frontage of the house without detection, Pouchi, who until now had been cowed by the roar of the shotgun, suddenly burst out from the porch and flew yapping towards the left-hand gate. Recognizing help when he saw it, the General gave a roar of welcome. "Good boy, Pouchi. Find him! Find the scoundrel."

Genuinely alarmed for Gabby's safety, Millburn acted promptly. Grabbing up a large stone he hurled it at a clump of trees near the right-hand gate. As it struck a tree and fell, the yapping dog changed its course and scampered across the intervening flowerbed. The triumphant General ran after it. "Good boy, Pouchi! Flush him out!"

The moment dog and master vanished among the shadowy trees, Millburn put his head down and flew down the opposite drive. "Gabby!" he hissed. "Where the hell are you?"

He was halfway to the gate when a shaken figure emerged from the shrubbery. Grabbing the Welshman's arm, Millburn kept running. He had just reached the gate when there was a roar of fury, followed by a stab of light and an explosion from the clump of trees. As both men ducked, pellets rattled among the dry leaves behind them. Gabby let out a yelp. "He's mad! Stark raving mad!"

Millburn dragged him through the gate and down the pavement towards the car. Bundling him into it, he threw the car into gear and ignoring the danger of collision, backed at full speed away from the house. As he braked and turned the car across the road, the General reached the gate. Giving another Imperial bellow, he threw the shotgun to his shoulder and fired. Pellets rattled against the side of the car and glass showered over the startled Millburn. Spinning the wheel, he put his foot down hard. "Jesus," he muttered. "This is worse than Happy Valley!"

They were a mile away before Millburn eased off the accelerator and turned to the shaken Gabby. "You hurt?"

Gabby who had miraculously held on to his tunic but lost his shirt, slid a finger beneath his buttocks and

116

felt gingerly. "I think I've got a few pellets in me." His voice rose indignantly. "The old bugger would have killed me. You realize that?"

As relief welled up in Millburn, so did anger. "You've done it to me again, haven't you? What was it going to be —bath salts, whisky, and bed? You never told me their old man was a homicidal maniac."

The resilient Welshman was recovering fast. "What are you moaning about? You got what you came for, didn't you? I saw you go into Hilary's bedroom."

Millburn had never felt more vindictive. "But you weren't so lucky, were you, boyo?" He grinned at the glare he received. "I warned you all that giggling was probably just wet knickers and wishful thinking. Maybe the next time you won't be so quick to keep the hot numbers to yourself."

## 13

Staines and the Brigadier were talking beside the french windows when Davies was shown into the library at High Elms. As the young lieutenant announced him, the American General turned, then gave a wry grin.

"Davies! What the hell are you still doing in uniform? I thought you'd have been sent your dungarees by this time."

Uncertain what undercurrents might be lying beneath the humour, Davies decided to accept it at face value and ran his eyes over the General's uniform. "They issue smart dungarees in your outfit, sir."

Staines grinned again. "We don't do badly, do we?" He thrust out a big hand. "If you don't like yours when they arrive, I'll send you a pair. At least they help morale."

With the man's handshake firm, Davies began to feel the interview wasn't going to be the ordeal he feared. "I'm sorry things went the way they did, sir. But

117

the boys did their best. If it hadn't been for that one damn shell the operation would have been a complete success."

Staines dropped his bulk into a chair. "I know that, Davies, and so do my staff. In fact I'll let you into a secret. I don't think there's another unit around that could have done such a precision job. Even getting there undetected was a small miracle."

Generosity on this scale exceeded Davies' wildest hopes. At the same time it increased his embarrassment. "Thank you, sir. But I hope it hasn't made any difficulties for you."

Staines gave a shrug. "That depends on which side of the fish pond you're standing. If the Brigadier's partisans get fifty or so of our boys back, I won't miss my share of drinks over here when Christmas comes. But if you've got Congress in mind, I might not be so popular when Lambert's finished with me. I had a telex cable this morning saying he's already done his first hatchet job. And there's plenty more to come."

Davies could not hide his dismay. "But won't your Congressmen take into account the prisoners we've freed?"

"The one's who're backing us will. But the hawks who want the Japs finished first are going to have a field day. Can't you see Lambert's headlines? RAF KILL AMERICAN PILOTS. RECKLESS MISSION TO HUSH CRITICS. Whether we like it or not we've given him the chopper to kill the chicken."

As Davies sank heavily into a chair, the Brigadier's quiet voice made both men glance at him. "I feel the same responsibility as Davies, General. We can't undo the accident but you have my word that every effort will be made to get as many men as possible back to the U.K."

The Texan lifted his big shoulders. "I'm not blaming you. It was a great idea. But now it's backfired on us, I'm thrown into the ball game myself. If we don't counter Lambert's campaign smartly, our entire air strategy over here could be affected."

Eager to re-burnish his unit's international reputation, Davies was looking at a large map that was lying folded across the desk. "The brigadier says you already have something in mind, sir?"

"That's right. By luck we've an operation due in a week that will hit the headlines of every paper in the States. I thought if I could get you involved, we could knock Lambert out cold before he can do too much damage. So I spent all last night arguing with the U.S. Army and the Navy. Lucky for us they share my view of your mission yesterday; in fact they're full of praise for it. Add to that your Rhine Maiden reputation and I managed to get you into the team. But don't think it was easy because originally this was meant to be an all-American occasion."

As attentive as an excited terrier, Davies watched the big Texan unroll the map. It proved to be a large-scale representation of the French Cotentin peninsular. Anchoring the map with two glass ashtrays, Staines motioned Davies to his elbow. "If you agree to play in this game and you pull it off, we're right back on base again. So don't say no until you've got all the facts. O.K.?"

Seeing he had the small Air Commodore's undivided attention, Staines turned back to the map and dropped a tobacco-stained forefinger on a point near the north-western tip of the peninsula. "X marks the spot! Up above the cliffs here near Omonville the Heinies have almost completed a large radio-location station. Apart from giving early warning of air raids, its job will be to scan and plot all Allied shipping movements along the Channel in the Plymouth-Southampton area. A Yank task force is going to blow it up. It's going to be a big operation. At least 3,500 troops are taking part. Your job, if you take it on, is to provide air support. In turn you'll receive high cover from our 8th Air Force Thunderbolts. If the job's a success, the news value will be sensational. FIRST AMERICAN TROOPS INTO EUROPE . . . INVASION IMMINENT . . . you can see the headlines in every newspaper from New York to Los Angeles. Best of all from our point of view is the publicity the RAF will receive as the British unit who gave our boys protection. Every Mom in the States will send the

British an extra food parcel and Lambert's campaign will get a lethal kick up the ass." Staines turned and gazed up at Davies. "Well. What do you think?"

Davies coughed and drew away from the cigar smoke as if blaming it for his hesitation. "What exactly would our role be again?"

"Ground support. That way all the Army and Navy as well as any war correspondents present will see you doing your stuff. You'll ground strafe any Heinie reinforcements who might be rushed up while our boys are blowing up the station. That shouldn't be too difficult. The station stands on an isolated site on the cliffs and there's only a narrow support road leading up to it."

Davies asked the obvious question first. "But why can't you attack it from the air?"

"That's easy. We don't want to." Seeing Davies' expression, Staines threw a grin at the Brigadier. "Remember the Dieppe raid of '42? Its purpose was to blood the British and Canadian troops and to probe the enemy's coastal defences. Now it's our turn. Someone up top has decided our divisions stationed in the U.K. must get some battle experience before the invasion. Also it's important we know what new defences the Heinies have up their sleeve. This radio station gives us the perfect excuse to launch a raid on this coast without anyone guessing we have other motives. With all the intelligence the station is intended to feed back, a raid of this size will seem completely justified."

Davies' face cleared again. "But won't the fact we haven't tried to bomb it look suspicious in itself?"

"No. Fortunately for us, our B.17s did have a crack at the early installations before this scheme was mooted and found the bunkers took everything they could hand out. Since then our agents have discovered they're nine feet thick and can only be destroyed by charges planted inside. So one way and another we don't think the Heinies will get on to us."

Knowing Davies better than the American and reading more from his expression, the Brigadier thought it prudent to add a few words of his own. "Apart from your unit's reputation, Davies, which has persuaded the American Army and Navy to fit you in, we do feel you're well equipped for the role. You can carry 250-lb. bombs, rockets, even anti-personnel bombs if you think them necessary. You've also got machine guns and 20mm cannon for strafing troops and tanks if the Germans can get them to the station in time!" A sensitive man, the Brigadier made it clear he appreciated what was being asked of the Air Commodore. "We're fully aware of the risks involved in ground support. However you will be patrolling the road, which is some distance from the station itself. And it is going to be impressed on the assault troops that the elimination of flak posts is a top priority."

Although Davies' face cleared somewhat, it still betrayed a conflict of emotions. Pride that 633 Squadron, the élite unit of his own creation, should be invited into an all-American operation was there in full measure. At the same time the small Air Commodore was too much of a professional to let pride take precedence over commonsense, and his doubts showed as he glanced back at the Texan.

"I appreciate your confidence in us, sir. But as the real purpose is to restore the RAF's image over in the States, wouldn't a couple of Typhoon squadrons do as good a job and also present smaller targets for ground fire?"

Staines frowned. "I'm going to have to recap, Davies. Someone in our Joint Air Staff decided for political reasons that Lambert's propaganda had to be countered and so your squadron was thrown in at the deep end. Because the operation needed my permission, I was thrown in too. Now the scheme has backfired and given Lambert a new stick to beat the RAF with. So now you, me and everyone else concerned with weakening the Heinies' Air Force before the invasion, has to clear up the mess and quick. Otherwise God knows what damage will be done."

Davies countered frown with frown. "I know all that, sir. But Typhoons are specially designed for ground support. If they do as good a job, won't that reflect just as well on the RAF?"

"Goddamn it, Davies, you keep on missing the point, never mind the facts of life. Armies, Navies and Air Forces hate one another's guts. Yours do and ours do. Half the time they're expecting us to bomb and strafe them instead of the Heinies. So imagine their faces when I come along and ask them to use RAF ground support. Now they know I'm a Fifth Columnist! I had to argue all night, Davies, and pull every conman's trick in the book before they agreed. But what chance would I have had if I'd suggested using a couple of unknown Typhoon squadrons? I got you in because of your reputation but even then it was touch and go."

A realist, Davies saw he had no choice. "All right, sir. We'll take it on. What's the date of the raid?"

Staines' rugged face betrayed his relief. "Good man. Granted the weather's favourable, a week today. The assault craft are due on the beaches at first light. I know it's short notice but that can't be helped. The raid was originally scheduled for the middle of September, so we're lucky to get into the act at all. You can be ready, can't you?"

"We can be if we get all the operational details in time."

"That'll all be taken care of this week. It'll probably mean your going down to Portsmouth to meet the Army and Navy but that can't be helped. I'll fix up a briefing session as soon as I can and we'll meet there. Keep everything between the three of us until I give you the green light. In the meantime I understand you'll be getting a few interim details from your own Intelligence."

The Brigadier nodded as Davies glanced at him. "We've asked our French agents to take a few photographs. They're working on it now."

Davies turned back to the Texan. "I take it there's an alternative date in case the weather plays up?"

"That's right. The following night. If that also proves rough it's off until the spring. The weather men reckon it'll be too hazardous later in October."

Davies was thinking of the recent inclement weather. "Let's hope the weather settles down before then."

The big Texan's grunt betrayed the importance he attached to the operation. "Amen to that." He turned his chair towards Davies. "Smoke?"

Davies saw he was holding up his cigar case. Remembering that the last time he had smoked one of the American's massive cigars he had survived without injury, and feeling it was a gesture that sealed the entente, the small Air Commodore took one. Applying a match with confidence, he let out a strangled cough. "My God!"

Staines looked innocent. "Something wrong?"

It was a full six seconds before Davies could vent his accusation. "This isn't the brand you were smoking before."

"That's right." The Texan was grinning. "The war's getting rougher all the time. Leave it if it's too strong for you."

Davies would have died rather than make such an admission. Drawing on the miniature airship again, he emitted a cloud of acrid smoke and unsteadily rounded the table to collect his briefcase. His effort to suppress a fit of coughing showed in his reddened eyes and halting voice. "They just take a bit of getting used to, that's all."

Staines winked at the Brigadier who, relieved at the outcome of the meeting, was hiding a smile. "O.K. Davies. We'll get you briefed as soon as we can— certainly before the weekend." As Davies saluted and reached the door, the big American's quizzing voice made him glance back indignantly. "Maybe by that time you'll have got that smoke finished."


The pretty Waaf opened Moore's ante-room door. "Pilot officers McKenny and Ross are here, sir."

"Good. Send them in, Tess, will you?"

Ross, entering the room first, looked uncertain as he approached the desk. McKenny, pale-faced and with a large plaster showing beneath his cap, had the expression of a man who had just had crippling news and was still stunned by it. The handshake they both received from the smiling Moore put Ross at ease but made no impression on McKenny, whose thoughts seemed to be in another world. Moore studied him for a moment before he invited the two men to draw up chairs.

"It's good to have you both back. The truth is I didn't expect you until tomorrow. I thought the West End might have tempted you to break your journey."

Although a man who found small talk difficult, Ross made the effort if only to counter McKenny's black mood. "Wouldn't you have minded, skipper?"

Moore's eyes twinkled as he sank back into his chair. "Officially, yes. Unofficially, I might have blamed it on the transport system." His tone changed as he turned to the silent McKenny. "How's your head, Paddy?"

The question had to sink through McKenny's preoccupation before he responded. "It wasn't much, skipper," he muttered. "There's no fracture or anything like that."

"So the M.O. says. All the same he'd like you to have a couple of days off." As McKenny gave a start, Moore turned to Ross. "As you're part of the same team and you got the same ducking, I don't see why you shouldn't have a couple of days as well. Only hang around the station. I might be needing every man I have quite soon."

McKenny's face clouded again. Curious to know the verdict on the operation, Ross failed to notice it. "Was the job a success, skipper? Or did St. Claire's accident foul it up?"

Moore's shrug gave nothing away. "We released a train load of prisoners. So I don't think we did too badly, do you?"

"I know, skipper, but what about the ones we killed? How are the Yanks taking it?"

"As far as I know, the Yanks are taking it very well. I had half a dozen phone calls yesterday afternoon asking me to congratulate you all on what you did. You'll find details on your flight notice board."

The freckle-faced Ross grimaced. "They're being generous, aren't they?"

"Very generous so far," Moore said truthfully.

"I don't suppose you've heard anything more about St. Claire and Simpson?"

"Nothing that didn't come out at the de-briefing. It looks as if they have a chance but only a slim one. Arthur Heron was wounded but he should be all right in a few weeks."

"So if St. Claire and Simpson bought it, we lost four men?"

A man who felt his squadron losses without showing it, Moore gave a terse nod. "That's right. And one way and another I think we were lucky. Particularly over you two." To Ross's dismay he picked from his desk a de-briefing report that the two men had filled in half an hour earlier. "This report from Adams says you think your port engine must have had an oil pipe nicked when you attacked that flak wagon. Are you sure of that? Because it took a hell of a long time to run dry, didn't it?"

Ross was careful not to glance at McKenny as he answered. "We can't think where else it can have happened, skipper."

Moore, who had been secretly watching McKenny, now turned to the Irishman. "Then you didn't run into any other flak on your way home?"

Once again it took McKenny a moment to realize he was being spoken to. "We'd have put it on the report if we had, skipper," he muttered. "Everything's down there."

"You're quite sure of that?"

"Yes. Of course I am."

Moore gazed at him, then shrugged. "I suppose stranger things have happened. But it does make you the luckiest couple on this side of the Channel. All right, I'll tell Adams he can send in your report with the rest of them. Congratulations on getting back safely and have a rest for the next couple of days. That's all."

Both men rose but only Ross turned for the door. "Can I have a word with you, skipper?" McKenny muttered.

Moore sank back into his chair. "Of course. Sit down."

At the door Ross paused and threw an uneasy glance over his shoulder before disappearing. Moore pushed a packet of cigarettes across the desk. "What's the problem, Paddy? You're looking right under the weather. Is it that bang on the head or is something else troubling you?"

McKenny made certain the office was empty before answering. Resentment that service life should force him to take Moore into his confidence made his voice sullen. "There was a letter waiting for me when I got back today. From my fiancée."

Wondering if he was going to get at the root of the Irishman's troubles at last, Moore played his cards carefully. "She's the pretty girl who's a nurse, isn't she? In Lincoln?"

"Yes. She's a staff nurse there. But she'll be leaving soon. She's joined a nursing unit that's going to the Middle East. They were expecting to go in November but this letter says they'll now be leaving in the middle of October."

"Is she the reason you wanted leave so badly last week?" Moore interrupted.

Although McKenny nodded, he avoided Moore's eyes. "I wanted to try to talk her out of it."

"I take it you didn't?"

"No."

Moore picked up a pencil from his desk and studied it a moment before speaking. "This is happening all over the world, you know, Paddy. Single men sent abroad have to wait four years before they see their girls again. So yours isn't a special case."

The Irishman's sudden passion made Moore's eyes lift. "It's special to me, skipper. If I can see her again, there's still the chance I might change her mind."

"You know they need nurses in the Middle East, Paddy? Pretty badly from what I hear. She probably knows that too."

McKenny's expression made it clear he could not care less what the Middle East needed. "I must have one more chance, skipper. You said I can have two days off. Then why can't I spend them in Lincoln?"

Moore was studying him closely. "Is this your only reason for wanting to see her? Or is there something else?"

The Irishman's outburst made Moore wonder for a moment if he were right. "Only reason? Christ, she's my fiancée and she's going abroad for God knows how long. And I'm in aircrew with only one chance in three of surviving the war. What other reason do you need?"

Deciding he must be reading more into the affair than he should, Moore sighed and sat back. "All right, Paddy. You win. When's your next train?"

The change in the man was almost miraculous. "I can catch a connection in Highgate at 20.30."

"Then you've got plenty of time to get ready. But I want you back at 24.00 hours tomorrow. Not a minute later. Is that understood?"

The Irishman was already halfway across the room. "I'll be back, skipper. I appreciate it. Thanks."

As he ran out into the corridor, Moore entered the anteroom. The Waaf, gazing with surprise at the slammed door, turned to him with raised eyebrows. "What did you do, sir? Give him a thousand pounds?"

Moore's smile was wry. "Tess, I'm going to ask you a question and I demand a straight answer. Am I getting too old and crotchety to appreciate the agony of young love?"

The girl ran her eyes down his youthful figure and giggled. "Hardly, sir. I'd say you understood it very well."

Moore grinned at her and then withdrew thoughtfully into his office. "Thanks, Tess. I was beginning to wonder."

Ross was waiting anxiously in the corridor. "What was all that about?" he asked as McKenny hurried towards him.

He received a cheerful slap on the shoulder. "Come outside and I'll tell you."

Puzzled at this change of mood, Ross obeyed. "He didn't bring up that business about the engine again, did he?"

127

McKenny laughed. "No. He believed the fibs we told him. All we spoke about was leave."

"Leave?"

"Yes. I've got until midnight tomorrow."

"You mean to go to Lincoln again?"

"That's right."

The Scot whistled. "How did you pull it off?"

In a rare good humour McKenny winked at him. "I think he's pleased with the job we did."

He was leading the navigator down a path that led to the junior officers' billets. "What time's your train?" Ross asked.

"8.30 from Highgate."

"Then we've time for a drink before you start getting ready, haven't we?"

Shaking his head, McKenny continued walking. "I want to get ready first. If there's still time we can have a drink before the transport leaves."

Heartened by the Irishman's change of mood, Ross followed him into their billet. As McKenny stripped off his tunic and began removing his shoes, the Scot dropped on the bed opposite him. "I suppose you'll be seeing Joan," he ventured.

McKenny grinned. "What do you think I'm going for?"

With moments of good humour a rarity these days, Ross decided to exploit this one to the full. "Has this something to do with that letter you got today?"

Unlacing a shoe, McKenny paused, then appeared to make a decision. "Yes. She's written to say she could be leaving Lincoln in a couple of weeks."

Hardly able to believe he was enjoying the Irishman's confidence, Ross proceeded with great care. "Where is she going, Paddy?"

McKenny dropped his second shoe before replying. "She's going with a nursing unit to the Middle East. The latest date of sailing is the middle of October."

Without being certain why, Ross was feeling relief. "Is that what's been worrying you lately?"

Turning to drape his tunic over a hangar at the head of his bed, McKenny took a moment to reply. "What do you think?"

"But why haven't you told me before?"

"What was the point? You couldn't do anything."

Ross found that hard to deny. "Are you going to try to talk her out of it?"

"If I can, yes."

"Do you think you can?"

There was no answer from the Irishman who still had his back to Ross. Unable to see the effect of his question, the Scot asked it again. "Do you think you can, Paddy?"

McKenny let out a sudden curse and slumped down on the bed. "No," he muttered. "I haven't a chance in hell."

Ross was showing dismay at this relapse. "Why not? Can't she get out of it?"

"She can get out of it if she wants to. But she doesn't."

"Why? Does she feel it's her duty?"

McKenny's laugh was harsh. "That's one way of putting it."

In his eagerness to help, Ross made his fatal blunder. "Have you talked to Father McBride about it?"

McKenny glanced up sharply. "What can he do?"

"He might offer to talk to her."

"You think that would make any difference?"

"It might. Isn't it worth trying?"

McKenny's eyes were suddenly full of dislike. "You still believe in fairies, don't you? That a priest has only to open his mouth and the walls of Jericho come tumbling down. I suppose you'd like me to go down on my knees and pray as well?"

The Irishman's hostility was bewildering Ross. "What's wrong with prayer? You've turned to it often enough in the past."

"That's right. And where the hell has it got me?"

Ross thought he understood. "If people make decisions that hurt others, Paddy, you can't put the blame elsewhere."

"You mean you can't put the blame on God. Right?"

The young Scot's voice did not falter. "If you want to put it that way."

"I do want to put it that way. He claims to have made the world and everything in it. He claims to be omnipotent. So he has to take the blame for all the suffering in it. He can't have his cake and eat it."

"That's ridiculous. People were given free will. If they use it to start wars and cause misery, they're the ones who must shoulder the blame."

"So God isn't to blame for this shambles? It's you and me and all the other guys?"

"In a way, yes, I suppose it is."

"Then why don't you set a good example? I know how you hate dropping bombs on women and kids. If this is all about free will, why don't you use yours and quit?"

"That's a stupid question."

"No, it isn't. If you're right about free will, everyone of us ought to stop killing one another."

"You know as well as I do that the people who started this war won't quit. They have to be stopped."

"You mean they act as if they're possessed?"

Ross fell into the trap. "Perhaps they are. By the power of evil."

McKenny's grin mocked him. "Then they're not free agents, are they? They're just pawns in a power game. Which brings us back to the question—why doesn't God put an end to it? You're prepared to fight evil—why isn't he? I thought he was supposed to love his children."

Unused to theological arguments, Ross was losing his way. "I've just told you—God can't interfere without taking away our free will. We have to clean up our own mess."

"But you've just agreed the power of evil is involved. Where's the free will in that?" When Ross remained silent, McKenny's voice rose contemptuously. "You and your kind make me sick. You know why? Because you haven't the guts to put the blame where it belongs. And in my book that's cowardice."

It is doubtful if anything but an attack on his

religion would have provoked Ross into retaliation against McKenny. "At least we know now why you attacked those transports, don't we? Joan has decided to nurse in the Middle East and so you hate the world, the Germans, your friends, even God himself. Have you ever thought that's the way children act when they can't have what they want?"

McKenny stiffened. For a moment it looked as if he might strike Ross. Then, muttering something beneath his breath, he snatched a towel from his locker and made for the washroom. The slam of the door made the unhappy Ross wince.

## ————— 14 —————

The wind, keening down the narrow country lane, made the two cyclists strain on their pedals. Dressed in the ubiquitous blue of the French farm labourer, both men were in their middle thirties. One, Pierre Lefray, was powerfully-built with a square, dogged face and a thatch of brown hair. His companion was thin to the point of emaciation, with hollow cheeks and lank black hair. A Breton like his friend, Jean Arnaud was a product of the slums of St Nazaire, cynical, tubercular, and fanatical in his hatred of the German invader. The narrow lane ran up a steep hill and the exertion of climbing it against the wind was clearly taxing him, yet his cycle was a full length ahead of Lefray's. As they passed a large proclamation carrying a legend in both French and German, he glanced back and gave a shout. "We're in the prohibited area now. So keep your eyes open."

Pierre Lefray contented himself with a nod. Vigilant before, the two men now glanced back over their shoulders every few seconds. Reaching a gate almost at the hill crest, they hurriedly swung it open and carried their cycles over the muddy entrance into a field. Hiding them in the thick hedge, both men crouched down to recover their breath and study the view before them.

Fields, divided by stone hedges, swept down the hillside to a distant beach. The sea was a grey line at the edge of an equally grey sky. The view was desolate except for a curious complex of buildings that towered into the sky a mile or more to the men's right. Reaching back into the hedge, Arnaud pulled out a small, telescopic camera and a pair of binoculars from his saddlebag. Stuffing the camera into a pocket he focused the binoculars on the installation.

A massive squat blockhouse leapt into vision. It supported a tall steel mast that terminated in a large, rectangular aerial. Two smaller dish aerials stood a hundred yards or so at either side of the parent building. Other blockhouses, all massively constructed, formed an irregular pattern inside a perimeter wall. Outside the wall pillboxes were cunningly sited to give maximum covering fire. The entire complex was surrounded by tank traps and dragon's teeth.

Arnaud passed the binoculars to Lefray. At the bigger man's grunt of shock, Arnaud gave his street-Arab grin. "There's a minefield, too. Two hundred metres in depth right up to the strong points."

Lefray was watching grey uniformed figures moving inside the perimeter wall. "It must be important to them. Why the hell can't London bomb it? Surely it would be cheaper in lives."

"They already have. But those blockhouses are three metres thick."

"All the same, it's going to be an expensive job. Louis says the beach defences are the worst he's seen along this coast."

Arnaud's shrug betrayed his cynical indifference to death. "At least the Yanks'll learn what to expect when the invasion comes." Straightening, he pointed at a tall oak whose branches reached out over the field. "That must be the tree Etienne told us about. Let's get the job over."

His thin chest was still rising and falling rapidly from his earlier exertions. As a sudden fit of coughing doubled him up the good-natured Lefray tried to take the camera. "Let me handle it. I know how to use that thing."

His deep-set eyes feverish, Arnaud pushed him roughly aside. "The hell you will! You'll obey orders or you'll be in trouble when we get back."

The chastened Lefray followed Aranud to the base of the oak and helped him on to its lower branches. He then ran back to the gate to keep watch on the road.

Gasping with his exertions, Arnaud was halfway up the tree when a shout from Lefray made him freeze. Listening, he heard the hum of an engine through the sound of the wind and the rustle of dry leaves. Glancing around him, he edged into a large fork in the branches and made himself as inconspicuous as possible.

At the gate Lefray was watching an Sdk/2 armoured car making its way slowly up the hill. Its purpose was clearly surveillance: an officer with binoculars was standing up in the turret scanning the surrounding fields. Behind him were the menacing barrels of a 20mm cannon and a machine gun. Slipping back through the gate Lefray took cover behind the hedge.

The armoured car's engine took on a sterner note as the hill steepened. Thirty yards away a flock of starlings broke cover from a tree with a clatter of wings. Able to hear voices now, Lefray threw an anxious glance at the oak. To his horror one of Arnaud's blue-trousered legs was visible through a gap in the branches. Cursing the impulse that had made him take cover at the wrong side of the gate, Lefray was considering a dash past it when the armoured car reached the gate and halted.

Gazing frantically along the hedge, Lefray saw a clump of bramble and edged towards it. In the lane a door slid metallically back. As boots clattered down on the lane Lefray pulled an automatic pistol from the waistband of his dungarees and sank down behind the bramble.

The gate rattled as a corporal climbed over it and jumped down into the mud. His expression told his views of an officer who delegated such jobs to his subordinates. Picking his way gingerly to one side of

133

the gate, he rubbed one muddied boot against the other as he surveyed the field before him. Peering through the bramble, Lefray saw that Arnaud's leg was still visible.

He ducked back as the soldier began moving towards him. As the footsteps came within a few paces of him, he braced himself. Then they halted and he heard the sound of a man relieving himself.

An impatient shout came from the lane. Grunting something, the corporal adjusted his clothes and started back towards the gate. Aware it was the most dangerous moment of all, Lefray was frantically trying to decide whether a suicidal attempt to rescue Arnaud would have any point or purpose if discovery came when a jackdaw broke out from the hedge and flew squawking past the corporal's head. With a start the German turned his head and watched it fly towards the cliffs. By the time he looked back his eyes were fully occupied by the glutinous mud that surrounded the gate. Stepping gingerly through it, he swung a leg over the gate and dropped out of Lefray's sight. His relaxed voice as he addressed the officer told the Frenchman all was well. A moment later the armoured car drove away. Waiting until it had cleared the hill crest, Lefray ran forward. "Are you all right?"

Arnaud's reply was caustic. "All right? You think I'm a bloody chimpanzee? The wind's nearly killing me."

"We were lucky. You had a leg showing." The anxious Lefray watched Arnaud edge out along an upper branch. "Don't fall, for God's sake."

A curse followed almost immediately as Arnaud, in lifting the camera to his eye, almost lost his balance. Wrapping an arm around a branch, he braced himself and tried again. In all he took six photographs before pocketing the camera and climbing down. Leaving his observation point at the gate, Lefray joined him.

"You think the light was good enough?"

Short of breath after his exertions, Arnaud's reply was curt. "We'll have to find out, won't we?"

Lighting foul-smelling cigarettes, the two men moved behind the clump of bramble and waited. Once they heard the sound of a passing horse and cart and the murmur of voices. It was followed ten minutes later by the armoured car. This time it did not stop at the gate but continued down the hill.

Although by this time Arnaud was shivering with cold, still the two men waited. Dusk was now closing in and shadowing the distant radiolocation station. Once more the patrolling armoured car returned and disappeared over the hill crest. This time Arnaud gave Lefray a nod and the two men dragged their bicycles from the hedge. Before wheeling them out on the lane, they stood a moment listening. Then, running forward, they began free-wheeling down the hill. Dusk closed around them and in a few seconds they disappeared.

"Was this Staines' idea, sir?" Henderson asked.

Davies gave him a sharp look. "Yes. Why?"

No one could be more blunt than Henderson when he felt the occasion demanded it. "Then I think he's picked the wrong squadron for it. This is a Tiffie job."

"What makes you so sure of that?"

"The job itself. Ground support. Isn't that what Tiffies are for?"

Davies had the expression of a man defending a shaky position and knowing it. "The job might call for a long patrol over the target area. Typhoons couldn't stay out that long."

"They could go over in relays, couldn't they?"

With a snort of exasperation, Davies turned to Moore. "I suppose this is your opinion too?"

The three officers were the only men present in the Operations Room that day. Acutely aware of his responsibility, Davies had asked for full security measures to be taken and two S.P.s were on guard outside.

Challenged into giving an opinion, Moore chose the most tactful one possible. "If we were talking in purely military terms, sir, the answer would have to be yes."

Davies scowled at the admission he was forced to make. "Well, we're not talking in purely military terms. Staines wouldn't have stood a snowball's chance in hell of getting the Yanks to agree to any other squadron but us. So for Christ's sake let's cut out the quibbles and make the best of it. If we can do a good job here, the publicity will be tremendous and a crisis will be averted. In the long run that could be more important than sinking a couple of Nazi battleships."

Henderson gave a long-suffering sigh. "All right, sir. We'll do our best, of course."

"Good man. That's the spirit." Looking relieved, Davies turned back to Moore. "I shall want you and Adams to come down with me to Portsmouth when they convene the briefing. You'll get plenty of warning."

Moore nodded. "You say our job will be to patrol the coastal road?"

"That's right. If Jerry doesn't get his reserves up in time, it'll be a doddle. Even if he does, you ought to be able to handle 'em easily enough if our Intelligence hasn't misled us."

"I'd like a preliminary look at the road and the station, sir."

"I'd rather you didn't. Jerry might get suspicious if he sees too many kites flying over the station."

"I can get round that easily enough. I'll take a flight path that will make it seem I'm photographing the Cherbourg docks."

Davies frowned. "I've already had Benson on the blower. They'll be sending a photo-reconnaissance Spitfire over the station as soon as the weather improves."

"I'd still like to take a look at it myself, sir." Moore said quietly. "It could make quite a difference on the day."

Davies gave in testily. "Oh, all right. Only you're not going alone. You'll take a minimum of four kites. And you'll stay at maximum height. That's an order."

"If I take men with me I'll have to give them some reason for the trip," Moore reminded him.

He received a scowl. "You see how you're complicating things."

"Can't I just tell them we're checking on all the radiolocation stations? There's nothing unusual in that

136

to stir their curiosity. In any case my men won't talk. I'll take three of my most experienced crews."

"Mind you do that," Davies grunted. "If anything was to leak out we'd all be crucified."

## 15

The young S.P. standing in the doorway looked embarrassed. "Sorry to bother you, sir. But Maisie says it's urgent."

Eyes still dazzled by the light, Ross stared at him. "What time is it?"

"11.20, sir."

"And you say she's waiting in the guardhouse?"

"Yes, sir. Shall I tell her you're coming?"

Ross swung his pyjama-clad legs to the floor. "All right. Tell her I'll only be a couple of minutes."

The S.P. nodded and disappeared. Ross, who was still feeling the effects of the crash, began dressing. With McKenny not due back until midnight, he had left the Mess early and been in bed by 10.30. As he slipped into his tunic he wondered what possible reason the girl could have for wanting to see him at this hour.

Most of the blacked-out billets were silent as he hurried past them, although muffled sounds of gaiety from the Mess ahead told him Millburn, Gabby and company were still in action. A chill in the night air made him wish he had put on his greatcoat. The shortcut took him past the Intelligence hut and the enquiring bark of a dog and a chink of light in a window told him Adams was working late.

He found Maisie inside the guardroom talking to the duty corporal. The corporal, a mechanic from the airframe section with the furrowed brow and doleful expression of a retriever, was clearly disappointed by his swift arrival. Guard duty, hated by all and sundry, was seldom relieved by the presence of an attractive

137

woman. He moved reluctantly away as Ross crossed the room. "What is it, Maisie?"

The girl, who was wearing a fawn mackintosh thrown over a skirt and blouse, gave the corporal a bright smile. "Thanks for getting him for me, love. Ta ta." Before Ross could question her further she took his arm and drew him outside. As she closed the door, her expression changed.

"We've got your friend over in the pub, love. Paddy McKenny."

Ross gave a start. "Paddy! What's he doing there?"

She gave him an impatient push towards the station gates. "I'll tell you everything later. Let's get there first."

Ross had a quick word with the sentry at the gates, then hurried down the dark road after the girl. "What's going on?" he muttered. "When did he get to your place?"

She was already halfway to the inn. "Just over an hour ago. A taxi brought him."

The darkness made it difficult to read her expression. "What do you mean—brought him?"

She pushed open the wicker gate. "You'll see in a minute."

The heavy front door was unlocked. Closing it, she switched on the light and gave a shout. "Joe! Bernard Ross is here."

The white-haired Kearns came hurrying into the hall. Shirt-sleeved and wearing an apron, he was clearly relieved to see Ross.

"Hello, lad. Maisie will have told you. We've got your pal upstairs."

Ross's forebodings were growing. "Upstairs? What's the trouble?"

Kearns gave a grimace. "He's in a bad way, lad. We've been worried about him."

Ross started immediately up the stairs. Hesitating, Maisie turned to the innkeeper. "I'll finish washing those glasses if you want to go up with him."

"No, lass. You were with the lad when he was talking. I'll see to things down here."

138

The girl followed Ross up the crooked staircase. Although the Scot was not tall, the ceiling beams made him duck his head. As he reached the landing, Maisie pushed past him and opened the door of a front bedroom. Leaving the room in darkness, she motioned Ross inside.

His first impression was the acid smell of spirits. Although the light from the landing was shining into the room, the bed was in shadow and it took him a moment to recognize McKenny lying there. The Irishman was asleep and his heavy breathing told the rest. The puzzled Ross turned to the girl.

"How did he get here in this state?"

She drew up a couple of chairs and accepted the cigarette he gave her. "He must have been drinkin' on his way back because they found an empty bottle of whisky on him. So maybe he wasn't incapable all the way. But he was bad when he got to Highgate. They looked at his identity card and put him in a taxi for the camp. Lucky for him, the driver was old Bert Leeson. We sometimes use him on Sundays when the buses aren't running. He's got a son in the Army, and thinking Paddy might get into trouble at the camp, he dropped him off here to see if we could pull him round first."

Ross glanced at the bed. "I take it you didn't have much luck?"

As the girl drew hard on her cigarette, he noticed her expression for the first time. Normally a bold and breezy girl who had a riposte for every pass made at her, she had a look of disquiet that puzzled him. "That's the funny thing," she muttered. "After I got some black coffee down him, he started talkin' all right. Almost too much. But then he suddenly went off again. That's when we thought we'd better get in touch with you."

Her face held his attention. "What do you mean —almost too much?"

She glanced away. "Joe didn't hear him. He was too busy lookin' after the bars. But it scared me, I can tell you."

"Scared you?"

For a moment she looked defiant. "It would've scared anybody, the things he was saying."

"Was it about his girl?"

"At first it was." Maisie paused. "Did you know she'd broken off their engagement and is going abroad?"

Ross nodded. "That's why he'd got this two-day pass. He was hoping to talk her out of it."

"Well, he didn't," Maisie muttered. "He didn't even see her. Apparently she'd been on night duty this week and was sleepin' when he got to the hospital. When he asked the matron to wake her up, she told him she insisted her nurses got their full sleep or they'd be in no condition to work." In the half-light Maisie's eyes were huge with disbelief. "Can you believe it? He's fightin' for his country, with a last chance to see his girl, and the old cow wouldn't wake her up. I don't blame him for what he did. I'd have felt like shooting the old bugger."

Ross was erect in his chair. "What did he do?"

"The way he told it, it was all jumbled up, but I gather he went berserk and tried to find her by throwin' open doors in the nurses' quarters. So the old bitch put three orderlies on him and had him thrown out."

Ross was actually experiencing relief. "So that's what happened."

"It's enough to make any man turn to the bottle," Maisie said. "All the same, I can't understand some of the things he said to me afterwards."

Her tone brought back the Scot's apprehension. "What things?"

"Horrible things. I'm not religious myself, 'least not more than most people, but I can tell you he scared the life out of me."

"What did he say?"

"Oh, horrible things about God and how he hated him. He got himself into a terrible state. I thought once he was going to hit me."

Ross cleared his dry throat. "You know the reason, don't you? He's blaming God for it."

"For losing his girl? But why should he do that?"

140

"I can't think. But he is."

Womanlike, Maisie was immediately captivated. "Just think how he must love her. Nobody's ever gone off God for me. When did all this start?"

"He's been moody for weeks, but I only found out two days ago."

Maisie was gazing with respect at the sleeping McKenny. "There can't be many men who feel that way about women. It reminds me of that film they made about the moors up here. The one with the chap called Heathcliff. What was its name?"

In his concern for McKenny, Ross had to concentrate on her question. "You mean *Wuthering Heights?*"

"That's the one. He must have hated God too for keepin' the two of them apart. I remember wondering afterwards if a man would ever feel that way about me." Maisie's lowered eyes were almost sullen as she drew hard on her cigarette. "Sometimes I had the idea Gillie was that kind of man. You know—the kind nothing can stop. But it looks as if when you're dead, you're dead."

Coming from a girl he had always seen as a cheerful extrovert, the sentiment came as a surprise to the religious Ross. About to protest, he rose to his feet instead. "I suppose I'd better try to wake him up. Can I have some black coffee?"

Maisie nodded and crossed over to the door. "I won't be long, love."

Sitting on the bedside, Ross shook the Irishman's shoulder. The only response was a groan. He shook again, harder. "Paddy! Wake up!"

This time, to his surprise, McKenny's eyes opened. At first they were blank. Then recognition seeped into them. "Bernie?"

"Yes. I've come to take you back. Can you walk?"

The Irishman lifted his head from the pillow, then dropped back with a groan. "I feel sick," he muttered.

Pulling and heaving, Ross managed to get him into the bathroom and over the water closet. For a full

141

five minutes the Irishman retched and vomited. When at last he staggered back, Ross swung him over the wash basin. Although the cursing McKenny tried to strike him, Ross doused his head and neck with cold water. Finally he rubbed him with a towel and steered him back across the landing. When Maisie entered a minute later the drenched and trembling Irishman was sitting on the bed. She pushed a cup of black coffee into his hands.

"Drink this, love. You'll soon feel better."

The bitter coffee made the pilot grimace. His bloodshot eyes roamed round the bedroom. "Where are we?"

"You're all right, love. You're in the pub."

"How did I get here?"

"Bernie'll tell you later. If I were you I'd go back with him now and get a good night's sleep. You'll feel better tomorrow."

With the girl's aid, Ross got the Irishman down the stairs and out on to the path. At the wicker gate she read his glance. "Don't worry. Neither of us will tell anybody."

Reaching back, he gave her an impulsive kiss. "Thanks, Maisie. You're really something."

Her dark eyes were on the unsteady McKenny. "It's little enough for what you do for us, love."

The night air appeared to fuddle the Irishman's senses again and on reaching the guardhouse Ross was forced to call on the young S.P. for assistance. Supporting McKenny between them, they half-carried him to his billet. To Ross's relief they passed no one of authority and five minutes later he thankfully lowered the Irishman down on his bed. He threw the S.P. a dark look as he straightened. "Not a word of this, young Conroy, or we'll take you out and bomb Berlin with you."

The young S.P., who unlike most of his breed had a hero-worship for the squadron's aircrews, gave him a conspiratorial smile. "Anyone can fall and twist their ankle, sir, can't they?"

Ross grinned back. "For an S.P. you've got a lot of imagination, Conroy. Remind me to recommend you for a DSO."

As the delighted youngster went out and closed the door, Ross began to undress McKenny. At first he believed the Irishman had fallen asleep again but as he began unlacing his shoes, McKenny cursed and tried to kick him away. "I want a drink."

Ross pushed him back. "You've had enough. Get your head down!"

For an answer he received a swinging fist on the side of his head. "I said I want a drink."

"We haven't got a drink. So shut up and keep still."

Pushing him away with surprising strength, the Irishman lurched towards his cabinet. "Who says we haven't?" Yanking the door open, he turned triumphantly with a bottle of gin in his hand. "What's this? Scotch mist?"

Ross tried to take it from him but was pushed violently away. Dropping on his bed, McKenny unscrewed the cap and tilted back the bottle. About to use brute force on him this time, Ross saw the bottle was almost empty. A few seconds later there was a curse and the crash of glass as the Irishman flung the bottle across the billet. Muttering something Ross could not catch, he fell back with his wet hair on the pillow. Deciding this time he would leave well alone, the Scot was beginning to undress himself when he heard an ugly laugh.

"The bastard's won. Did you know that?"

For a moment Ross was puzzled. "Who's won?"

"That God of yours." As he glanced back, Ross saw the Irishman's head had lifted from his pillow. With the bruise dark on his face, his expression was almost evil. "I'll tell you something else. He plays dirty too. He didn't even give me a chance to see her."

Turning, Ross hung up his tunic. "Go to sleep, Paddy. Things'll look better in the morning."

"Those bloody priests have got you taped, haven't they?" McKenny sneered. "Upside down and sideways.

There isn't a God, you superstitious fool, and there's never been one."

Ross began unlacing his shoes. "Then he didn't prevent you seeing Joan, did he?"

"Oh, yes he did. An' do you know why? Because he's bloody vicious and ruthless."

Ross walked across and laid a blanket over him. "I'm putting out the light now."

There was a curse and then, with the swift change of mood that characterizes drunkenness, McKenny reached up and fumbled for his hand. "Good ol' Bernie! Nobody like you, Bernie. You're all right. It's just you've got so many weird ideas and . . ."

As the Irishman's voice dropped into a mumble, Ross released his hand gently and threw another blanket over him. He then sat on the bedside and waited until the man's breathing steadied before climbing wearily into bed. Expecting to fall asleep almost immediately, he kept on hearing McKenny's taunts and accusations and when sleep did finally come to him, it was fitful and disturbed.

## 16

From 35,000 feet the coast of France was like a low cloud clinging to the edge of the sea. The dome of sky was a cold blue and the brilliant sun made McKenny's eyes throb in spite of his smoked glasses. He was flying J-Jimmie, the squadron's photo-reconnaissance Mosquito fitted with an F.53 camera. Behind J-Jimmie the exhaust gases were streaming out like the wake of a ship.

Three other Mosquitoes were arrayed beyond the Irishman's port wingtip. Flying in fingers four, they belonged to Moore, Young and Millburn. The morning after McKenny's return to the station, the day had dawned clear and bright. With the Met. people anticipating excellent visibility until the early afternoon, Moore had not wasted a moment. The four Mosquitoes had been air-tested before breakfast and on their way towards Cherbourg by 08.30.

It was an early call that could hardly have been more unfortunate for McKenny. With only six hours' sleep behind him, the Irishman still had alcohol in his blood. Fearing at one time he might have to report him unfit, Ross had feverishly plied him with black coffee and douched him twice beneath a cold shower. The result was success only as far as the pilot's ability to fly was concerned. His mood remained as black as a towering thunderhead.

In spite of the urgent preparations Moore had to make, McKenny's condition had not gone unnoticed by him, and he had questioned both the Irishman and Ross before allowing them to make their air-test. Careful to say nothing about McKenny's experience in Lincoln, the young Scot had vouched the pilot was fit enough to carry out the operation. In other circumstances Moore would have taken no chances and grounded the crew. As it was, with the operation needing his two photographic specialists, it was a difficult decision to make. In the end, after giving McKenny a reprimand which he had taken in sullen silence, Moore had given him permission to fly.

With time for questioning at a premium and Ross covering his friend with half-truths, Moore had no way of knowing it was a mistake. Perhaps because of the bitterness that compounded it, McKenny's hangover was not clearing. His head still throbbed with hammer blows and his mood was as unstable as fulminate of mercury. In addition the residual alcohol was affecting his blood vessels. His hands and feet ached intolerably from the bitter cold and as it affected his nerve centres, the rows of dials before him kept blurring. Sitting beside him, the uneasy Ross noticed how the Irishman kept turning his oxygen fully on to clear his vision.

Flying at point in the fingers four formation, Moore was gazing down on the congealed sea where the wake of two ships, probably mine layers, looked like the excrement from two caterpillars on an enor-

145

mous leaf. He was wondering what the German response would be. There was no doubt the four Mosquitoes were being monitored: at this height half a dozen radio-location stations would have picked them up fifteen minutes ago. And fifteen minutes was a long warning if any of Jerry's latest FW.190 A-6s were in the neighbourhood. Intelligence had discovered he was using a new fuel additive that greatly increased his fighters' rate of climb. It meant, if the 190s had been despatched immediately, they could already have reached 20,000 or thereabouts. After that their power curve would rapidly fall away but they could still be a deadly threat if the Mosquitoes dallied too long over the coast.

The question was whether the enemy would risk his 190s encountering Allied fighter patrols to intercept four Mosquitoes whose great height made it obvious they were not going to launch an attack. He might turn a blind eye to them or, uncertain why they were tracking along the coast at that height, he might decide to play safe and intercept. Equally, with the morning so clear after weeks of poor weather, he might even think them an excellent excuse to test his air defences. With no need to keep radio silence, Moore had a word with his crews. "Starfish Leader. Keep your eyes open for bandits. We might be tempting them into a little practice."

The experienced crews had already been searching every corner of the brilliant sky until their eyes watered but could see no tell-tale contrails. Below, the Pointe de Barfleur slid beneath their starboard wingtips. By leading the flight in a westerly direction that would take it across the tip of the Contentin peninsula, Moore was hoping the Germans would believe they were doing a reconnaissance of the important port of Cherbourg.

Ahead the peninsula reached out into the Channel like the leg of a huge animal. Smoke puffs began opening out like evil blossoms as the coastal batteries, stretched to their extreme range, began to put up a probing barrage. Moore changed course and altitude, flew straight for thirty seconds, then swung 20 degrees to port again. Feeling their aircraft yaw in the rarefied air, the pilots opened formation to lessen the danger of collision.

The smoke puffs multiplied as they neared Cherbourg. Hoppy's needle-sharp eyes could see ships, tinier than matchsticks, lying alongside wharves and jetties. At the end of the port's long mole the submarine boom stretched across like a knotted hair. As A-Apple rocked to an explosion, Moore changed course again and dropped five hundred feet.

To further the deceit, the Mosquitoes circled Cherbourg twice before heading west again. As they swept along the northern coast, Moore's hope was that the Germans would assume the reconnaissance was over and they were making for home.

Ahead, the Cap de la Hague looked like the rounded back of a sea monster. Beyond it could be seen the Isle of Alderney. Below, the countryside was well-wooded but as the Cap drew nearer the hills and cliffs took on a more barren aspect. After winding through wooded hills, the communication road the Mosquitoes were detailed to patrol had now emerged a couple of miles behind the cliffs and was running parallel to them. As Moore's eyes followed it, Hoppy leaned forward against his straps. "There's a cloud ahead, skipper. It could foul things up."

The cloud the Cockney was pointing at was a haze of stratocirrus. As it drifted below the crews saw it was thin enough for the coastline to be traced through it. At the same time all of them knew it would fog up details of the radiolocation station on the camera film.

The station was now dead ahead of them, standing on a barren hillside a mile from the sea. "What are you going to do, skipper?" Hoppy asked.

Moore was trying to estimate the height of the cloud. 24,000 feet . . . possibly a couple of thousand less. If 190s had been scrambled as soon as the monitors had picked up the Mosquitoes, they could already be at that height or even above it. A cool strategist, Moore decided that with photo-reconnaissance Spitfires already briefed to take photographs he had no right to risk his crews' lives. He would content himself with a survey of the area he was detailed to patrol.

He gazed down again. Hazy though the view was, he could pick out the salient features. A support track ran from the coastal road to a cluster of mounds at the cliff edge that he took to be the gun battery. Below the battery was a rocky bay with a semi-circle of sand. Although the beach ran westwards, the cliffs straightened and grew steeper as a hill range ran out into the sea. Eventually a rocky promontory, reaching almost to the water's edge, separated the beach from a large, sandy bay that indented the coast for another two kilometres. The radio-location station stood on the hillside above this beach. Still further west, where a shallow valley ran between low cliffs, was a third and smaller bay.

As Moore lowered his binoculars, Hoppy, who had been scanning the coast road, turned to him. "Is that all we're supposed to do, skipper? Just patrol that road? It looks like a piece of cake."

Moore's comment was dry. "It could be a tough old biscuit on the day, Hoppy."

Back in J-Jimmie McKenny was showing increased impatience when no order came from Moore. "We haven't come all this way for nothing, have we?"

Ross nodded at the haze below. "Moore knows I can't get photographs through that."

"Then let's go beneath it. We're doing no good up here."

Ross stared at him. "We can't go down there. Jerry could be waiting for us."

In his present self-destructive mood, any challenge was fuel to McKenny. "So what? They keep saying they want his fighters destroyed, don't they?"

Knowing how acute the Irishman's hangover was, Ross made the mistake of not taking him too seriously. "Don't tell me you feel like being a hero. Not after the state you were in last night."

The pilot's masked face turned towards him. "I can't do anything right these days, can I?"

"Not when you keep on disobeying orders. If you go on this way you'll either get us shot down or court-martialled."

"I thought you were the Christian soldier who

wanted to win this war and give evil a kick up the backside?"

Suddenly aware how dangerous the Irishman's mood was, Ross ignored the gibe. "Have a word with Moore and ask what he wants. That's the simplest answer."

"Why bother about Moore? God'll always take care of you, won't he? Or aren't you so sure about the Old Guy anymore?"

Ross was apprehensive now. "Stop clowning about, Paddy. If we disobey orders, Moore will jump on us with both feet."

McKenny needed nothing more to curse and peel away from the formation. Moore's voice rapped out sharp and urgent in the men's earphones. "Get back into formation, Zero Three! At the double!"

In J-Jimmie, now in a thirty-degree dive, Ross was staring at McKenny in disbelief. "Have you gone crazy? You can be court-martialled for this."

Once more they heard Moore's authoritative voice. "McKenny! This is an order. Get back into formation!"

McKenny's response was to switch off the R/T. "We've come all this way: we're taking those photographs," he told Ross. "So get your camera ready!"

The altimeter needle was swinging rapidly back round the dial. 27,000 feet . . . 25,000 . . . 23,000. As he watched the film of cloud leaping towards them, Ross felt his hand sweating. If there were any Focke Wulfs climbing up to intercept, they would be licking their lips at the dish being offered them.

For three seconds the sunlight dimmed, then J-Jimmie was through the haze and the cliffs were sharp in detail. Levelling off at 22,000 feet, McKenny nodded tersely at the camera. Deciding that now the risk had been taken it might as well serve a useful purpose, Ross began filming. By this time the flak was heavy from both the coastal defences and the radio-location station, and twice McKenny had to steady the Mosquito as explosions threw it off course.

As the buildings fell behind, Ross decided one pass was enough and climbed back into his seat. "We've been lucky so far. Now let's get out of here."

149

For a moment it seemed the aggressive Irishman would make another run over the station. Instead he muttered something and turned towards the sea. With the sun shining through the tenuous cloud, it had a glare that hurt the eyes. As Ross squinted up at it through his tinted goggles, he saw a black speck suddenly darken beneath it. Another speck appeared a second later. As he gave a yell of warning, tracer flashed past their starboard wing.

In spite of his hangover McKenny's combat reflexes were good. Before the Focke Wulf pilot could make his correction, he swung J-Jimmie violently to port. The 190 banked after it and for a few seconds, with their relative speeds reduced to a low vector, the Focke Wulf seemed to be swinging almost lazily in the sky. In his mirror the fascinated Ross could see its stubby wings, long cupola, and a halo of yellow light around its radial engine.

With combat joined, McKenny's training cleared his mind of everything but the task in hand. Survival depended on keeping the curve of pursuit so severe that the enemy pilot, who had to turn inside the curve to line up his guns, would either black out from the g-forces or break off his attack.

J-Jimmie's wings tilted more and more as McKenny increased the angle of turn. As elevators took the place of rudder, the Irishman drew the column back into his chest, forcing the aircraft into a circle as tight as a death ride in a fun fair. Ross felt the unnatural weight of his head pressing down on his spine, the drag on his eye sockets, and the leaden weight that was sinking into his bowels. Behind them, the German pilot fired one abortive burst before settling down grimly in pursuit.

It was a classic air combat situation in which the manoeuvrability of the aircraft decided who should live or die. It so happened McKenny and Ross had the good fortune to be in a twin-engined aircraft that had the manoeuvrability of a fighter. As the Irishman increased his turn until the Mosquito's wings were almost bowing with the strain, the 190, forced into an even steeper bank to line up its guns, suddenly faltered as its pilot

150

blacked out from the crushing g-forces. Before Mc-Kenny could voice his triumph there was the sound of a pneumatic drill pounding metal as the second 190 took over from the first whose pilot was recovering a thousand feet below.

For Ross, helpless to do anything but cling to his straps and pray, the next few minutes were a mad confusion of spinning sea and sky. From the glimpses he caught of diving aircraft and black crosses, it appeared an entire flight of 190s had dropped on them and some calm cell in his mind told him to prepare to die. The sudden sight of Mosquitoes and Spitfires diving past made him wonder if he were having hallucinations. A moment later sea and sky levelled off and in the way of aerial combat the sky was abruptly empty of aircraft. As the sweating McKenny sank back in his seat, the bewildered Ross turned to him. "What happened?"

The Irishman jerked a sullen thumb upwards. "Moore came down to help. And then a crowd of Spitfires arrived. They're chasing Jerry back to Berlin."

Glancing up Ross saw Moore's trio of Mosquitoes a thousand feet above. As McKenny began climbing towards them, the Scot's anger exploded.

"What made you do a crazy thing like that? If those Spitties hadn't been around we might have all been killed."

He expected another gibe but the shock of combat had temporarily exorcized the Irishman's inner demon and he made no comment as Ross raged on.

"That's the third time you've nearly killed us. If you want to commit suicide, jump off a cliff or shoot yourself. But stop trying to do it when I'm flying with you."

The glance McKenny gave him was full of sullen contrition. Reaction made Ross neither notice nor care.

"I've had you. Right to the top. If Moore doesn't ground you I'm going to ask for another pilot. And when they ask me why, I'm telling them everything."

With his expression hidden by his mask, McKenny swung into position alongside Millburn. Gabby was gazing across at the jagged holes that the second 190 had punched into J-Jimmie. "What do you think came over him, boyo? You think he was drinking poteen last night?"

Millburn, who for all his carefree behaviour on the ground was a highly professional pilot, growled his disgust. "I hope the skipper takes the hide off the sonofabitch."

Henderson, who was standing thoughtfully at the window of his office, turned as Moore entered. "Hello, Ian. Sorry to disturb you but I had Davies on the phone a few minutes ago. Among other things he read out an extract from the *New York Daily Mirror* that Staines has passed over to him."

"How was it?" Moore asked. "As bad as we expected?"

Henderson scowled. "Worse if anything. Lambert says we knew from the beginning there was a risk to the prisoners. And that the entire operation was politically motivated. What the bastard doesn't say is that if he hadn't been carrying out a poison-pen campaign against the RAF, the operation wouldn't have been necessary in the first place."

When Moore only nodded, Henderson showed a bitterness rare in one so phlegmatic. "We pull off one of the most skilful low-level operations of the war. We free maybe two hundred American aircrews and give a massive boost to the morale of the partisans. And all we get for it is a bollocking. And Davies still wonders why I don't like playing politics."

"Did he have any news of the other operation?" Moore asked.

The Scot nodded moodily. "He's full of it. He's certain this time Lambert is going to be dumped right on his arse. I wish I was as confident."

"Is he going to be on the HQ ship?"

"Yes. Plus dozens of American top brass, war correspondents, and Lambert." Henderson could not help the malicious thought. "I hope they use the same Operations Room or whatever they call it in the Navy."

152

"Did he say when he wants Adams and me to go to Portsmouth?"

"That trip's off." When Moore gave a start, Henderson continued: "Apparently one of the major naval units taking part in the operation has been under refit in Scotland and there's been a hold up. Nothing serious but to avoid a last-minute rush when it reaches Portsmouth, two Yank officers have flown up to Scotland to hold the briefing there. As we're on their flight path back, Davies has arranged for them to drop in here as well."

"Good. When do you expect them?"

"Sometime tomorrow afternoon. So make sure Adams and your two flight commanders are within call, will you?"

As Moore nodded, Henderson's tone changed. "What's all this I hear about McKenny? There's a rumour going round he disobeyed your orders this morning and nearly dropped you all in the brown stuff. Is it true?"

Moore, who had ordered his flight commanders to say nothing about the incident until he had interviewed McKenny, guessed the source of the rumour. On landing he had gone straight over to the Irishman and the words they had exchanged must have enabled the mechanics to put two and two together.

"I'm afraid it is. I've just had him in my office."

"What happened exactly?"

Moore told him. When he finished Henderson looked shocked. "That's blatant insubordination! What are you going to do? Court-martial him?"

"I'm not sure yet," Moore said quietly.

"Not sure?"

"No."

Knowing that in spite of Moore's affability, he could be ruthless with conduct that endangered his crews' safety, Henderson was looking as much puzzled as indignant. "Why not?"

"I had a word with Ross beforehand. He wouldn't deny or confirm what happened this morning but he did tell me what happened to McKenny in Lincoln

153

yesterday. And I suppose in fairness one must take it into account."

"Lincoln?"

Moore gave details of the hospital incident. The frowning Henderson rubbed his chin. "It's rough, I'll give you that. Bloody rough in fact. But it still doesn't excuse his going haywire and risking all your lives. Men are getting Dear John letters all the time. You forgotten the Yanks are over here?"

"I agree. But I can't help feeling there's something else behind it."

"What else?"

"I don't know."

"Doesn't Ross have any ideas?"

"He says he hasn't."

The big Scot made an impatient gesture. "Insubordination's too serious a crime for excuses, Ian. I know his country isn't at war, that he didn't have to fight, and the rest of it, but I feel you still have to make an example of him."

Moore's good-looking face turned expressionless. "I've got it in hand. I'll decide if a court martial is called for after he's seen the M.O. again. I also want to make a few more enquiries. In the meantime he's been grounded."

Aware how adamant the young squadron commander could be when his mind was made up, Henderson gave no more than a grunt of disapproval. "All right, he's your responsibility. But as I'm still the C.O. around these parts, I don't want you making any decision until I've seen the M.O.'s report myself and heard the result of your enquiries."

McKenny slammed the billet door and made for his locker. Ross, who had been anxiously waiting his return, sat up on his bed. "Well! What happened?"

The Irishman cursed and jerked open his locker door. "He's grounded me."

Ross showed no surprise. "What about a court martial?"

"He's going to make up his mind about that after I've seen the M.O. again."

154

The young Scot sank back in relief. "Then you're all right."

A half-bottle of gin in his hand, McKenny stared at him in dislike. "How do you work that out? You think the M.O. is going to find something wrong with me?"

"It's not that. Moore's a decent officer and if he was going to court-martial you, he'd have done it right away. I think he's sympathetic about what happened in Lincoln yesterday."

"Why did you tell him about that? I don't want his sympathy."

"I had to tell him something. You nearly got the flight wiped out this morning."

"You're talking as if he's let me off. He's still grounded me."

"He couldn't do much else, could he? Not after you disobeyed his orders in front of both his flight commanders."

McKenny's look of dislike grew. "You're glad about it, aren't you?"

A man who hated lying, Ross could not help his brief hesitation. "Of course I'm not."

"Yes, you are. You were getting scared to fly with me. It stood out a mile."

Ross saw no point in more lies. "Is it surprising after the way you've been acting lately?"

McKenny tilted the bottle and took a long drink. Ross watched him uneasily. "When are you seeing the M.O.?"

"In twenty minutes."

The Scot gave a start. "Then you're crazy. If he finds out you've been drinking this time of the day, you'll be in even worse trouble."

"How can I be in worse trouble?"

"Don't be a fool, Paddy. If you play your cards right, you could be flying again in a few weeks."

McKenny lowered the bottle. "You'd love that, wouldn't you? If you're smart, you'll keep a bottle of gin in that locker."

Ross ignored the comment. The Irishman's taunting gaze remained on him. "Although, come to think of it, it doesn't make any sense, does it? Not when you're the one who's supposed to believe in God and all his Angels."

Ross's young face set. "Don't start all that again."

"Why not? It fascinates me. If God is so wonderful and good to his children, what are you so scared about? All he'll do if we're hit is put a magic carpet underneath you and lower you to the ground."

"Stop talking bloody nonsense," Ross gritted.

"Why is it nonsense? Don't you believe he can do it?"

Ross rose to his feet. "I'm going to the Mess."

"What's the matter?" McKenny jeered. "Can't you face the truth?"

Ross took a deep breath. "It's time you faced the truth, Paddy. Because of this girl you've gone to pieces and turned against everything and everybody. But it's not that easy to lose God, is it? It's twisting your guts out so much you want to destroy my faith too. Isn't that what all this is about?"

For a moment the Irishman went very pale. Then his harsh voice echoed round the billet. "You need a home truth or two yourself, Bernie. The Church has conditioned you to genuflect, eat biscuits, and act out the rest of the bullshit but none of it helps when the shit's flying about. I know it doesn't—I saw your face this morning. You won't admit it because of the implications but it's a fact just the same. You've no more faith than I have."

The young Scot had also turned very pale. "I believe in God, Paddy. I believe in his mercy and his love."

"But not in his protection, right? And what about his mercy? He didn't show much to St. Claire and Simpson the other day, did he? Or to Lester and Thomson. And according to you they were also fighting against evil." There was a look on McKenny's face that made Ross shudder as the Irishman leaned forward. "I'll tell you something, Bernie. If this is the way God behaves to people who're fighting his war, I'd rather ask the Devil for help."

Ross crossed himself involuntarily. The gesture

156

brought a jeer from McKenny. "Look at yourself, you stupid bastard. You're as superstitious as an African pygmy."

It was an effort for Ross to keep his voice steady. "You won't destroy my faith, Paddy. No matter what you say or do."

The Irishman tossed the bottle of gin on to his bed and went to the door. Hand on the latch, he turned and gave another laugh. "You want a bet? Wait and see."

---

# 17

Moore was in No. 1 hangar standing alongside a stripped-down engine of A-Apple when a flushed young ACII stiffened in front of him. "Your sergeant's been looking for you, sir. She says you're wanted in the Intelligence Room."

Tight security was in deployment around Adams' "Confessional" as Moore approached. S.P.s were standing outside the windows and a third was on guard at the door. The reason was obvious the moment Moore entered. Apart from Davies, Henderson, Adams and the two flight commanders, two American officers were present. One was a naval commander; the other an Army colonel. All were gathered around Adams' desk, which had been cleared for the occasion.

Davies' slight testiness told Moore he was excited. "What happened? Your sergeant didn't know where you'd got to."

As composed as always, Moore glanced at the two Americans. "Sorry, sir, but I didn't hear the aircraft fly in. I've been over in No. 1 hangar. I've had a bit of trouble with my starboard engine recently and Chiefy asked me to take a look at it."

Grunting something, Davies turned back to the two American officers who had straightened from the

157

desk. "Gentlemen, this is our Squadron Commander, Wing Commander Moore. Moore, this is Commander Runcorn of the United States Navy and Colonel Tilsey of the United States Rangers."

Moore shook hands with each man in turn. Runcorn, slim and dark, was a man in his early forties with observant eyes. Tilsey was a fair, good-looking man of athletic appearance who looked a few years younger than his compatriot. As Davies gave Moore's name, Runcorn stubbed out a cigarette. Adams, watching the introductions, noticed the Americans' eyes flicker over the ribbons Moore was wearing. The behaviour told him both were acquainted with Moore's record and had respect for it.

With introductions completed, Davies wasted no more time. "Before we start talking about the job we've got for you, I want to impress on you all the need for security. You won't mention a word of this outside this room, not even to one another. Is that absolutely clear?"

As all the squadron personnel nodded, Davies glanced at the Americans before turning to the two flight commanders. "If you were wondering why representatives of our major ally are present, it's not just because they're involved but because it is their operation. We are going to be the only British unit taking part, so you will realize we're being given quite an honour. I know you'll play your part by being worthy of it."

The puzzled glance Young exchanged with Millburn added to the tension of the moment. Motioning them both nearer the desk, Davies picked up a pointer and prodded a huge photograph lying there. "Here is the Americans objective. One of Jerry's largest radiolocation stations, powerful enough to scan every ship that passes down the Channel and to pick you up almost before you leave your airfield. It isn't new to you: I let you fly over it yesterday so you could take in its main features. What you didn't know is that it's not going to be bombed but raided from the sea by the Americans. I won't say any more because that's why our American colleagues are visiting us. But you'll see in a moment that you are taking part in an extremely important operation. Now I'll hand you over to Commander Runcorn and Colonel Tilsey."

As the two Americans glanced at one another Runcorn picked up the pointer and handed it to Tilsey. Grinning at him wryly, the good-looking colonel walked over to a large map of the western seaboard of France pinned to a blackboard behind the desk. His accent told Adams, who prided himself on voice identification, that he came from the South West, probably California.

"Firstly, gentlemen, I would like to say how glad we are that your squadron is taking part in this mission. By this time it's something of a household name in the States, so we feel it's an honour we're in this job together."

Winking an eye at the absent Staines, Davies accepted a cigarette from Henderson. With the courtesies over, Tilsey got down to business.

"From the nature of the target you might be visualizing the kind of raid the British carried out on Bruneval in 1942. A drop of paratroopers, a surprise attack, and withdrawal in assault boats before enemy reserves could arrive. Although this station is more ruggedly built and has better defences we might have thought on the same lines if we hadn't other reasons for the raid. With the invasion of Europe on the horizon, we need battle experience that we can disseminate among our invasion troops and up-to-date knowledge of the beach defences we're likely to face. This raid should satisfy all these objectives while also getting rid of a station that because of its range could warn the enemy of our pre-invasion shipping movements. In other words we're really doing a Dieppe job like the Canadians and British did in 1942. At the same time we can justify to the enemy the forces we're deploying because of the exceptional defences of the station. Has anyone any questions so far?"

"How long does the tide give you ashore, Colonel?" Henderson asked.

"Three hours. Three and a half at the most. So we have to move fast."

"Exactly how strong are the station defences?"

The American waited while Adams pinned up an artist's impression of the station on a second blackboard. "In effect it's a cluster of strongpoints supporting the aerial masts for good measure. Round them is this perimeter wall and armed pillboxes. Outside the perimeter is a minefield. In addition," and Tilsey's pointer returned to the map and ran along the cliffs, "there is a gun battery here. We're assuming it's part of the coastal defences but its positioning shows they've also had the station's defence in mind. Add to that heavy beach defences and you'll see we have a pretty hard nut to crack."

"What about enemy reserves?"

"Intelligence tells us they have an infantry unit of unknown size on manoeuvres somewhere around Bricquebec. They also have a squadron of tanks in Les Pieux. Add to that the strength of the station itself and it means we're having to put tanks ashore as well as light artillery."

Young was making thumb measurements on the map. "What about Cherbourg? We're pretty close to it, aren't we?"

"Yes, but most of the defences there are static ones, heavy artillery and the like, although of course they might rush some infantry towards us. The main Panzer defences of the peninsula are down in St. Jores where they can be moved quickly to any coast under attack. However, as they couldn't possibly reach us under three hours, the local reserves in Les Pieux seems to be our main threat."

"How are you figuring to cross those minefields, Colonel?" Millburn asked.

"We've got thirty B.17s flying in ahead of us. We're not expecting them to damage any strongpoints but they should hand out a few headaches and blow gaps in the minefields for our tanks to exploit."

Millburn, who had shared a few beers with Young at lunchtime, went beyond his brief, to Davies' displeasure. "If it's anything like Dieppe, you're going to lose a lot of men, Colonel."

Tilsey nodded. "You could well be right. But our troops have been in England a long time now and they

160

need battle experience. What other way is there of getting it?"

The American's frankness and modesty was clearly impressing his British audience. They encouraged a twangy quip from Teddy Young. "You could always teach 'em to fly and lend 'em my Mosquito. You wouldn't hear me fretting if I could put my feet up for a year or two."

The Australian's levity brought a glare from Davies but before he could intervene the young Colonel laughed. Expecting more formality from the British, both Americans appeared delighted at the relaxed atmosphere. "I'll tell them that. You never know—some might take up the offer."

"Any time, sir," Young grinned.

As Davies coughed, Tilsey got back to business. "Our total strength will be around 3,500 men of which 800 will be Rangers—our equivalent of your Commandos. We're also shipping thirty-odd tanks along. We've been training down in Cornwall for the last couple of months, so we're in reasonable shape. Our first job, which will be done by the Rangers, will be to destroy that coastal gun battery and any other gun emplacements that block the way. Then we shall put tanks ashore in a gap in the cliffs two miles west of the station. In the meantime troops will be coming ashore and clearing the cliff defences. If all goes according to schedule we'll then be able to launch an attack on the station from three sides. When we take the station the strongpoints will be destroyed from the inside by plastic explosives. While all this is going on our engineers will be studying the gun battery and the coastal defences we've knocked out. When they've got all the information they need, we pull out our tanks and troops and come home. That's our side of it. Now I'll pass you over to Commander Runcorn who'll tell you what our junior service will be doing to sabotage our plans."

Grinning at the crack, the slim, dark naval officer exchanged places with Tilsey. "Good afternoon, gentlemen. Our junior service would first like to add its own appreciation and pleasure that your squadron

161

is sharing this operation with us." As laughter broke out Runcorn laid his pointer on the map of France. "For operational purposes the landing sites have been given the following code names. Blue Beach, here, is a bay beneath the gun battery where the Rangers will land. White Beach, to the west, is a larger, sandy bay where the main bulk of the infantry will come in. Further west still is Red Beach. It stretches across a gap in the seafront through which we're hoping our tanks can deploy. Reference maps of these sectors giving their exact positions have been given to your Intelligence Officer, who will distribute them later. O.K. so far?"

As men nodded, the naval officer went on: "Our task force will consist of destroyers, infantry landing ships, assault craft, gun-ships, and minesweepers. Our HQ ship will be the destroyer *Brazos*. Our first job will belong to the minesweepers who will clear a passage through the fields and mark it. In the meantime we'll be embarking troops. The minesweepers will then return and lead us to a point seven miles off the enemy coast. As the radiolocation station isn't operational yet, hopefully we'll arrive there undetected."

At this juncture Adams hesitated, then raised a hand. "What about the other monitoring stations along that coast? Won't they pick you up?"

Runcorn nodded apologetically. "Sorry, I forgot to mention that. Fortunately the normal radar site is far less stoutly constructed, and a couple of days beforehand your air boys and ours are going to carry out a blitz on them. As you know, it happens periodically, so shouldn't cause too many German eyebrows to raise, but to be on the safe side we're also going to blitz sites in the Pas de Calais and Fécamp areas. In addition, in the same area, we've got aircraft flying up and down the coast carrying some kind of jamming device. They'll start operating only at the last minute to avoid alerting the coastal defences prematurely. That side of it is a bit too complicated for me but our scientists assure us it should work."

As Adams nodded, Runcorn turned back to his

main audience. "Once there our destroyers will fan out to protect the convoy and the landing parties. These parties will embark at 05.00 hours and try to hit the beaches at first light. In the meantime the destroyers will be laying smoke and bombarding the coastal defences. They can't hope to do much more with four-inch guns than harass the batteries and strongpoints but they can also turn their guns on any reserves coming up to aid the station. Naturally all ships will remain in position throughout the operation and re-embark the troops when it is completed. We don't know whether the Heinies will commit the Luftwaffe during this time but if they do we've got twelve squadrons of Thunderbolts to take care of us. Any other questions so far?"

For a couple of minutes Young and Millburn had been exchanging puzzled glances. Young beat the American to the question by a short head.

"It's all clear but for one thing, sir. What are we supposed to do?"

Before Runcorn could answer, Davies moved forward. "Perhaps you'll let me answer that, Commander?" When the naval officer nodded, Davies took his place before the map. Aware of the insecurity of his position, his voice was sharp as he ran a finger along the coastline.

"As you see, there's only one main road in these parts and it runs a mile or so back from the station. So if Jerry rushes up any troop transports or tanks, this is the way he must come. Your job will be to stop him. And if any of his tanks try to take the short cut across the cliff top, you stop him there as well. All right?"

Unaware of the deeper issues at stake, Young was looking flabbergasted. "You mean it's a ground support job, sir? But why us? It's a cut and dried job for Typhoons."

By this time Davies had a craw full of Typhoons. "What the hell gives you that idea, Young? You can carry more stores than Tiffies and just as important you can stay longer over the battle area. That could be crucial." Seeing Young opening his mouth, Davies moved in quickly. "You won't have any worries about enemy aircraft. The 8th Air Force will be giving you top cover."

The Australian muttered a chauvinistic quip at the grinning Millburn. Remembering how little the two flight commanders knew, Davies got his temper back under control.

"You've been chosen because you're the most flexible and highly-trained unit we have. Moreover"—and Davies felt it was safe to go that far—"the Americans know your reputation and wouldn't be using you unless they felt you were the right men for the job. As I said earlier, you're being paid a high compliment."

Prompted by his mid-day beer, Young could not resist blowing a raspberry at Millburn. With the sound coming out louder than the Australian intended, those who knew Davies expected a sharp response. Instead Davies craftily used the gesture as a distraction. "You want to watch that drinking at lunch time, Teddy. All that wind could do you a mischief at 20,000 feet."

The two visiting Americans joined in the laughter. Moore, aware of Davies' dilemma, made a tactful intervention as it ceased. "Might I make a suggestion, sir? As we don't know how heavy the enemy response will be, wouldn't a couple of Typhoon squadrons on stand by be a good insurance? Then we'd be in no danger of letting the Americans down if Jerry springs any surprises."

Standing alongside Adams, Henderson muttered his approval. "That's not a bad idea. It's something the Yanks might accept."

Watching Davies' expression as he glanced at the two Americans, Adams felt certain the Air Commodore felt the same way. When Runcorn gave a nod, Davies turned back to Moore with some gusto.

"We'll work on that idea, Moore. It has promise. All right, let's leave the rest until next week. For security reasons we're not briefing the crews before Monday. By that time they'll all be down south at Holmsley, which will be your base during the operation. I've already arranged for a Bombay to pick up your maintenance crews and their stores on Monday morning. In the afternoon Commander Runcorn and Colonel Tilsey have kindly agreed to pay us another visit when they'll give us and the crews a final, detailed briefing. Any more questions until then?"

When no one spoke Davies turned to the two Americans. "Then that only leaves me to thank you two gentlemen for coming today." He glanced at Henderson. "I think before they leave we ought to crack a bottle of Scotch, don't you?"

The Scot grinned as he produced a full bottle from a drawer in Adams' desk. "I thought you never drank before dinner, sir."

Davies' sense of humour was nothing if not astringent. "I wish I could say the same about you, Jock."

As the laughing men separated into small groups, Moore found himself alongside Tilsey. The young Colonel's bearing and handling of the briefing had impressed him. "Might I ask what part you're playing in the operation, Colonel?"

"I'm in charge of the Rangers. We're the ones landing at Blue Beach below the battery."

"That means you're spearheading the raid, doesn't it?"

"Not really. You could say the B.17s are doing that."

Never one to seek the limelight himself, Moore found the good-looking American's self-effacement likeable. "I know it's none of my business but it does seem you're making this hard for yourself. Wouldn't it be cheaper in lives to probe a more normal stretch of coast and clobber the station again with Lancasters or Forts? At least we should be able to keep knocking the aerials down."

"Hardly. If we went in without a definite objective the Heinies would smell a rat and our own Press would crucify us for throwing away lives. Besides"— the American's shrug was fatalistic—"I'm only a colonel and ours isn't to reason why."

Moore pursed his lips, then nodded. "No, I suppose not. Anyway, good luck."

Tilsey toyed with his glass a moment, then gave a

wry smile. "I'll come clean with you, Moore. Originally I was one of those who resisted the idea of using anyone but our own men. Now, having seen your outfit, I'm glad I was talked round. I think you'll take good care of us."

With the telephone to his ear, Adams gave a start and sank into his chair. Sue Spencer, packing maps and photographs into a large crate, paused to listen.

"How many, sir? That's very good, isn't it? You're right—they're doing a fine job. I take it you've no further news from the Red Cross?" Adams listened for a few seconds, then nodded. "I see. Thanks for keeping us posted, sir. I'll inform the C.O. right away."

Replacing the receiver, he was about to pick it up again when he felt the girl's eyes on him. "That was the Brigadier. The first of the American escapers has got back. Five of them—smuggled over from a Belgian fishing port. It's quicker than anyone dared hope, so there's an excellent chance there'll be more within the next few weeks."

"That's good news, Frank," she said quietly. "The crews will be pleased too."

Knowing the news she hungered for, Adams did not keep her waiting. "There's also word from the Red Cross. They've confirmed the deaths of Lester and Thomson."

As her face paled, Adams went on quickly: "But they've no news of Tony and his navigator. They've been asked to carry on the search, of course."

Without a word she turned and continued to pack the crate. Feeling clumsy and inadequate, Adams cleared his throat. "It could be good news, Sue. If they'd been killed in the crash their identification tags would have been found. As it is, the partisans could have pulled them out of the aircraft and taken them away with the Americans."

For a moment she sat very still. Then she crossed the Nissen hut and picked up a pile of de-briefing forms from a table. "Don't humour me, Frank. You know as well as I do that if their aircraft caught fire and exploded, their discs could have gone anywhere."

Adams opened his mouth, then closed it again. Since St. Claire had gone missing, the element that sustained life seemed to have drained from her. She had lost weight and the dark shadows under her eyes betrayed her grief. Yet when Adams had suggested she took leave or even a few days off duty, her reaction had been almost hostile. He had the feeling that, consciously or subconsciously, she was determined to go on working for St. Claire as well as herself.

She returned to the crate, hesitated a moment, then turned. "Shall I tell you something, Frank?"

"What?"

"At times like this it's almost a relief."

Adams pretended not to understand. "A relief?"

"Yes. Aren't you shocked?"

Adams shook his head. "No."

"I am. I hate myself for it. Yet that's how I feel." When Adams said nothing she went on. "If Tony had been here I'd have gone half-crazy for the next two nights. Now that's all over."

Adams cleared his throat again. "Do you think it's going to be that dangerous?"

"Don't you?"

"Not necessarily. If the flak posts get knocked out early—and the Americans are giving them top priority —it shouldn't be too bad if they keep to the road."

"You know them better than that. They'll help the Americans in every way they can."

Adams was afraid she was right. "Moore's not going to throw their lives away. He's too responsible a squadron commander."

"I know that. But he's also not the kind of man who'll let the Americans have losses if his intervention can help them."

"It might never happen," Adams muttered. "Let's hope it doesn't."

She was gazing through the window as if she had not heard him. "Every man in this squadron is as important as Tony. And yet I'm feeling relief because this time I know he's safe. I'm selfish, aren't I, Frank?"

Adams sighed and removed his spectacles to clean

them. "No. As I said once before, you're human like the rest of us."

"That's just another way of saying I'm selfish."

"No. We can't bleed for everyone or we'd bleed to death."

To Adams' horror her shoulders began shaking. "We should bleed for everyone. Otherwise we're nothing. Oh, God, Frank, I wish this war was over. I'm terrified what it's doing to me."

## 18

The aged MG sports car contained two drunken pilot officers and their girl friends. With its hood down, the wind was buffeting their faces and ruffling their hair. Both girls squealed as the car skidded round a corner and rocked violently before straightening again. The driver, not yet twenty-one, glanced back over his shoulder and gave a yell of pride.

"Isn't she a beauty?"

The second pilot, equally youthful, gave his girl friend a wink. "She's not bad. But I still think that old jalopy I had last year could go faster."

"Don't talk bull, man. This'll do eighty if I push her."

"Then start pushing her. Otherwise it's going to be closing time before we make the Saxon Arms."

The driver put his foot down and the note of the engine rose a full octave. The country road ahead was flanked by trees and high hedges. The sun had long set and dust was stealing over the fields. A couple of crows, settling down for the night, cawed indignantly and rose with a clatter of wings as the car roared past.

The driver reached out and put his arm around the waist of the girl beside him. As she snuggled against his shoulder, he began singing lustily. A second later the other pilot joined in. The girl at the back was showing alarm at the speed they were travelling but quietened when she was also pulled into her boy friend's arms.

Fifty yards ahead the road swung into a sharp left-hand bend. With his attention diverted by the girl alongside him, the driver failed to see it until the girl let out a warning scream.

It was the last sound any of them were to hear in their young lives. A second later the car leapt across the road and slammed into a tree with an impact that could be heard a mile away. Two bodies catapulted out, crashed into the hawthorn hedge, and hung motionless. Two others lay mangled among the jagged wreckage. In the silence that settled over the countryside, the only sounds heard through it were the hiss of hot metal and the dripping of petrol.

Moore was in No. 2 hangar when Henderson found him. With the move south scheduled for the morrow, he and his two flight commanders had been busy all day checking their specialist officers were sending everything needed for the operation. All heavy equipment, including bombs and rockets, had already been despatched by road transport. The Bombay, due at Sutton Craddock the following morning, would airlift the more fragile equipment and it was these items the ground crews were now packing into crates. The men had been working hard all day, and with only a privileged few knowing the reason for the move, rumours were rife and complaints many.

Teddy Young was the first to notice Henderson as the big Scot steered his bulk through the orderly chaos. "The Old Man looks in a paddy. I wonder what's up."

Henderson came to a halt in front of them. "Did any of you give your lads permission to go out this evening?"

Moore glanced at the two flight commanders, who shook their heads. "No, sir. The station's on standby."

169

"That's what I thought," Henderson said grimly. He turned to Young. "No one asked you for a quick trip into Scarborough or Whitby?"

The ginger-headed Australian looked puzzled. "They know better than that, sir. What's the problem?"

"The problem is two corpses on a mortuary slab in Highgate. Jennings and Stuart. Killed instantly in a car crash."

Young's jaw dropped. "You serious, sir?"

"Too bloody serious. The police have just phoned me. The M.O.'s gone off to identify them."

Young dropped on to a packing case. "I heard Jennings was going to buy a jalopy. They must have gone over the fence and picked it up. The stupid young bastards."

Henderson turned to Moore. "You realize what this means? With Heron wounded, Illingworth sick and McKenny grounded, even if we use our reserve crews we're going to be two kites shy. We might get away with one but two—hell, Lambert will crucify us."

Moore guessed the way the Scot's thoughts were running. "Are you asking me to lift McKenny's suspension?"

Henderson scowled. "You don't think I like it, do you? But has anyone got any other ideas?"

Teddy Young gave a resigned shrug as Moore glanced at him. The young squadron commander stood deep in thought for a moment, then moved away. "I'll go and have a talk with McKenny."

With all passes cancelled, the Mess was crowded when Moore entered. Although the bar was as busy as usual, he could see that news of the car accident had preceded him. The aircrews were gathered into small groups and there was a total absence of their usual gaiety. The irony did not escape Moore as he caught sight of Ross talking to Hopkinson and Stan Baldwin at the bar. Men could die in combat almost daily and their comrades would mourn them in wine and laughter. Yet when they were killed in commonplace ways the shock was felt by all.

Ignoring the questions put to him, he pushed his

way towards the young Scot. "I want a word with you, Ross. It won't take a minute."

He led Ross into the corner where the piano stood. With St. Claire missing, Lindsay absent, and the only other pianist on the station, Illingworth, down with 'flu, it was the quietest corner of the room.

"I've got a problem, Ross. As you must have heard, Jennings and Stuart have just killed themselves in a car crash. Yet we've an operation scheduled for the day after tomorrow that calls for full squadron strength. If I were to rescind McKenny's suspension, would you be willing to fly with him?"

Ross's surprise disguised his apprehension. "Are you giving me a choice, skipper?"

"In fairness I must. How do you feel about it?"

"How important is the operation?"

"It's very important. If it wasn't, I wouldn't be letting McKenny off the hook."

"Then it's O.K. I'll fly with him."

The young Scot's willingness to do his duty made Moore join Henderson in damning the political side of the operation. "You don't have to, Ross. No one will think the less of you if you refuse. In fact no one will know."

"It's all right, skipper. Have you had a word with Paddy yet?"

"Yes. I've just left his billet. I told him if he put one foot wrong I'd skin him alive. He swore on the Bible he'd behave. Can I trust him, Ross? Don't cover him because he's your friend. His life as well as yours could be at risk if he acts like a damn fool again."

Ross cleared his throat before replying. "I think he'll be all right, skipper. I know it hurt him like hell to be grounded."

"That's what I'm banking on. He knows this is his last chance. All right, Ross. You'll both join the rest of the boys in the morning. If we can't get your kite cleared in time, you can take either Jennings' or Stuart's aircraft. We've no problem there, worse luck."

Ross checked him as he moved away. "Are you going to tell Paddy, skipper, or shall I?"

"You leave that to me," Moore told him. "It'll give me another chance to warn him of the consequence if he wanders off the straight and narrow."

## 19

His chubby face pink from the effort, the young aircraftsman Ellis heaved a box of camera gun films from the 25-cwt. Bedford, lowered it to the ground, and sat heavily down on it. Towering over him was a huge Bombay transport that had flown in just after dawn. A second Bedford in the process of being unloaded was standing at the opposite side of the aircraft.

As the young ACII mopped his face, a lanky Leading Aircraftsman ducked under the tail of the Bombay and approached him. The newcomer, wearing a filthy pair of overalls and a shoestring of a tie, was clearly an old sweat. "What the 'ell are you doing, Ellis? Takin' a holiday?"

"I'm bushed," the youngster muttered. He gazed up resentfully at the huge aircraft. "What's all this about anyway? Where are we going?"

The old sweat gazed furtively around, dropped on the box beside him, and pulled a fag end from the pocket of his overalls. Lighting it, he sucked in smoke greedily. "The Middle East, mate. A pound to a penny."

The ACII looked shocked. "You mean the desert? But what about all the things we're leaving behind?"

"That's the way the mob does things. Some stupid bastard wakes up and then it's all rush an' panic. We'll probably get our kit in a couple of months' time, full of flies and sand."

"I don't want to leave England," the youngster wailed. "I've got a girl here."

172

McTyre gave a lascivious grin. "They've got girls over there too, mate. Real women—all tits and bottom. I had an oppo' once who did a tour round Alexandria. They used to go to a café where they put on shows for the lads. You know what the women did?"

Ellis shook his head. Leaning towards him, McTyre gave the gory details. When he finished, the cherubic-faced Ellis looked both fascinated and horrified. "He must have been pulling your leg!"

McTyre shook his head triumphantly. "Naw. I've heard the same thing from other bods who's been there. In a couple of weeks you're goin' to see things that'll make your hair curl."

"I still don't want to leave England," the youngster muttered.

McTyre gazed up with distaste at the grey October sky. "You must be off your marbles, mate. Who's your girl friend? Mae West?"

A yell from the second transport made him glance round. A corporal had ducked beneath the Bombay. "What the hell are you doing, McTyre? Havin' a game of cards?"

Ellis jumped to his feet as the corporal strode towards them. Nipping out his fag end, McTyre rose more slowly. "Listen to the bastard," he muttered. "He's been sittin' on his arse for the last half hour while I've done all the work, and now he's yelling for action. Roll on the revolution, mate!"

While 633 Squadron was preparing to move down to Holmsley, a week of intense activity was being culminated on the south coast of England. For days massive air patrols had kept the skies clear of enemy reconnaissance aircraft while 3,500 American troops arrived and settled into specially prepared camps in the Portsmouth/Southampton area. At the same time hundreds of tons of equipment, guns and ordnance were loaded on to supply ships assembled in local docks and on to tank landing craft.

Other sections of the Services were equally busy during this time. Minesweepers, whose task would be

173

to clear a channel to the enemy coast, began assembling off Southampton. Four American destroyers positioned themselves in the Portsmouth roads. The HQ ship *Brazos*, straining every steam pipe and rivet to make up lost time, arrived only forty hours behind schedule. Thunderbolts of the 8th Air Force touched down at selected airfields and prepared themselves for a showdown with the Luftwaffe. High-ranking officers of all services and a large coterie of war correspondents began to arrive at an hotel on the outskirts of Portsmouth where a reception hall had been converted into a Communications Centre.

The 6th October dawned cloudy but bright. In the early evening the first of the American troops began to file on to their assault craft. As each vessel filled up, it moved out into the Solent. The minesweepers lifted anchor and began their perilous outward journey. Although for the majority of the assault force the 6th was only a day of discomfort, for some men the operation had already begun.

633 Squadron, the only British unit involved, flew their Mosquitoes into Holmsley airfield in the New Forest during the morning. The Bombay transport, carrying ground crews and specialist officers as well as essential spares, arrived half an hour later. To unaccustomed eyes the scene would have appeared chaotic as the Station Warrant Officer, known to one and all as "Bert the Bastard", bawled orders and men ran around as if chasing their tails. Yet the chaos had an order of its own and by the late afternoon, to the indignation of its permanent residents, 633 Squadron was in full possession of the airfield. Evidence of this was provided by McTyre. The old sweat had brought with him a kitbag of tea, sugar and tinned milk, and before darkness fell was doing a roaring trade dispensing tea at 2d a cup from one of the dispersal huts.

To their surprise and gratification, the aircrews and non-flying officers were billeted in a small hotel that stood just off the Lyndhurst-Bournemouth road. All the crews had been given a briefing by Moore and Adams just before leaving Sutton Craddock and in the late afternoon received their promised visit from Runcorn and Tilsey, who were doing a tour of the operational squadrons. After being given all the latest intelligence, the crews were allowed to stand down on the condition they did not stray outside the hotel grounds.

In the meantime, to the anxiety of those responsible for the operation, the weather began to deteriorate. The wind started to freshen and rain squalls began sweeping in. To the troops who, for logistic reasons, had already been embarked on their assault vessels, discomfort turned to distress as more and more of them became seasick. In the large Portsmouth hotel, tension grew apace during the night as the half-hourly weather reports came in. Among the high-ranking American officers and the war correspondents who crammed the Communications Room, the huge figure of Staines and the bearded face of Lambert were conspicuous. A few British liaison officers were also present, among them Davies. Made even more aware of the importance of 633's role by a VIP phone call he had received just before midnight, the small Air Commodore was suffering an anti-climax as the night wore on. 10.00 hours was the absolute deadline for a decision if the convoy was to sail on the 7th and yet by dawn the meteorological reports were still unfavourable. With the first two weeks in October the absolute limit for amphibious operations in the Channel, Davies was in a dispirited and testy mood when the Met. Officer returned yet again to the Communications Room. Although everyone was too tired to notice it, this time he was showing some excitement.

"I've some good news for you at last, gentlemen." As weary heads jerked up, he went on: "Our latest reports indicate the winds will start decreasing during the forecast period and will veer west-south-west in the late afternoon. The rain and the poor visibility should gradually clear during the day and the swell will moderate."

The Chairman of the Executive Committee, a distinguished-looking American with a tanned face and white sideburns, rose from his chair. "What does all that mean? That we can go?"

The Met. Officer's reply had all the caution of his

breed. "We have reason to hope that by the time the convoy reaches its station across the Channel, conditions should be reasonable to fair, sir."

The Chairman grinned at his expectant officers. "When translated, I guess that means yes. So get the machinery moving, gentlemen."

A cheer sounded, followed by a rush of feet as officers scrambled for telephones. Back in the small hotel near Lyndhurst, Henderson grabbed up his bedside telephone the moment it began ringing. "Yes. Henderson here."

"I've good news, Jock. It's on."

Henderson, who, between cat-naps, had been listening to the rain squalls lashing against his window, was surprised. "They're taking a hell of a chance aren't they?"

"Not according to their Met. boys. They predict reasonable weather by this evening."

"Let's hope they're right," the Scot said dryly.

"They usually are. Jock, listen! Lambert will definitely be covering the operation in the *Brazos*. Staines is also going out, which means you'll be right under the microscope. So tell your boys to do their best, will you?"

"They usually do, sir."

"I know that. But this support job is becoming more important by the minute. The C.-in-C. himself phoned me just before midnight, so you'll see how big the political snowball has grown."

The Scot almost asked if it was expected that his men flew their aircraft straight into the enemy strongpoints, then checked himself in time. "They'll be told to do their best, sir."

"Good man. You don't need to rush them off their feet today. You've plenty of time."

Henderson was the last man to flap when there was no need. "You can leave all that to me, sir. Do you still intend going aboard the *Brazos?*"

"What a damn silly question, Jock. Of course I do."

The Scot had his reasons for feeling a trifle malicious that morning. "You do realize the Luftwaffe might come out in strength?"

Davies' yelp made the phone rattle. "If Staines can go and Lambert can go, I think I can go too, don't you?"

"Yes, sir. But then why can't I come along as well?"

"Oh, Christ, don't let's have that again. You know why. You should be glad: we'll all probably be seasick. Now I'm going to get a couple of hours shuteye before things get under way."

In fact the operation was already under way. With the all-clear given, minesweepers returned to their dangerous task of clearing and marking channels across to the Normandy coast. As the news filtered down to the rank and file, men shook off their malaise and looked again to their responsibilities. Sailors hurried about ships checking everything from Oerlikons to ship hoists. Tank crews examined their armour again; artillerymen checked their pieces. Unit commanders repeated briefings while infantrymen cleaned their firearms for the fourth, fifth, or sixth time. In short, with the prospect of action only a few hours away, the task force became a fighting unit again.

The aircrews of 633 Squadron began the day less arduously. Aware they would get little sleep the following night, Henderson allowed them to stay in bed until 09.00 hours. After a leisurely breakfast, they were transported to the airfield to airtest their Mosquitoes. As each aircraft landed, mechanics swarmed around it to carry out final checks. Lastly, trolley trains arrived carrying 250 MC bombs and wing rockets. When armourers had finished hoisting these into position, each of the fifteen Mosquitoes was ready for its dangerous and exacting role.

With great care being taken in every step of the preparation, the autumn afternoon was fading before the final Form 700 was signed. When at last the crews were driven back to their hotel they discovered Henderson had organized a first-class meal for them. The irony was not lost on the crews and grins ran round the tables as the deep voice of Stan Baldwin, the only coloured man in the squadron, could be heard remarking to his pilot, Paddy Machin, that it was the best Last Supper he had ever tasted. Coffee was taken in an adjacent room where Henderson, Moore and Adams gave the men a final talk, an interview that provided an opportunity for last-minute questions. The bar was then opened until 21.00 hours with drinks strictly rationed. When it closed Henderson had a quick word with Moore and his two flight commanders and then addressed the men. "All right, lads, that's it. An early night will get shut of those bags under your eyes. You'll be called at 04.00 hours sharp."

With good-natured grumbles the crews filed off to their rooms. When the last man had gone, Henderson closed the door and turned to the two flight commanders who, along with Moore, had remained behind.

"This'll only take a few minutes. As Moore has already told you, this isn't just a highly responsible operation for us, it has strong political overtones as well. So it's important we do our best to stop reinforcements reaching that station. But that doesn't mean any of you play Tom Mix and attack the strongpoints or gunposts. The Yanks don't expect it and neither do we."

The Scot's eyes shifted to the impeccably-dressed Moore. "If you have any problems or need support, don't hesitate to call for it. You'll get a quick response because both Davies and the Typhoon squadrons will be tuned in on your wavelength."

"Are you joining Davies on the *Brazos,* sir?" Millburn asked.

The disgruntled Scot shook his head. "He won't let me go in case I'm wanted here when you come back. But I'll be standing by in the Ops. Room. All right, I'll see you in the morning."

The party of men took the lift up to their rooms on the second floor. Reaching his room first, Moore drew Millburn to one side. "Take it easy tomorrow. Don't think that because they're Americans down there you have to go in and spike Jerry's guns single-handed."

Millburn grinned. "I'll be a good boy, skipper."

"Mind you are. I don't want half my squadron littered over the cliffs."

Shouting goodnight to one another, the men dispersed. For ten to fifteen minutes the corridor was silent. Then a door creaked open and the furtive figure of Millburn and Gabby appeared. Motioning to one another to keep quiet, they tiptoed to the end of the corridor and disappeared.

Five minutes later, looking disappointed, they tiptoed back and entered a smoke-filled bedroom. The shirt-sleeved figures of Teddy Young and Hopkinson were sitting on the bed with a cabinet laid on its side in front of them. Opposite were the New Zealander Larkin and Frank Day. A bottle of gin and a dozen bottles of beer littered the floor nearby. As Millburn and Gabby entered, Hopkinson was shuffling a pack of cards in preparation to deal. Young, a glass of gin in his hand, turned to the newcomers with a grin. "I thought you two were hoping to bed down with those waitresses?"

Millburn helped himself to a beer. "This bum navigator of mine lost his way again. He got us into the laundry room."

The perky Hopkinson jerked a thumb at the ceiling. "They're on the top floor. In the last two rooms."

The American stared at him. "How do you know that?"

"I asked the night porter." As Millburn made for the door, the Cockney grinned. "I wouldn't bother. He said one sleeps with the secretary and the other with the receptionist."

"Those two poofs?"

"That's the way it goes, Yank. The ones near the camps get too much and those out in the sticks have to take what they can get."

"But they've got camps round here. Camps of red-blooded Yanks."

Gabby joined in the chorus of cat-calls. "You know why your lot get more than your share, don't you? It's those fat wallets of yours. Take 'em away

179

and you'd be more frustrated than a pisspot on a Welsh Sunday."

"*I'd* be frustrated? I'm on the same pay as you, remember? RAF starvation pay. And have you noticed me short of dames?"

"That's the line you shoot 'em," Gabby declared "A couple of oil wells and a half a dozen ranches. You're the biggest conman in the business."

The American gave a wicked grin. "And who kept rubbing that scratch he got over the Frisians, so he could show off his war wound to his girl friend? Go on, boyo—who?"

As Gabby glared at the American for this revelation, Young gave Hopkinson a wink. "I don't know why you guys don't stick to horses. At least you don't have to bullshit 'em." He slapped a pocketful of change on the cabinet. "All right, get your starvation pay on the table. You might not be needing it tomorrow night."

In other rooms men were reacting differently to the ordeal on the morrow. A few lucky ones, Stan Baldwin and Machin among them, were already asleep. Roberts and Preston had finished a half-bottle of gin that Preston had sneaked into the room and with the sharp edges of life pleasantly blurred were now dozing off. Butterfield and Foster, both soccer fanatics, had found an argument about the relative merits of Dixie Dean and Stan Mortensen a useful prelude to sleep.

Others were finding sleep more difficult. By mutual consent Smith and Paget had given up the effort and were playing a game of pocket chess. Monahan and Evans, both ex-students, were reminiscing about their days at college and the girls they had known. Matthews was wondering if he would ever achieve his ambition of becoming a jazz drummer, while his navigator Allison, ex-£2-a-week clerk from Gateshead, was wondering how his widowed mother was managing on the money he sent her weekly. In their pre-battle behaviour, most of the crews were running close to form.

Among the exceptions was Moore. A complex man, sensitive and intelligent on the one hand, painstaking and disciplined on the other, the squadron commander left nothing to chance before an operation and so was usually able to rest with a satisfied mind. Finding sleep difficult tonight, his first thought was that there must be some technical or tactical point he had overlooked but although he racked his brains for a full hour he could think of nothing significant.

He wondered if McKenny could be the reason. After the Irishman's behaviour, all Moore's military instincts had demanded the pilot remained grounded, not least to safeguard Ross. Yet Moore could be a pragmatist when the occasion demanded it, and he could not feel guilty for a decision that had been forced on him by demands outside his control.

His thoughts moved on to Harvey and then, by chain reaction, to the girl Harvey loved, Anna Reinhardt. Since the Yorkshireman had been wounded, Davies had received only one item of news about her— that she had escaped from the Ruhpolding valley after the Rhine Maiden establishment had been destroyed. As soon as the news had reached Moore he had visited Harvey in hospital. He had arrived just before Harvey's most serious stomach operation and Moore was not the only one who believed the news had saved the Yorkshireman's life.

Lying there in bed Moore could see the girl as she had appeared at their first meeting in the Black Swan: oval-faced, dark hair swept up in a French roll, dressed like a queen in a black dress with no jewellery except an emerald brooch. A beautiful woman who was to prove as capable and courageous as any man. Moore had no illusions about his feelings for Anna Reinhardt. She was all he admired in a woman and hardly a day had passed since she was dropped into Occupied Europe that he had not remembered her.

He wondered where she was now. With enemies searching everywhere for her, she might already be in a prison cell. A German girl, a traitor in Nazi eyes, in the hands of the Gestapo. As he winced, Moore knew it was a nightmare that must have haunted Harvey throughout the long weeks he had spent in hospital. Although he had shared the thought with no one, Moore was glad Harvey had not returned to the squadron in time to take part in the present operation. Secretly he often wished the Yorkshireman's injuries would ground him permanently. With Anna operating as an SOE agent behind the Nazi lines, the odds against the couple meeting again were heavy enough. With Harvey flying in a squadron reserved for highly-specialized and dangerous missions, at times they appeared hopeless.

Another man finding it difficult to sleep was Ross, who was sharing a room with McKenny. Until an hour ago the Irishman's relief at the lifting of his suspension had seemed a guarantee in itself that he would behave responsibly the following day. Yet when the two men had come up to their room, all Ross's misgivings had returned. During their absence someone must have noticed their room did not contain its obligatory Bible because one copy had been laid on each bed. The sight of them had brought about an immediate change in McKenny. Cursing, he had snatched up his copy and flung it down the room where it had struck the corner of a desk and fallen to the floor with is binding split open.

It was a sight that had made Ross cross himself. From McKenny's glance he had expected a new onslaught of taunts and ridicule. Instead the Irishman had turned away and climbed into bed without comment.

Although greatly distressed by the incident, Ross had been equally relieved it had not led to a quarrel that could have disastrous consequences on the morrow. The sense of duty that had made him volunteer to fly again with McKenny in no way meant the home-loving young Scot had aspirations to glory. For him the golden sands of the Galloway coast, the mist-shrouded peaks of Ailsa Craig and Arran, and the green Heads of Ayr around which he had often walked with a bonnie lass called Maggie Andrews were all he wanted out of life. These last few weeks they had never seemed more precious and he desperately wanted to see them again.

It was this yearning that had committed Ross to the act that was now denying him all chance of sleep. Terrified of another quarrel with McKenny, for the first time in his young life Ross had not knelt down at his bedside and prayed. Instead, like a man ashamed of his faith, he had crept between the sheets and silently said his prayers there.

After the taunts and threats McKenny had made, Ross found this act full of frightening implications. Turning his head towards the Irishman's bed, he listened. Believing McKenny was asleep, he tip-toed to the window and drew the blackout curtains aside.

Although the night sky was still overcast, here and there stars were shining through breaks in the clouds. The wind had dropped and had a plaintive sound as it sobbed in the eaves. Gazing out into the darkness, wondering what the dawn would bring, Ross had a sense of loneliness as sharp as a wound.

A voice at his elbow made him start violently. "What's the matter, Bernie? You looking for fairies?"

Ross tried to smile. "I couldn't sleep so I was checking on the weather."

McKenny glanced out. "It won't be perfect but it's improving. What's the time?"

"Half-eleven."

"Then the convoy will be on its way."

"Yes, I suppose it will."

"I'll bet a lot of them will be seasick. There's bound to be a heavy swell after all this wind."

Ross was finding comfort in the Irishman's amicability. "I'm glad I'm not crossing with them. I get sick on a boating lake."

McKenny's eyes had lifted to a large break in the clouds through which stars could be seen. As he gazed up, his mood changed. "A hell of a lot of them are going to die on that beach tomorrow. And I'll bet a week ago half of them had never heard of it. It doesn't make any sense, does it?"

Caught unawares, Ross could only shake his head. In the dim light McKenny's face had turned bitter. "Look at those stars. They don't give a damn, do they?"

Ross was feeling a familiar dryness in his throat. "They're only stars, Paddy."

The Irishman's hard stare turned on him. "How can you of all people say that? They're God's stars.

183

And they'll look down on all those bodies rocking in the surf tomorrow and they won't give a damn. You don't learn very fast, do you? That's what life's all about. Total cosmic indifference."

Ross wanted to protest but his courage failed him. As if ashamed of his outburst, McKenny pulled the blackout curtains back into place. "We'd better get some sleep or we'll be bushed tomorrow."

Back in bed, Ross lay listening. When he was certain McKenny was asleep, he slipped out and went down on his knees. His prayers were feverish and full of shame and yet when at last he crept back between the sheets it was as if a load had fallen from him and he fell asleep almost at once.


Far away across the Channel the American convoy was standing in readiness off the enemy coast. Troops embarked on their landing craft were watching the eastern horizon for the first sight of dawn. Some were still retching from seasickness. Others were whispering to their comrades to hide their nervousness. All were totally isolated in their thoughts.

Banks of mist drifted over the restless sea. Through them the ghostly hulks of tank landing ships could be seen. Occasionally men felt drizzle touch their faces. The muted throb of engines came through the splash of waves. On the Rangers' landcraft, craft that carried Colonel Tilsey, a sergeant pointed eastward at a fog bank that was turning grey. Following his eyes, men swallowed to lubricate their nervous throats.

Less than a minute later the sound of aircraft engines could be heard. As the roar grew into deafening thunder that swept overhead, the spell that had gripped the convoy was broken. Men straightened their chilled bodies, cheered, and waved their arms at the invisible B.17s.

The thunder moved southward and became a heavy grumble. Feeling their heartbeats in their wrists and temples, the assault troops waited. A brilliant light lit up their white faces. As the parachute flare sank downwards, the horizon that until now had been a solid wall of darkness was bisected into cliffs and sky.

A flash ran across the night clouds, followed by a dozen others in rapid succession. The explosions, sounding like heavy doors being slammed, held a brutal threat that made more than one man cross himself. Bows awash with speed, a destroyer came sweeping through the ranks of bobbing ships. As an officer yelled orders through a megaphone, a hundred engines roared into life and the landing craft started for the beaches. Operation Crucible had begun.

## 20

Flying line astern with A-Apple in the lead, the fifteen Mosquitoes crossed the English coast near Highcliffe and dropped immediately down to the wavetops. Men on an inshore fishing boat were buffeted by air displacement as the line of screaming engines and fishlike bodies hurtled past. A startled gull, rising from the swell, struck the windshield of T-Tommy and slid off in a tangle of blood and feathers. To the west the visibility was poor as the night made its reluctant retreat. To the east the sky was rapidly brightening over the Isle of Wight.

With fuel reserves an urgent consideration, all Mosquitoes were carrying auxiliary tanks. As a further conservation measure they were flying at economical cruising speed without boost. To confuse the enemy's radar scanners, Moore had led them in a short dog-leg after leaving Holmsley. Now he was taking them so low over the Channel their slipstreams were scuffling the grey wavetops.

The lighthouse and Needles of the Isle of Wight had barely fallen behind before they ran into a rain squall that reduced visibility to half a second's reaction time. With radio silence in force, the crews' response was based on the high level of training Moore had given them. Instead of increasing the interval between aircraft, they closed up almost nose to tail. It was a manoeuvre only superbly-experienced and confident crews could have attempted. While each pilot shared his attention between the Mosquito ahead and the tossing sea below, navigators strained their eyes to pierce the grey curtain that swept horizontally past.

The squall died two minutes later. In A-Apple, Hopkinson touched Moore's arm and pointed. Far ahead, sheets of light that resembled a summer electric storm were illuminating the horizon. The cessation of the flashes a minute later told the crews the destroyers were lifting their fire to allow the beach parties to land. With the Mosquitoes now halfway across the Channel, which was a hundred miles wide at this point, navigators were keeping an eye open for flak ships. Although fewer ships guarded this wider section of the Channel than the Dover Straits, there had always been the danger one might have spotted the convoy during the night and alerted the coastal defences. In fact this had not happened but now it was daylight, and with bitter experience of the massive firepower these floating gun platforms contained, crews kept a wary eye open in case one should be on the move and cross their flight path.

The reappearance of flashes ahead told the crews a duel was now being fought between the naval escort and the coastal defences. Daylight was advancing fast and eight minutes later a dark line began to separate sea and sky. Ships, hull down on the horizon, grew into toy vessels and then into towering hulks of camouflaged steel. Columns of water were erupting around them and over to the right a heavy explosion followed by an enormous mushroom of smoke marked the death of a destroyer.

Shivering the waves with their slipstreams, the Mosquitoes weaved their way through the assault craft while each man gathered his own split-second impressions. Landing craft, full of huddled men, heading for the beaches. . . . A body floating face down in the surf. . . . Canisters of smoke, intended to conceal, blowing away in the dawn breeze like tattered rags. . . . Men running clumsily across glistening shingle.

. . . Two rag dolls sailing into the air as a shell exploded. Ominous lines of tracer sweeping like whip lashes towards the aircraft as the cliffs flashed past.

Staring back through the perspex blister, Hopkinson was trying to take a count of the aircraft. "I think they've all got through, skipper."

When Moore judged his aircraft were out of range of the coastal light flak, he led them in a tight orbit and gazed down. On Blue Beach to the east, Tilsey's Rangers appeared in charge of the situation. Uneven ground around the gun battery had enabled them to close in, and as Moore watched, a tongue of fire from a portable flame-thrower licked out and enveloped one huge bunker.

Straightening from his orbit, Moore flew west along the coast road. From his height of 2,500 feet he could see over both sides of the hill behind the radiolocation station and although he knew reinforcements must already be on the move, at present both ends of the road were empty of traffic.

With the station now only a mile or so to his right he could see the damage the B.17s had done. Outhouses and billets had been reduced to rubble, the perimeter wall was broken in a dozen places, and the cliff top outside was pock-marked with craters where mines had been detonated by exploding bombs. The main buildings and strongpoints, however, appeared intact, as did the three aerials of the scanners. The burnt-out wreckage of four B.17s testified to the ferocity of the defences.

That most of the heavy flak towers were still operational was soon evident from the murderous fire now pouring upwards. The brightening sky was peppered by white and black puffs of smoke as the radar-controlled guns followed the Mosquitoes along the cliffs. Young swore an Australian oath as his Mosquito almost turned over to the concussion of a 37-mm shell. To lessen fire Moore swung sharply to port and led his file of aircraft as far inland as visibility of the coast road would permit.

White Beach, where the main body of the infantry was pouring ashore, fell behind. Ahead was Red

Beach with its shelving valley where landing craft were putting armour ashore. Seeing the road ahead was clear, Moore was about to lead his patrol back along the battle area when his earphones crackled. "Guard Dog Leader. Do you hear me?"

Moore would have known Davies' voice anywhere. "Guard Dog Leader to Ramillies. You are loud and clear."

Davies sounded as excited as a schoolboy on sports day. "What's the position on the road?"

"So far it's clear in both directions."

"Good. Now listen. There's a foul-up on Red Beach. Do a recce, will you, and report back as quickly as possible."

Relieved that Davies had broken radio silence, Moore called in Teddy Young. "Take over and keep patrolling the road, Teddy. I'll join you in a few minutes."

As Young led the squadron into a tight 180-degree turn, Moore put A-Apple into a shallow dive. Picking up speed he crossed the cliffs two miles to the west, and headed back over the sea towards Red Beach, where two tank landing craft had their ramps down on the beach. One had been hit and had dense smoke pouring from its quarterdeck. The other had a crippled amphibian lying at the foot of its ramp which men were struggling to drag aside. On the beach itself tanks and gun carriers ran in a drunken line towards the gap in the seafront that was their only escape route. Three of the vehicles were ablaze and trapped soldiers were trying to find cover behind others from murderous fire that was sweeping the bay.

Higher up the beach a dozen or so Americans were crouched behind a shingle ridge that lay at one side of the gap. As A-Apple swept towards it, a soldier jumped up dragging a Bangalore torpedo behind him. He had not run five yards before a hail of bullets cut him down. A comrade jumping up to give aid was killed before he cleared the top of the shingle.

Before A-Apple swept past Moore spotted the obstacle and the origin of the murderous fire. Conscious the gap in the seafront represented a weakness in their defences, the Germans had bridged it with a thick concrete wall. A camouflage net, ripped almost in half by shell fire and fluttering in the morning breeze, explained why aerial reconnaissance had failed to detect it. The gunfire came from two large bunkers built into the low cliffs at either side of the wall.

As A-Apple flashed over the gap, one of the flak posts gave it a vicious burst of tracer before concentrating again on the pinned-down soldiers. Hopkinson's Cockney voice echoed Moore's thoughts. "If their tanks can't break out, skipper, they'll never be able to take that station."

Back on the HQ ship *Brazos* the usual muddle of communications that seems to plague all large-scale military operations had kept Davies ignorant of the reason for the debacle on Red Beach. Now, as the details reached him, he forgot his earlier orders for the Mosquitoes to concentrate only on the support road.

"Ramillies to Guard Dog Leader. The problem's a reinforced wall blocking the gap. Can you distract the gun posts for a minute or two?"

Moore, who had already decided on his line of action, acknowledged tersely. "Message received, Ramillies. Guard Dog Leader to Zero Seven, Zero Eight, and Zero Eleven. Join me on Red Beach at the double."

Zero Eleven belonged to McKenny and Ross, Zero Seven to Machin and Baldwin, and Zero Eight to Millburn and Gabby. All three Mosquitoes arrived in less than a minute and formated behind Moore who was orbiting over the road. A few words were all the experienced crews needed. McKenny and Machin banked away, swept out to sea, and came back on a reciprocal course towards Red Beach. Thirty seconds after their departure Moore and Millburn, flying almost wingtip to wingtip, aimed their Mosquitoes at the distant gap in the coast. The tactic was to be the diversionary one used against the flak wagons in the Ardennes. In the few seconds left for reflection before the action began, the usually chirpy Hoppy sounded apprehensive. "If I mess this up, skipper, I'm going to kill a couple of dozen Yanks."

Moore's reply hid his own apprehension as the

slopes of the shallow valley flashed past. "They'd die anyway if we leave them there, Hoppy. But you won't mess it up."

"Let's hope you're right," the Cockney muttered.

Opening the bomb doors, Moore could feel them quivering beneath him. Alongside him the doors of T-Tommy opened at almost the same moment. "Main switch on, skipper," Hoppy said. "No. 1 bomb tail-fused."

The second pair of Mosquitoes were less than two miles away and approaching from the sea at a combined speed of nearly six hundred miles an hour. As the bomb doors opened, the enemy gunners accepted them as a threat and both heavy and light automatic guns swung upwards to cover them. At 1,000 yards the two Mosquitoes began firing with their 20-mm cannon and although for the sake of the American soldiers as well as the second pair of Mosquitoes the shells were aimed wide, the ground gunners took the fire as further proof the two aircraft were a major threat and gave them their full attention.

It was an opportunity the pinned-down American soldiers did not miss. Dragging Bangalor torpedoes behind them, two men jumped over the ridge and hurled themselves to the foot of the wall. Two more followed a few seconds later. It was a display of zeal that none of the Mosquito crews wanted but there was nothing they could do to recall the men.

The ground fire was both fierce and accurate. With his diversionary task completed, Machin broke away, a thin trail of white smoke coming from his port engine. To Ross's alarm, McKenny held on course for three more endless seconds which gave time for both bunkers to fire on them. For a moment the Mosquito seemed to stagger in mid-air. Then J-Jimmie recovered and joined Machin in circling round as if to make a second attack.

As a decoy ruse, the manoeuvre worked perfectly. With the enemy gunners fully occupied, the second pair of Mosquitoes sweeping towards the opposite side of the wall were allowed an almost uninterrupted run-in. Neither Hoppy nor Gabby was using their bomb-

190

sights; at zero height they were a handicap rather than an asset. Instead, with the bomb releases in their hands, they were watching their pilots intently.

The Mosquitoes were flying so low their slipstream was shivering the dry gorse and ferns that lined the valley. As gorse gave way to sand, Hoppy held his breath. Moore, whose eyes were fixed on the left-hand bunker, saw it flash into his windshield and gave a shout, "Now!" Hoppy pressed the bomb release and the 250-pounder plunged down, bounced once, then buried itself in a mound of sand little more than ten yards from the bunker.

Forty yards to the right Millburn and Gabby had a similar success with their own attack. Yet because both crews entered the bunkers' field of fire the moment they swept over the wall their need to take violent evasive action prevented them being certain their bombs had not bounced over the wall and landed near the pinned-down Americans. Necks twisted to watch as they swept out of range, all four men were mentally counting: "Eight . . . nine . . . ten . . . eleven. . . ."

The two explosions came within a second of one another, hurling fountains of sand upwards. When the smoke blew away it looked from above as if little damage had been done to the massive bunkers. What no outside observer could see, however, was the effect of the concussion inside them. With blood oozing from their mouths and eardrums, men were sprawled in grotesque postures beside their guns. Of the four American soldiers who had reached the wall, two were dead and the other two half-stunned. The rest of the advance party, however, did not waste their opportunity. Running forward with demolition equipment, they quickly had charges planted beneath the wall. Orbiting above, ignoring the vengeful flak from other gun posts, Moore saw explosions throw rubble high into the air. As tanks and mobile guns began moving eagerly forward, there was a yell in the R/T from Millburn.

"We've done it, you guys! They're on the move again."

Relaxing, Moore gazed back and saw only two Mosquitoes were orbiting with him. His terse question quietened the American's jubilation. "Where's Machin?"

Hopkinson pointed seaward where an aircraft trailing white smoke could be seen making towards the convoy. Moore lifted his mask. "Zero Seven! Are you all right?"

Machin's voice sounded far away. "Our port engine's running hot, skipper, and we're losing revs with the other. I'm trying to ditch near the ships."

In the meantime there had been another breakdown in communications on the *Brazos* that had prevented Davies hearing the outcome of the action from Moore. When he received it from Army sources his delight at his squadron's important contribution showed in his semi-abandonment of Signals procedure. "Ramillies calling Guard Dog Leader. Good work, Moore! Everyone here is as relieved as hell. Now get back to that road and away from the flak!"

Before Moore obeyed, he noticed that the American assault troops had broken through the lighter cliff defences and were now massing behind bushes and in hollows. His guess was that now the tanks had broken out of Red Beach, the assault on the station itself would wait until the armour arrived to spear-point it, a move that would reduce casualties both among the remaining minefields and within the perimeter wall itself.

As the three Mosquitoes swept eastwards to join the rest of the squadron, Gabby pointed at a huge pall of smoke that hung over the cliffs ahead. His quip was aimed at Millburn.

"It looks as if they've finished off that gun battery. You know something, boyo? They must have some of our Commandos with them."

The jubilant Millburn laughed. "You're seeing something today, you little punk. Hard-nosed Yankees on the prod. Maybe they won't bother to get back into those boats. Maybe they'll go straight on to Berlin."

Gabby grinned maliciously. "Maybe they still will. Straight into prisoner-of-war camps."

About to answer, Millburn caught sight of American Rangers hurrying westward along the cliffs. Having

neutralized the powerful gun battery, which both reduced the enfilading fire sweeping White Beach and
took pressure off the fleet at sea, Tilsey was now leading
his men forward to tighten the noose that was closing
around the radiolocation station. Millburn jerked a
thumb at the Rangers. "See that? It's going to be over
in half an hour. This invasion when it comes will be
like taking candy from a kid."

Gabby sniffed. "It doesn't take much to make you
cocky, does it?"

"Jealousy will get you nowhere, boyo," Millburn
grinned. "Nowhere at all."

Millburn's jubilation was shared by almost every
officer on board the *Brazos*. Apart from the hold-up
on Red Beach, now satisfactorily resolved, every step
in the operation was on schedule. The only question
men were asking themselves—and it seemed like looking a gift horse in the mouth—was what had happened
to the German infantry and tank reserves? Allowing
for almost any contingency they ought to be within
sight by this time.

To older soldiers who had experienced German
military efficiency it was the one mystery that threw a
shadow over the operation. As a consequence some
men actually showed relief when Davies, after clapping
his hands over his earphones to shut out extraneous
noise, glanced round at them. "My men report tanks
and infantry ahead." He leaned over his microphone.
"Ramillies here. I want map references of those tanks
and their number. Over."

Men crowded closer as Davies listened. When he
finally glanced at them there was not a cough in the
Operations Room. His gnome-like face seemed to have
sharpened and there were two red spots high up on his
cheekbones.

"It seems as if our Intelligence has been wrong,
gentlemen, unless the enemy has brought up reinforcements during the last two days. My men report dozens
of tanks moving up the road from the south-east and
equally heavy infantry reinforcement behind them."

"What are you saying?" The question came from a
greying, two-star general. "That we're in a trap?"

Davies hesitated. "It's too early to say that, sir. But this report does suggest your tanks will be heavily outnumbered."

---

# 21

The tanks were coming up the lane like a column of bulldogs with their teeth bared. A pennant was fluttering from the leading vehicle's turret. As the Mosquitoes came screaming over the hill, tank commanders ducked their heads and watched the aircraft stream past and soar into a climbing turn. The troop transports that were following halted and grey-clad soldiers swarmed into the thick hedges that flanked the road.

Although his instinct was to attack immediately, Young knew it was vital first to alert HQ of the threat and he dipped a wingtip to gain a better view. The tanks appeared to be a mixture of Panther Ds and Tiger Is, both extremely formidable fighting machines and in another class to the light armour the Americans had been forced to bring. It was their number, however, that startled the Australian. They stretched down the hill and beyond it, giving the impression an entire armoured regiment was on the move.

The explanation, had Young known it, was simple. For many months the Germans had been disturbed by the French Maquis' activities and the almost daily reports they were known to be giving the Allies about German defence dispositions. With the forthcoming invasion making it vital this information was stopped or, even better, rendered incorrect, new and elaborate security measures had been introduced. Only one-third of the armour available on the Western seaboard was now left visible to prying eyes: the rest was hidden in innocuous shelters or specially-constructed underground parks. Unfortunately for the Americans, the local hideout for the Panzer Group defending that area was a large turf-covered bomb dump only seventeen miles away. With the huge coastal guns needing large reserves of ammunition, even Arnaud's efficient partisans had assumed the well-guarded dump was what it seemed and so had gravely underestimated the enemy armour available.

It was the Tank Commander's reluctance to throw his forces in piecemeal that had delayed his response. Instead of advancing immediately with his visible reserve, he had made a rendezvous point and waited there until his main force of armour had joined him. In the meantime, knowing an infantry division was on manoeuvres near Rocheville, he had put in a request that a contingent should be rushed up at once. After appraising the American raid, German HQ had granted his request and the troop transports had caught up with his column five minutes ago. A second contingent of troops was standing by on red alert.

This brief delay had in no way worried the Tank Commander. Indeed, to give the Americans time to extend themselves and so become sitting ducks for his heavy counter-attack had seemed good military strategy. What he had not expected was the wall at Red Beach to be breached so quickly. Even this news had not shaken his confidence because he knew his armour not only outnumbered but could also outgun the lighter amphibious armour of the Americans. His concern at this stage, then, was not the outcome of the battle but whether he could reach the radiolocation station in time to give it support.

Expecting an immediate attack by the aircraft, the tanks had halted like the transports behind them. With the Mosquitoes peeling away and then orbiting above, an observer with romantic tendencies might have imagined the two units were paying tribute to one another before engaging in mortal combat.

If it was a tribute, it was a short-lived one. Finishing his report, Young wasted no more time. "Leader to Red Section. Line abreast and pick your target."

Like a line of cavalry changing direction, the Mosquitoes banked round and came swooping down on the road. At the same moment tank turrets spun round and automatic guns began pumping out shells. Weaving to make themselves a difficult target, the Mosquitoes launched their first rockets at 900 yards range. Seconds later they opened fire with their 20-mm. Hispanos. One rocket struck a Panther on its most vulnerable spot, just beneath its armoured skirt. The puff of smoke that erupted from the turret gave no real hint of the shambles inside as the warhead exploded. The fireball that burst out five seconds later and rose to a hundred feet above the column gave a better indication of the kill. A second rocket struck a Tiger's starboard track and immobilized it. Bright flashes along the column denoted hits by the 20-mm. shells.

The more manoeuvrable LMGs of the tanks raked the Mosquitoes as they swept across the road. Before they could attack again the tanks slewed round on their tracks and made for the hedge that stood between them and the cliffs. Built without a Bocage earthwork, it proved no obstacle to the heavy armour. Crushing it aside, the tanks broke out on the open cliff top and the danger caused by their high concentration was over.

To the west Moore had heard of the crisis on his R/T. As he led his small flight past the embattled station to join his main force, he saw that some American tanks had crossed the minefields and were already nosing through the station perimeter. On the northern flank exploding mortar shells suggested the American infantry were also closing in. The battle for the station, then, appeared to be going well. At the same time Moore was under no illusion how quickly the situation could change if the heavy tanks Young reported were to reach the scene.

The flashes of rockets and tracer, the pock-marked morning sky, and the drifting smoke ahead told him he was less than a minute from them. In T-Tommy behind him, Millburn was showing uncharacteristic concern. "Where the hell have all these Jerry tanks come from? We were told they'd have less than twenty."

"Jerry's always smarter than you think, boyo. If those tanks break through, it'll be that prisoner-of-war camp for sure."

Millburn gave a muted curse. In the Mosquito opposite him, McKenny had turned to glance at his starboard wing. Jagged holes disfigured it and part of the aileron was shot away. Alongside the Irishman, Ross was showing reaction. During the shell-shocked seconds it had taken him to launch his decoy attack on the gunpost, all McKenny's self-destructive impulses had surfaced again. Teeth clenched and lips drawn back, he had made the young Scot believe he intended to crash the Mosquito against the bunker. When he had levelled off only a few feet above the spitting guns, Ross's eyes had been tightly closed and his body rigid with fear. His voice betrayed that fear now.

"Why didn't you break off sooner?"

McKenny shrugged. "That wall was important. Any fool could see that."

"That didn't mean we had to fly down the barrels of the guns. You should have broken off when Machin did."

"For Christ's sake, I can't do anything right these days. We got away with it, didn't we?"

"How many more times do you think we can get away with it? We've overplayed our luck already."

The Irishman threw him a mocking glance. "I didn't think you called it luck. I thought it was divine protection."

Ross found he was shaking with anger. "Stop sneering at me, Paddy! Stop it!"

McKenny's laugh chilled the young Scot. "What will you do if I don't? Get out and walk home?"

In A-Apple ahead Moore was in contact with Davies. "Have you called up the Tiffies yet, sir?"

Davies sounded anxious. "They're on their way, Moore. Is it bad?"

Blue Beach was directly ahead of Moore and he could see American soldiers running westward along the cliffs. Alerted that heavy tanks and infantry were on their heels, Tilsey's men were making for two stone hedges that ran across the fields to the cliff edge. Moore could only hope the Rangers carried adequate anti-tank weapons. Troops caught out in the open by tanks were like meat caught in a meat grinder. "It's very bad, sir," he told Davies. "We're going to need all the support we can get."

Half a mile or so from the gun battery the Rangers had destroyed, the German tanks had halted to allow their infantry to catch up with them, a respite that gave the Rangers another minute to reach cover. Jumping behind the low stone hedges, the Americans lined up their anti-tank weapons and waited.

Ahead of them the German infantry, veterans from North Africa, were all experienced in working with armour. Packing behind the tanks, they thumped their rifle butts on the steel plating to indicate their readiness. Through the explosions and general din of the battle, Tilsey's Rangers heard the cough of engines and the chilling, never-to-be forgotten grinding of tracks as the giant tanks rolled forward once more. Only here and there could their grey hulks be seen. Panthers flanking their advance were laying smoke that the prevailing wind was sweeping across the battle zone.

Young's Mosquitoes had taken full advantage of the short delay. Their rockets were darting like fiery lances into the dark smoke. Aware that the armour of both the Panthers and the Tigers was thinner at the rear and also that the Tigers' petrol tanks were carried there, they were attacking from that quarter whenever possible. Moreover the arrival of the German infantry made the tactic reap even grimmer rewards.

Leading his small flight down the cliffs, Moore joined in the attack. Flying at almost zero height he launched his first rocket well within safety range at a Tiger that loomed out of the smoke. An orange flash followed by a balloon of fire brought a cry of success from Hopkinson. A couple of seconds later a blast of heat flung the Mosquito upwards.

A hundred yards away Millburn was attacking with the urgency of a man who knew his compatriots would be overwhelmed unless the armoured advance could be checked. The rocket he released flew off the armoured skirt of a Panther in a ricochet of sparks. Cursing, Millburn held his dive until smoke was swirling past the cockpit blister. Grey-clad figures appeared, their faces lifted apprehensively. Thumbing his firing button Millburn opened up with both cannon and machine guns. Men stumbled and fell and the Panther slewed round as a 20-mm shell blew a section off its track. Holding his dive until the last second, Millburn pulled out less than a dozen feet above the tank. Gabby's indignant voice attacked him over the intercom. "What're you trying to do? Frighten the bastards to death?"

With the tanks drawing within range of the first stone hedge, American bazooka teams were now in action. Columns of black smoke signalled a couple of hits but the tough German armour kept on rolling forward. As Moore circled back for a second attack, the sight of a burning Focke Wulf 190 falling past him told him another battle was being fought overhead. Although by this time the German High Command had satisfied itself the raid was only a local one, they had decided the Americans must have their noses bloodied or they would return for the invasion with a dangerous confidence. Accordingly squadrons of 190s and 109s that for the last few months had been used only in defence of the Fatherland were now descending in swarms on the covering Thunderbolts.

The battle both on land and in the air had now reached the stage where all seemed confusion to those taking part in it. In the air men were assailed by sights and sounds the human senses are ill-equipped to withstand: parabolas of lethal tracer, shell bursts of jagged steel, the scream of engines and airfoils, the judder and crash of cannon fire. Behind the hedges Americans, firing desperately at the juggernauts advancing to crush them, had eardrums and lung tissues ruptured by the blast of shells. In the tanks Germans were loading guns, firing and loading again in a hell of sweat, din, and cordite fumes. For all of them time lost its meaning. Even fear withdrew into the background, although its hideous presence was never far away. The dominating emotion was urgency: the urgency to kill before one could be killed.

In J-Jimmie McKenny was fighting like a man to whom life had lost all value. As he traded cannon fire with Tigers and Panthers at point-blank range,

199

Ross, conscious of the need for desperate counter-attack, was denied even the relief of condemnation as the ferocious attacks continued.

In A-Apple Moore was growing concerned about the ammunition problem. Already three of Young's flights had reported they were low on rockets and 20-mm shells. The thought of having to withdraw and leave the troops below to their fate distressed Moore and he took A-Apple up to 1,500 feet to reappraise the situation. From that height he could see American tanks moving about in apparent freedom within the station perimeter. A quick check with Davies confirmed that the station was now in American hands and that explosive charges were being laid within the blockhouses. Within minutes, if all went well, the withdrawal to the landing craft could begin.

Heartened by the news and the possibility his squadron might still be in at the death, Moore gave his attention again to the threat from the east. As the smoke-covered cliffs swept back, Hopkinson gave a start. "Take a look over there, skipper! Aren't those Jerry tanks down on the beach?"

---

## 22

Moore saw that the Cockney was right. Somewhere back along the eastern cliffs the Germans had found a way down to the sand and their light tanks were racing along it towards White Beach.

Tilsey was already reacting to this threatened outflanking of his frail defence line. Rangers were sliding down the cliffs and taking cover on the blunt promontory Moore had noticed earlier. With the tide high, it reached out to within ten yards of the sea. If the tanks were allowed to pass this neck of beach, they would be in a position to pour enfilading fire on the infantry landing craft and menace the withdrawal of the entire task force. Shells bursting among the tanks and on the promontory told Moore the Rangers and the armour were already engaged.

Away on Moore's left the Typhoons had arrived. He could see their heavily-muscled shapes diving in and out of the smoke. Welcome though their arrival was, it only compensated for the troops Tilsey was being forced to draw out of his defence line. Trying to estimate how many Mosquitoes he dared pull out, Moore lifted his mask. "Guard Dog Leader to Zeros Six, Eight and Ten. Join me over Blue Beach."

Young, sounding weary, answered him. "Day and Clifford have bought it, skipper."

"Then send me No. Eleven."

Without waiting for the aircraft to arrive, Moore banked round and attacked. He received the full attention of the tanks that were heading along the beach in ever-greater numbers. Scoring a hit on one that crippled its tracks, Moore opened fire with cannon and machine guns on the infantry following the armour. As he swept towards the cliffs a sudden fork of tracer made him bank steeply away. Grimacing at the startled Hoppy, he tried to pin-point the source of the gunfire.

It proved to be a flak post half-buried in a high sand dune. Deciding it was too well-protected to make an attack worth while, Moore gave a warning to the three Mosquitoes now formating behind him. "Keep clear of that flak post half a mile east of the promontory. Follow me."

Circling out to sea, the four Mosquitoes separated and came at the tanks line abreast over the surf. Shells laid a curtain of steel before them. All four aircraft released a rocket apiece and then banked steeply away. Two scored direct hits: two missed their targets. The rocket that lanced out from McKenny was heading straight and true for a Panther when a fault in the projectile made it veer away at the last moment. As it harmlessly showered a tank with wet shingle, the flak post on the cliffs picked on J-Jimmie and raked it with tracer.

It was a provocation the cursing Irishman could not resist. Soaring into a tight turn, he headed back for the cliff. Realizing his intention, Ross gripped his arm. "Moore told us to ignore it!"

It is doubtful if McKenny heard him. Hands gripping the control wheel as if it were the throat of an enemy, he aimed the Mosquito's nose at the concrete bunker. As a sheet of tracer swirled towards them, Ross made his last appeal. "Paddy, for God's sake! It's suicide."

A second later J-Jimmie seemed to halt in mid-air as the tracer struck her. At the same moment McKenny fired two rockets. One struck the bunker but failed to penetrate the reinforced concrete. As McKenny banked steeply away there was a massive rat-tat-tat on the underside of his armoured seat. Forgetting the navigator enjoyed no such protection, McKenny failed to notice the agonized jerk Ross made against his straps. The gun post was swinging back into the Irishman's sights and his sole obsession was to destroy or be destroyed.

This time he opened fire with his cannon and closed to point-blank range. Ironically, the smaller projectiles were more effective, penetrating the visor through which the bunker's LMGs were firing. As the gunfire abruptly ceased, McKenny went into a climbing turn and glanced at Ross triumphantly.

"What do you mean—suicide? We've knocked it out, haven't we?"

Ross did not reply. As his eyes cleared from the fight, McKenny saw the Scot was sagging limply against his seat harness.

"What's wrong, Bernie?"

When Ross again made no response, McKenny reached out and tried to tug him round. For a moment the Scot's limp body resisted, then it lolled towards him. There was fear now in McKenny's voice.

"Bernie, can you hear me? How bad is it?"

The young Scot was trying to speak. Instead blood spurted from his mouth and ran down his overalls. His left leg began kicking spasmodically. A moment later his head fell back and his dead eyes stared up through the perspex blister. McKenny's cry was one of pure terror. "For Christ's sake, Bernie. Say something!"

In A-Apple Moore had noticed McKenny's reckless attack on the gun bunker but an American voice in his R/T had checked his reprimand.

"Brooklyn to Guard Dog Leader. Do you read me?"

Moore had already recognized Tilsey's voice. "I read you, Brooklyn."

"You got any bombs left?"

"Yes. Why?"

"Drop them on this headland. Try to block the beach."

It was a tactic fraught with danger. "We can't be that accurate with bombs. It could put your men at risk."

Tilsey was still cool enough for irony. "You could say they're at risk now. Drop your bombs."

Beside Moore the usually cheery Hopkinson was looking apprehensive. "Does he know what he's askin', skipper? If we kill any more Yanks we'll be at war with 'em."

The perils latent in the request were obvious enough to Moore but with the entire withdrawal threatened he could see no alternative. "Guard Dog Leader to Zeros Six, Eight, and Eleven. Bomb tip of promontory at ten-second intervals."

Warned of the forthcoming bombing, half of Tilsey's men were falling back to fresh positions along the low cliff face. Moore's guess was that Tilsey was staying with the rearguard. On the opposite side of the promontory, shells were falling among the tanks as the American destroyers reacted to this new threat to the withdrawal.

With J-Jimmie back in formation again, Moore led the Mosquitoes across the cliffs. His plan was to attack the promontory from its landward side in the hope that the forward plunge of the bombs would hurl debris over the neck of beach.

As he made for it he glanced down to see how the wider battle was progressing. The confrontation between the Rangers and the German tanks and infantry was reaching its climax as the weakened line of Americans fought gallantly to hold their positions. Hideous

203

tongues of flame licking through the smoke told Moore the tanks were within flammenwerfer range of the Rangers. Mosquitoes and Typhoons were still plunging in and out of the smoke like dolphins in a sea. A near collision rocked A-Apple as one Typhoon, its pilot intent on a marauding tank, missed it by less than thirty feet.

Glancing further west Moore could see great columns of smoke rising from the radiolocation station and landing craft lining up on the beaches. If the enemy's eastern thrust could be held for another twenty minutes or so, the mission could still be a conspicuous success.

Down on the beach Tilsey and his rearguard kept their positions until A-Apple with its bomb doors open could be seen approaching at 1,500 feet over the cliffs. Then, bending double, their boots slipping in the shingles, they ran back and took cover with the rest of their party behind a ridge seventy yards from the promontory. Moore's urgent voice reached down to Tilsey. "You're too close, Brooklyn. Drop back another hundred yards."

Ducking as a shell showered him with sand, the panting Tilsey crouched over the microphone his Signals corporal was holding out to him. "We're O.K., Guard Dog Leader. Just get those bombs dropped."

With the promontory sweeping towards him Moore had no further time to argue. Conscious he was flying well below safety height with a nose-fused bomb, he banked steeply away as his 250-pounder dropped. It burst on the western side of the promontory and threw up a shower of rocks. As A-Apple recovered and went into a climbing turn, Hopkinson gave a grunt of approval. "It might work, skipper, if we can get enough bombs down there."

But the tough German armour had recognized the threat, and reckless of their safety, tanks were making at speed for the neck before it could be closed. Pushing aside a clay boulder, a leading tank rounded the promontory and came in sight of Tilsey's men. In the exchange of fire that followed a bazooka shell tore off one of the tank's tracks and left it grinding impotently in the sand. Yet two others were already rounding the promontory and more were in eager pursuit.

Anxious for his colleagues below, Millburn chose to go in next. Although flak was heavy around him, the experienced American laid his bomb not thirty yards from Moore's. This time half a dozen large rocks rolled down on the debris-covered beach. Tilsey's encouraging voice crackled in Moore's earphones. "You're doing great, Guard Dog Leader. Keep it going."

Zero Six followed Millburn. It was flown by the two soccer fanatics, Butterfield and Foster. Realizing the outcome of the battle might depend on their making the breakthrough along the beach, the tanks put up their fiercest barrage yet. The youthful Foster, trying to concentrate on the low-level bar of his bombsight, saw chains of shells swirling towards him. He was just about to press the bomb release when a 75-mm shell burst full in the main fuel tank. Two seconds later all that remained of Zero Six was a rotating ball of fire that fell into the sea in a cloud of steam.

Moore's voice had a flat sound as he spoke to Mc-Kenny. "Let's try this another way, Zero Eleven. Tail-fuse your bombs, go in low, and drop them both together."

Moore saw Hopkinson wince. It was an order the squadron commander hated giving but if the beach was to be blocked, it was now clear that only pin-point accuracy would achieve it. If McKenny survived the gauntlet of fire at zero height, Moore's hope was that the tail-fusing of the bombs, with their eleven second delays, would enable J-Jimmie to escape the heavy explosions.

Had Moore seen McKenny's expression he would have realized that his concern for the Irishman's safety was academic. Brought back to the hell of sanity by Ross's death, the Irishman was waiting only for a chance of redemption. Before Moore had finished speaking his hand reached out and fused the two bombs. As he took J-Jimmie over the cliff top at 1,000 feet, Hopkinson gave Moore a puzzled look. "Didn't he hear you tell him to go in at low level?"

The explanation came two seconds later. As every

tank in the vicinity opened fire on him, McKenny pushed both throttles through the gate and went down like a meteor. A 75-mm shell blew off half J-Jimmie's tail fin and another set fire to its port engine but it is doubtful that anything could have stopped the Irishman in that moment of expiation. Trailing flame like a torch, the Mosquito struck the far end of the promontory and exploded, fuel tanks, bombs, and all. As scraps of aircraft, sand and boulders were flung upwards on the periphery of a huge ball of fire, A-Apple, a thousand feet above, shuddered to the massive explosion.

Hoppy's murmur was hoarse. "God in Heaven!" His pale face turned to Moore. "He meant that, skipper. Those bombs were nose-fused! Why?"

Below, the huge smoke cloud was beginning to drift away and the circling men could see that the neck of the promontory had been severed and tons of earth and rock were blocking the beach. After their initial shock, enemy tanks were on the move again and one was rearing up like a dog as it tried to pull itself over the rubble. When it slid back and crashed heavily on its side, it was clear that in spite of the German infantry who were already attempting to move the rocks, no tanks would round the promontory in time to affect the American withdrawal. However, the reaction of the American Rangers was not triumph as they rose from behind their bank of shingle. Like the airmen above, they seemed stunned by McKenny's sacrifice.

Moore led Millburn back over the cliffs. The sight that met them was heart-rending, for with their line weakened the Rangers were suffering greatly for their valour. With the German armour having broken through at last, anti-tank teams were still firing as tanks reared over them and crushed them with their pitiless tracks. Other Rangers, risking incineration from flamethrowers, could be seen running through the smoke and endeavouring to drop grenades down tank visors and turrets. Two things were being learned at heavy cost that morning on the bloody cliffs of Omonville. One was that the Germans were going to fight with their usual tough determination when the invasion came. The other was that the New American Army waiting in England for its day of destiny need fear comparison with no army in the world for its courage and fighting qualities.

Over on White Beach, with the Americans conscious it was a race against time, shuttles of landing craft were frantically ferrying infantrymen out to the waiting ships. Disregarding the dangers to their rearguard, destroyers were now pounding the advancing German armour and in a final effort to gain time, the American tanks were thrown into the battle. Outgunned and lighter-skinned than their German counterparts, they were doomed from the onset but went into combat like terriers harassing a stampede of bulls. Soon the cliffs above Blue Beach were dotted with their blazing hulks but there is no doubt their courageous sacrifice earned the Americans the extra few minutes necessary to ferry the last of their infantry out.

Above the bloody battle the surviving Mosquitoes and Typhoons had run out of ammunition one by one. No units had played their part with more distinction, as their heavy losses showed. The final and ironic tragedy for 633 Squadron came when Millburn and Moore, having sent their surviving aircraft home, were taking a last look at the shrinking perimeter to see if there was anything more they could do. As they swept over the wrecked radiolocation station, Millburn, who was flying fifty yards behind Moore, saw a single line of tracer soar up from a shattered bunker. Before he could yell a warning, the tracer ran the full length of A-Apple. A second later the Mosquito reeled and began to side-slip towards the cliffs. As it cleared them it seemed to recover for a moment, only to crash in a huge shower of spray in the surf a couple of hundred yards from the last of the American landing craft. Diving down, Millburn swept less than a hundred feet above the wreck. "See anything?" he yelled at Gabby.

The distressed Welshman shook his head. Millburn did another pass but neither man saw any movement in A-Apple. With the beach littered with wrecked vehicles and mounds that had once been men, there was nothing Millburn could do except send an emergency call to Davies in the *Brazos*. With heavy hearts and a last glance at the wreck, the two men started back for England.

## 23

By noon of that same day Holmsley looked like a battlefield. At the far end of one runway a tractor was feverishly dragging a crippled Mosquito out of the way of incoming aircraft. Seven other battle-scarred Mosquitoes were dispersed around the airfield. Having spoken to their ground crews, the weary pilots and navigators were now tramping towards Henderson, who was standing at the edge of the tarmac apron. Adams was at his elbow. The rest of 633 Squadron, plus the airfield's regular personnel, were waiting in anxious groups and watching the southern horizon.

Someone gave a shout and pointed an arm. Seconds later the uneven throb of engines could be heard. As a Mosquito appeared over the pine trees, crash wagons began throttling up and a siren gave a scream. With smoke pouring from one engine and huge holes in both wings, the Mosquito was keeping in the air with the greatest difficulty. Once clear of the pines it ignored the wind direction and sank down on the runway like a man at the end of a marathon. For fifty yards its landing appeared successful. Then its undercarriage collapsed and it crashed down on its belly. Two crash wagons and an ambulance accelerated as the aircraft skidded on to the grass and ground-looped with a snapping of spars and a shearing of metal.

Henderson took a couple of steps forward, then halted. "Half of my squadron scattered over a bloody cliff in France and the other half pranging itself on a satellite airfield. And all to nail a pack of lies from a paranoiac war correspondent."

Adams was sharing his bitterness. "This will be the end of it, surely."

The Scot was watching the first crash wagon scream to a halt with its nose only inches from the Mosquito's smoking engine. As white foam squirted out and killed the fire risk, he relaxed and turned to Adams. "It had better be or they'll be wanting a new C.O. as well as a squadron commander."

Adams winced at the reminder. By this time the first of the surviving aircrews were arriving. Visibly moved by their hollow faces and battle-stained appearance, Henderson moved among them. "You've done a great job, lads. And although I don't expect it means a damn to you right now, the operation was a big success."

The weary men showed no reaction. Stunned by the brutality of battle, they could feel only in personal terms. Larkin was the first to express the anxiety all were feeling. "What's the latest news of Moore and Hoppy, sir?"

"Better than we first feared," Henderson told him. "Air Commodore Davies says the Yanks picked them up and got them to the hospital ship. The last he heard they were both undergoing surgery."

It took a moment for his news to sink into the exhausted crews. Henderson's eyes were on a Mosquito that had just landed safely. Instead of taxi-ing to its dispersal point, it was jolting across the grass towards them. As its propellers jerked to a stop, Millburn and Gabby dropped to the ground. Releasing his parachute harness, the American, whose oil-stained right cheek was badly contused, began running forward. Henderson met him halfway.

"You two all right?" When Millburn nodded, the Scot went on: "You saw Moore go down, didn't you? What happened?"

No one was more anxious for news of the popular Moore than Millburn. "He wasn't a hundred yards ahead of us when an LMG got him. He didn't seem right out of control when he hit the surf. What's the latest news? Did the Yanks pick them up?"

"Yes. They're on the hospital ship having surgery. That's all Davies could tell me."

By this time Gabby had joined them. "Does that mean they're bad, sir?"

Anxiety made Henderson irritable. "I've just said —I don't know. We'll have to wait until the convoy gets back."

The survivors, who had clustered round Millburn to hear his news, were now looking as if the effort had drained them of their remaining strength. As Henderson's eyes ran round them, his tone changed. "I've never seen a crowd of men look so knackered. Forget the de-briefing—we'll handle it later. Go off and get yourself some grub and coffee."

Millburn remained behind as the crews trudged off. "Did Davies tell you about McKenny, sir?"

Overhearing his comment, Young moved back. Henderson shook his head. "He's one of those who got the chop, isn't he?"

"Yeah. But it wasn't an accident."

The Scot frowned. "What does that mean?"

Millburn told him. Henderson exchanged a shocked glance with Adams. "Are you telling me it was suicide?"

"What else could it be? Nobody goes in at zero height with nose-fused bombs."

"But why would he do that?"

The American shrugged. "Search me. If the tanks had gotten past that headland they'd have cut off our withdrawal for sure. But no one was asked to commit suicide."

"And you're sure that's what it was?"

"It had to be. Even if he'd dropped his bombs from that height, he'd still have blown himself to hell."

Henderson's bitter eyes moved to the surviving aircraft. Deciding it was all too much to take at one sitting, he gave a sigh. "It's been that kind of day, so I suppose it all fits. Do you expect any more kites in or are you the last?"

"We're the last," Millburn told him.

Henderson winced. "God Almighty." With an effort he pulled himself together and led the three men towards a distant Nissen hut. "Let's go and have a bloody drink."

Adams halted the staff car outside Sutton Craddock's Administration Block and made his way down the corridor to Henderson's office. He found the Scot just replacing the telephone receiver. At any other time he would have noticed the satisfaction Henderson was showing. "Can you spare me a few minutes?"

Henderson sat back. "As a matter of fact, you're just the man I wanted to see. What's happened? Have our spares and replacements arrived?"

Adams grimaced. "Nothing seems to have arrived." He nodded at the pile of requisition forms on the desk. "I see you're still signing them."

"I've been doing nothing else since we got back," Henderson grunted. "At this rate it'll be Christmas before we're back at full strength. The only consolation, I suppose, is that this time the job wasn't for nothing. Staines says that over in the States Lambert's campaign has collapsed like a house of cards. In fact we made such a good impression that he's been forced to join in the chorus and praise us."

Although seldom malicious, Adams could not contain his grin of pleasure. "So that's the end of it."

"It has to be, hasn't it? He can hardly switch round in a week or two and start slanging the RAF again."

"It must have lost him some credibility over there."

"I hope it's lost him his bloody job," Henderson muttered.

"Davies must be pleased."

"Davies? He's like a dog with two tails. Particularly after the C.-in-C.'s congratulations." Then the Scot's tone changed. "Harvey phoned me this morning. He's been down to Southampton to see Moore."

"What's the latest news?"

"Much better than we hoped. They think Moore

211

could be back on his feet in about two months. Hoppy's going to take longer but should be operational soon after Christmas. Guess what? Harvey's staying down in Southampton until the end of his leave."

"Why? So he can visit Moore?"

Henderson grinned. "Being Harvey, he made some other excuse but that's his reason all right. Funny, isn't it, when you think how he used to dislike Moore." It was then the Scot noticed Adams' expression. "What was it you wanted to see me about?"

"I've got news about McKenny," Adams told him. "I think it explains everything that happened."

Henderson showed immediate interest. "You mean why he committed suicide?"

"Yes, I think so."

The Scot motioned to a chair. "Then let's have it."

Adams sank down somewhat heavily. "I've just come back from Highgate. A Catholic priest there, a Father McBride, phoned me early this morning to ask if he could see me. He'd just heard about McKenny's death and thought we should hear the background story."

"A priest?"

"McKenny's priest," Adams explained.

Henderson's face cleared. "Go on."

"I think he got in touch with me because not long before the train operation I had a word with McKenny about his heavy drinking, and he must have mentioned my name to McBride. It seems McKenny had stopped attending Mass and Confession but wouldn't give McBride a reason. So eventually McBride had a word with Ross. Ross didn't want to talk at first but when McBride convinced him it was for McKenny's good, Ross told him about an ugly incident they'd had back in the summer. Do you remember the low-level raid we made on Rutenbreck?"

Henderson had to think. "Was that when we clobbered a machine tool factory?"

"That's the one. McKenny had a hung-up bomb and it fell on a row of houses. Both he and Ross saw women and children running out. One child was blazing like a torch."

"Did they mention this at de-briefing?" Henderson interrupted.

"They only said they'd hit the row of houses. They probably didn't want to think about the child."

"Go on," Henderson said again.

"Also back in the summer they were both witnesses when Taylor and Gibson were trapped in their crashed aircraft and burned alive." Inclined to digress when the psychological aspects of war were involved, Adams digressed now. "To an irreligious old sod like me, a few incidents like that seem more than enough to destroy anyone's faith in a just and kindly God. It makes me wonder how many men are going to come out of this war with any faith at all. To some that's surely going to be a far greater loss than an arm or leg. Yet because it's not a loss people can see, they're not going to get much sympathy or understanding."

Henderson shifted restlessly. "I've got the point. The priest believes these experiences caused his breakdown."

To his surprise Adams shook his head. "No. Perhaps because McKenny was a Catholic, McBride wasn't satisfied his faith could be undermined that way. I think he's wrong and that was the beginning of it, but that's neither here nor there. McBride went on making enquiries and eventually found out that McKenny's girl friend had broken off her engagement and was going overseas. Even that didn't satisfy McBride and he went to Lincoln to see the girl. You'll never guess what he found out."

Henderson's attempt at humour was only half-hearted. "Don't tell me she'd shot the Pope."

"Just the opposite. She'd turned religious herself."

The Scot's square face frowned at Adams. "What is this? Some kind of sick joke?"

"No. When you think about it, it makes sense. McKenny's girl friend was a Protestant and according to what she told McBride, she'd hardly given religion a second though since she went to Sunday school as a child. But sometime during the summer she got 'the Call'."

Henderson's eyebrows rose. "The Call?"

213

"You know—the sudden impulse to give up all earthly things and spend the rest of one's life serving God. In her case it meant joining a group of nursing missionaries who in a week or two are going out to a leper colony in West Africa."

"But McKenny told Moore she was going to the Middle East."

"That was to conceal what had happened to her. He didn't want us all to know she was giving him up for God."

The Scot was frowning again. "All right, I can see it would be a blow. But if he was such a religious kid at that time, how could her turning religious too cause him to break down?"

"Turning religious is one thing, having a conversion so complete that it ended their relationship is another. Although, unlike McBride, I believe other factors were already turning him against religion, it must have been a hell of a shock, and when he finally realized she was leaving him for God, he began to see God as his rival. His enemy, in fact. And it's not difficult to imagine what this would do to anyone as fundamentally religious as McKenny. In his pain he'd began turning against everything and everybody, including his best friend, Ross. Ross more than anyone because deep down he'd be jealous that Ross had managed to keep his faith intact." When Henderson slowly shook his head, Adams allowed his imagination a moment's indulgence. "It's a bit like the story of Lucifer, isn't it? One of God's brightest angels becoming his deadliest enemy."

Henderson gave a grunt. "That's a bit fanciful, isn't it?"

Remembering whom he was talking to, Adams felt his cheeks turn warm. "I suppose it is. But even in wartime it's not every day you run into something as profound and harrowing as this."

Henderson conceded a nod. "Then you think that was why McKenny committed suicide? To destroy Ross as well as himself?"

"Oh, no. Not to kill Ross. In one way they were closer than brothers. When I did the de-briefing, young

Evans said he heard McKenny over the R/T a few minutes before he killed himself. The reception was poor but Evans said he was asking Ross how badly hurt he was and sounded half-crazy on finding he was dead. Why he then crashed into the promontory is anyone's guess. It might have been revenge on God, an impulse of self-destruction, expiation for getting Ross killed, or simply a self-sacrificial act to save hundreds of American lives. I like to think it was the last two but who can ever say?"

Henderson pushed a telex form across the desk. "I know what the Yanks are saying. Both he and Ross have gone up for a posthumous Congressional Medal of Honour."

Adams removed his spectacles and began wiping them. "I'm glad. If medals mean anything, both boys deserve them more than most. Ross knew the danger when he volunteered to fly with McKenny again, and the damned war had already destroyed McKenny before it killed him."

For once Henderson did not find Adams' sensitivity an embarrassment. "It might be a good idea to keep this quiet, Frank. At least until the dust settles. But it's not all doom and gloom, thank God. Do you know who was on the telephone when you came in?" As Adams shook his head: "It was the Brigadier. He's got news of St. Claire and Simpson. They're both alive and well."

Adams was sitting bolt upright in his chair. "Is he sure?"

"That's what his agents have told him. The Resistance can't get either of 'em across yet but they'll be giving it a crack in due course. Do you want to tell Sue yourself?"

Adams jumped up. "Do you mind?"

"No. You're her Father Confessor. Off you go."

The interval between his leaving Henderson's office and reaching his "Confessional" was a blank to Adams although his thudding heart told him he must have run most of the way. When he threw back the door, the girl was filing photographs into one of the steel cabinets. Seeing his exhausted condition, she showed concern. "What on earth's the matter, Frank?"

Before Adams could get his breath back she suddenly halted and put a hand to her throat. The panting Adams nodded and entered the hut. "Yes. I've got news for you . . . Good news. Put those photographs down and come over here."

## ABOUT THE AUTHOR

FREDERICK E. SMITH joined the R.A.F. in 1939 as a wireless operator/air gunner and commenced service in early 1940, serving in Britain, Africa and finally the Far East. At the end of the war he married and worked for several years in South Africa before returning to England to fulfill his life-long ambition to write. Two years later, his first play was produced and his first novel published. Since then, he has written twenty-four novels, about eighty short stories and two plays. Two novels, *633 Squadron* and *The Devil Doll*, have been made into films and one, *A Killing for the Hawks*, has won the Mark Twain Literary Award.

# BANTAM WAR BOOKS

These action-packed books recount the most important events of World War II. They take you into battle and present portraits of brave men and true stories of gallantry in action. All books have special maps, diagrams, and illustrations.

| | | | |
|---|---|---|---|
| ☐ | 12657 | **AS EAGLES SCREAMED** Burgett | $2.25 |
| ☐ | 12658 | **THE BIG SHOW** Clostermann | $2.25 |
| ☐ | 13014 | **BRAZEN CHARIOTS** Crisp | $2.25 |
| ☐ | 12666 | **THE COASTWATCHERS** Feldt | $2.25 |
| ☐ | *12664 | **COCKLESHELL HEROES** Lucas-Phillips | $2.25 |
| ☐ | 12141 | **COMPANY COMMANDER** MacDonald | $1.95 |
| ☐ | 12578 | **THE DIVINE WIND** Pineau & Inoguchi | $2.25 |
| ☐ | *12669 | **ENEMY COAST AHEAD** Gibson | $2.25 |
| ☐ | *12667 | **ESCORT COMMANDER** Robertson | $2.25 |
| ☐ | *11709 | **THE FIRST AND THE LAST** Galland | $1.95 |
| ☐ | *11642 | **FLY FOR YOUR LIFE** Forrester | $1.95 |
| ☐ | 12665 | **HELMET FOR MY PILLOW** Leckie | $2.25 |
| ☐ | 12663 | **HORRIDO!** Toliver & Constable | $2.25 |
| ☐ | 12670 | **THE HUNDRED DAYS OF LT. MACHORTON** Machorton | $2.25 |
| ☐ | *12668 | **I FLEW FOR THE FÜHRER** Knoke | $2.25 |
| ☐ | 12290 | **IRON COFFINS** Werner | $2.25 |
| ☐ | 12671 | **QUEEN OF THE FLAT-TOPS** Johnston | $2.25 |
| ☐ | *11822 | **REACH FOR THE SKY** Brickhill | $1.95 |
| ☐ | 12662 | **THE ROAD PAST MANDALAY** Masters | $2.25 |
| ☐ | 12523 | **SAMURAI** Sakai with Caidin & Saito | $2.25 |
| ☐ | 12659 | **U-BOAT KILLER** Macintyre | $2.25 |
| ☐ | 12660 | **V-2** Dornberger | $2.25 |
| ☐ | *12661 | **THE WHITE RABBIT** Marshall | $2.25 |
| ☐ | *12150 | **WE DIE ALONE** Howarth | $1.95 |

***Cannot be sold to Canadian Residents.***

Buy them at your local bookstore or use this handy coupon:

Bantam Books, Inc., Dept. WW2, 414 East Golf Road, Des Plaines, Ill. 60016

Please send me the books I have checked above. I am enclosing $_____ (please add 75¢ to cover postage and handling). Send check or money order —no cash or C.O.D.'s please.

Mr/Mrs/Miss _____

Address _____

City _____ State/Zip _____

WW2—5/79

Please allow four weeks for delivery. This offer expires 11/79.